Aziz Mohammed is a Saudi literary author, born in Khobar City in 1987. His debut novel *The Critical Case of a Man Called K* was published in 2017 and was shortlisted in 2018 for the International Prize for Arabic Fiction, known as the "Arabic Booker." He was the youngest and the first debut author to be shortlisted in the history of this prestigious prize. He has since participated in the cultural programs of literary festivals, bookfairs, and cultural centers all around the Middle East as a literary author and cinema critic.

Humphrey Davies is an award-winning literary translator of Arabic into English. He received first class honors in Arabic at Cambridge University and holds a doctorate in Near East Studies from the University of California at Berkeley. He has won and been shortlisted for numerous literary prizes, and has twice been awarded the prestigious Saif Ghobash–Banipal Prize for Arabic Literary Translation. He has translated Naguib Mahfouz, Elias Khoury, Mourid Barghouti, and Bahaa Taher, among others. He lives in Cairo, Egypt.

T0352366

The Critical Case of
a Man Called K

Aziz Mohammed

Translated by
Humphrey Davies

hoopoe
AN IMPRINT OF AUC PRESS

First published in 2021 by
Hoopoe
113 Sharia Kasr el Aini, Cairo, Egypt
One Rockefeller Plaza, 10th Floor, New York, NY 10020
www.hoopoefiction.com

Hoopoe is an imprint of The American University in Cairo Press
www.aucpress.com

al-Hala al-harija li-l-mad'u K by Aziz Mohammed, copyright © 2017 by Dar Altan-weer, Beirut, Cairo, Tunis
Protected under the Berne Convention

Published by arrangement with Rocking Chair Books Ltd and RAYA the agency for Arabic literature

English translation copyright © 2021 by Humphrey Davies

ISBN 978 164 903 075 7

Library of Congress Cataloging-in-Publication Data

Names: Muḥammad, 'Azīz, 1987- author. | Davies, Humphrey T. (Humphrey Taman), translator.
Title: The critical case of a man called K / Aziz Mohammed ; translated by Hum-phrey Davies.
Other titles: Ḥālah al-ḥarijah lil-mad'ūw K. English
Identifiers: LCCN 2020043851 (print) | LCCN 2020043852 (ebook) | ISBN 9781649030757 (paperback) | ISBN 9781649030795 (epub) | ISBN 9781649030801 (adobe pdf)
Subjects: LCSH: Leukemia--Patients--Fiction. | Blue collar workers--Fiction. | LCGFT: Psychological fiction.
Classification: LCC PJ7948.A95 H3513 2021 (print) | LCC PJ7948.A95 (ebook) | DDC 892.7/37--dc23
1 2 3 4 5   25 24 23 22 21

Designed by Adam el-Sehemy
Printed in the United Kingdom

One

Week 1

THE MOMENT I WAKE, I'M overcome by a feeling of nausea.

I take a breath with difficulty, rub my eyes, stare out through a pall of sleep. There are dark spots on the pillow. I deduce from the way I'm breathing that they must have come from my nose. The left side of my mustache is stiff with coagulated blood and the blood in my nostrils is still moist. I jerk into consciousness, raise my head, and, in an instant, my pulse returns to normal. From the position of the sun in the window, I realize that I am, however you look at it, late. I turn over onto the other half of the pillow and close my eyes again.

I remember that before I went to sleep, just before dawn, I was reading a book and before that I'd taken a hot shower, which I'd read somewhere makes you sleepy. Before that, I'd had dinner, smoked, moved around from room to room, turned the lights on and off, got into bed and got out again, stood up and sat down, all to no purpose. Nothing different from what people do every night if they can't sleep. I've chosen a bad day to make do with just two hours' sleep, though any other day would be just as bad. From the midst of the chaos of the bedside table, the alarm clock's harsh bell keeps hammering away, like a nail being driven into my head.

It takes a few minutes for me finally to get out of bed. I turn over in my mind the fact that I'm late, without this impelling me to hurry. I piss, and from the color deduce that I'm dehydrated. I clean my teeth till the gums hurt, from which I deduce that I've cleaned them long enough. I wash the traces of sleep off my face and of blood off my mustache and the inside of my nostrils. I smell the familiar metallic smell. A little blood trickles down my throat, like a burning clot of old memories.

As a child, I was always getting nosebleeds and would become aware of the movement of the warm blood as it trickled down through the respiratory tract before I saw it fall onto my clothes and feet. The first moment of seeing it was always terrifying, even though there wasn't any pain. Nosebleeds often prevented me from joining in games with the other boys after school, especially on hot, sunny days, and even though I became an expert at stopping the bleeding (by, for example, holding an ice cube against the top of my nose or closing the open vein by pinching it with two fingers from the outside), the sun, in its fury at this land, could always make it flow again.

Now, though, it's winter. I check by looking through the window. The day is bright, the sun's rays falling on traces of recent rain. I dress in a hurry, my only concession to being late. As soon as I leave the house, the downpour resumes.

In the car, music blasts out the moment I turn the key. I silence the radio with the same violent movement that I used to reach out to the alarm clock on the dressing table. Not a thought enters my head throughout the journey. The front windshield wipers move right and left like a hypnotist's pendulum. Suddenly, I find myself at the overflowing parking lot and become aware again of where I am. I park far away and walk with hurried steps. It's cold and something urges speed.

A number of times, during the long walk toward it, I raise my head to look at the tower. The entire building is visible and it's easy to find your way to it from anywhere, but the entrance remains hidden and getting to it requires several twists and turns. The closer you get, the more you feel you will never enter.

Everything is the way it was yesterday, but the feeling of alienation the building inspires is so strong that somehow it all seems different.

Immediately after you cross the side entrance, a strong smell of paint erupts, which the unventilated corridor holds in place. At the end of the corridor there's an escalator, whose end is invisible from where it starts and which moves endlessly upward, as though it could take you to wherever you want to go, though in fact it takes you only to the elevator lobby, where you wait. This late in the morning, no one is waiting in the lobby but me. Empty or full, however, makes no difference to how long you have to wait.

The lobby's glass façade looks out over an exterior court-yard containing a garden, in which no one ever strolls, and wooden benches, used by smokers. I can always tell how late I am by the number of smokers outside: no one goes out for a smoke immediately after he arrives; he has first to have been noticed by those upstairs long enough to establish his presence. Who knows, perhaps the glass façade was made specifically so that people could fill their vision with such observations while waiting, and the moment the elevator arrives, rush into it, as though unable to bear the sight a moment longer.

I enter and press the button for the tenth floor. The door remains open for a while before closing automatically. I glance at my watch. I check the zipper of my pants, as I often forget about it. I contemplate my clothes from top to bottom, as though noticing for the first time what I'm wearing.

The second I reach the tenth floor, I hide my hands in my pockets and try to look like someone confident he's on time. I maintain this look as I cross the marble corridor to the administrative offices and open the glass door that keeps the department separate, then make my way along the narrow aisles between the rows of desks, taking care to avoid bumping into this person or returning that one's greeting, and finally sit down in front of the computer. I pull off the yellow sticker, knowing without reading it who wrote it and stuck it on the screen, then say good morning to the Old Man, who sits next to me, my voice sounding scandalously exhausted. A phrase from Kafka's *Diaries*, which I'm reading these days, keeps repeating itself in my mind: "At this sudden utterance some saliva flew from my mouth as an evil omen." When I hear the wan voice next to me return my greeting, I realize, as though discovering this for the first time since I woke, that it's just another ordinary day at work.

Nausea again, as soon as I set my eyes on the screen. Perhaps I'm still under the influence of the *Diaries*. It's only natural that if you overindulge in Kafka he'll get to you with all sorts of stuff. On the other hand, for a long time now I've experienced the same nauseating exhaustion, to a greater or lesser degree, in the early mornings. I remember it as an indefatigable visitor during my early adolescence specifically, maybe because things are always most noticeable at their beginnings.

After waking at six in the morning to go to school, I'd spend long minutes in the bathroom, resting my head on the lavatory bowl and almost dropping off, till startled by my mother's violent banging on the door telling me to hurry up and catch the bus. I'd give her all kinds of excuses so that I could stay home and, even though they were cloaked in the artifice that she could usually distinguish in my tone when I lied, the nausea and exhaustion weren't entirely invented. "Put up with it!" she'd reply; I remember the words well because she'd say them again, without thinking and very insistently, and I'd always be obliged to repeat my complaint, insisting from my side till I'd gotten rid of her suspicion that I was appealing to her for no good reason, or till I could overcome her assumption that I wasn't making an effort to "put up with it."

I was in first year middle school when, one day, they persuaded themselves that they ought to take me to the doctor. My father was with me and the room was small and cramped, or seemed so to me at the time. The doctor had large rough hands, with which he silently probed my body. After he'd examined me, he said everything was normal. Then he washed and dried his hands with movements that seemed to indicate irritation, as though he had neither the time nor the inclination to cater to complaints of this kind, and when he went around behind his desk to sit down, his gown dragged against the wall, making a terrifying scratching sound that was much louder than one would expect from such a contact.

We, my father and I, were seated on the other side of the desk in facing chairs, our feet almost touching. The silence was oppressive. All we could hear was the sharp pouncing of the doctor's pen as he wrote something in the file that there was no longer any call for him to write, as it was clear that the case wasn't worth a visit to him. Suddenly, my father pulled his feet in a bit. Maybe if he hadn't been there, the visit wouldn't have made such an impression on me.

"It's perfectly normal," the doctor repeated, in a tone that implied he finally had the time to punish me for wasting his, and the inclination to do so. "At his age, during adolescence, the cells divide faster than usual, causing the body to expend its energy on growth." Then he put down his pen and crossed his arms in front of him, as though cradling his disgust. "If every adolescent boy kept visiting clinics just because he felt a little tired and nauseous, the clinics would be filled with them and we'd be too busy to attend to the important cases." In his eyes, I was one of those spoiled children who complain at the slightest stress; it may well have been clear to him too that I'd grow up to be one of those men who are always grumbling about their jobs.

He kept on talking, his rigid arm making a rustling sound on the desk that indicated the suppression of a more violent movement. My father, for his part, was looking distractedly at its corner, with the expression of a man being informed that his spermatozoa are weak. At some point, without looking at me, he said, agreeing with the doctor, "Quite. He exaggerates." Those were the only words he uttered, and he did so in the quietest tone possible, as though it would have been easier for him to accept if I'd been afflicted by something major.

"But he's a healthy boy, and good-mannered," the doctor said, making amends for any impression his tone might have given that he was criticizing my father's genes or his child-raising practices. "And his body's sound and can take a beating," he went on, while continuing to look me up and down, with a smile of a kind that simultaneously complimented my father and indicated contempt for me. When my father smiled in response (something the doctor noted with a sideways, complicit look), his words began to take on a jolly character and all of a sudden he was offering advice and joking rebukes—"You have to be tough!"--supporting his pronouncements with his clenched fist while banging his rigid wrist on the desktop. When he sensed that his words weren't having a positive effect on me, he laughed, to make clear that what he was saying was partly in jest, though that didn't mean it wasn't also important. Then he turned to my father and smiled, deriving from the smile he received in return further delegated powers, as though the doctor was my father's censorious side, and even went so far as to say I should stop playing the invalid and worrying over nothing so that I didn't upset my mother. No, it couldn't be attributed to my father's genes, because in the end the two of them were one and the same—or so, more or less, I thought, as I stared determinedly at the floor, like someone plucking up the courage to flee.

Suddenly he stretched out his cold, coarse hand, perhaps to stroke my cheek, or to wipe that look off my face. I felt instinctively that he was reaching out to slap me and flinched in response and sat back in my chair, while they both let out a raucous laugh, a self-satisfied laugh that confirmed the conclusion the two of them had reached about me. It had been decided, once and for all, that the defect, whatever it might be, resided in my own nature. The doctor thrust his open palm toward my father in an apologetic gesture, as though to say this was a sickness that he couldn't cure, and in response my father did the same. They stood up together and shook hands warmly, their two huge bodies taut above me, as though they were shaking hands over something other than the end of the visit. At that precise moment, I realized, somehow, that this would stay with me for a long time: it was simply another of those changes that take place as you grow and that hold you in their grip for as long as you live. That's all it takes—a trivial moment like that, after which you realize, for the first time and forever, what anguish it is to be yourself.

Week 2

ANOTHER BAD DAY TO MAKE do with just two hours of sleep. I wake in a panic, drive like a drunk, and make it to my desk on time. I rip off the yellow sticker, crumple it into a ball on the desktop, and give my good morning salutation to the Old Man (as I shall call him here, in homage to my favorite Hemingway novel). He's the man who occupies the desk next to mine or, perhaps I should say, to be more precise, the computer screen next to mine, since after they increased the number of employees to beyond the department's holding capacity, they put a new desk between each two old desks. Now the place is full to overflowing with squashed-together, parallel rows of screens, each open to the next, like in the computer lab at a school. The only thing that interrupts their serried lines is the space allotted to the printer, which continually gives off noises, pushing out one sheet of paper after another and forcing you to rush over to it the moment you print anything so that your sheet doesn't get lost among other people's.

Continuous congestion and incessant movement keep the inside of the tower in a constant hubbub, although from the outside it looks unoccupied.

By good luck, or bad, my desk is located right next to the printer; in fact, the printer impinges on part of its surface area, to the degree that whenever anyone prints anything I can feel the heat from the sheets of paper close to my head. The pace at which the sheets are ejected helps me to gauge the rhythm of work in the department. Days when there's a crush on, I hold off on reading and surfing the internet as someone may rush over to the printer at any moment to pick up what he's printed, and someone else may come and stand behind him, and then another, and another, just like the line at the WC at the end of lunch hour.

This aside, my position provides good visual protection. Only the Old Man, if he were to stare at my screen, would be able to see that I'm writing about him right now, but I put my trust in his withdrawn nature, which ensures that he will forget my existence the moment he finishes responding to my greeting. He always answers without turning his head, to cut off any attempt to start a conversation with anyone, since nothing he might wish to hear from you could ever be more important to him than what's happening on his screen, and it's not his habit to abandon that screen at any time during work hours except to stand, stretch, and complain how cold the air conditioning is, on which occasion his voice will be suffused with something of the pallor that affects the vocal cords of those who go for long periods without speaking. Sometimes his clicking on the mouse seems pallid too, as if the sound it makes was coming from his throat.

It's his last month at work, though one might think he'd passed retirement years ago. His dark complexion, burned by the sun in ages past, has acquired a dullness from all its days between these walls. He wears a robe and headdress of faded white and lets the headdress hang down so that it hides both sides of his face, all day long; this makes it difficult for me to guess what his expression may betray as he stares at his screen. When I think about it, his appearance seems of a piece with the life of the old mariners and of the men who hunted for pearls in the depths of the Gulf, and that may indeed have been his profession before the oil cast him up at this desk. I still have no idea what role he plays in this particular department, next to the rows of shirts and pants, colored wraps, and even new robes, whose heads speak English as they deal with minute technical details. Perhaps he doesn't know either. I wonder whether he might have received instructions to keep sitting here and pretending to work till he completes his years of service with the company, simply because they have no grounds to throw him out. With his lean frame, rigid above his desk, he looks, in fact, like a rusty nail stuck in this vast machine in which he has spent some thirty years.

I, for my part, have worked here three years. Let's call it the Eastern Petrochemicals Company, after the Eastern Petroleum Company where one of Tanizaki's protagonists works; this is appropriate as we are in the eastern, oil-rich, part of this country (it's better not to give specific names or places as I don't know who may not barge in some day and read what I've written). It's a large company, with a guaranteed future, and that's what matters. As an IT graduate, it would make no difference if I were working in an electricity, gas, fertilizer, or any other crap company. I didn't put a lot of thought into choosing my college major either. My father died when I finished high school, and that timing played a part in directing me toward options with financial incentives. This specialization was said to be in demand in the labor market, and what more can anyone ask than to be in demand in the labor market? One has to earn one's living somehow: young people are suffering from unemployment, the house needs the salary, and are you better than Kafka? These are good enough reasons for me to make sure I keep my place among the white-collar workers.

In any case, it doesn't call for any great effort to remain an employee in this department—just the regular reports confirming the absence of weak points or breaches in the system, the continuous complaints that reach one from other employees working on more important things who don't have time for technical issues, and the updates whose ends one reaches just in time to find that their beginnings need to be updated again; and even when, by some miraculous coincidence, there is no work, things can be invented with which to task the employee should he ever be seen sitting empty-handed, unless he should take the initiative by asking for additional jobs, which is what he's supposed to do. "The employee should never let himself get used to doing nothing," say the experts here. "Then he will always be fully prepared when the need arises." These words of wisdom mean that jobs are thrown at you one after another, before you've finished the one before, so that you're always busy and prepared to be even busier, as though a single moment of idleness might ruin you.

My supervisor is devoted to maxims of that sort, just as he's wedded to an excessive caution and loves to repeat the American expression "You can never be too careful." His very appearance is irritating: he wears his pants high, almost above his navel, and as a result has to keep pulling them up as he walks so that they don't slip off his belly. He seems unaware how much his wide pants make him look like Charlie Chaplin. It may be that he thinks he possesses a contemporary look, and to confirm this thought, he keeps looking down at his Skechers, a stupid make of shoe that perfectly expresses his personality—bad taste, blind imitation, and an ever-present awareness that he isn't the right person for the position.

His one good quality is that he doesn't say much, contenting himself with sticking notes on your screen, and if you commit some terrible error, he says, "Hmm. I can't believe it." If you really blow it, you find him gazing at you in silence with a reproachful look, so you understand that your mistake has left him dumbfounded. Most of my mistakes dumbfound him, maybe because they're so hard to believe, even though he always does believe them and lives in the alert expectation of my making them. In fact, he even hopes that I'll forget certain tasks and makes up his mind not to remind me of them until the last day. If I forget to run the routine anti-virus checks as scheduled, he rolls his eyes back in their sockets till only the whites show, so that you think for a instant he's going to faint; just hearing the word "virus," on its own and irrespective of the context in which it occurs, is enough to make him lose his mind. And all this even though we haven't spotted a single virus that posed a real threat to the system throughout my years here. He persists in treating these routine checks as though a disaster will happen if they aren't run on schedule. When he comes to remind me of the time for the check, which I always forget, he stays and watches me till the scan is over, inspecting the progress of the work every two minutes, hovering around me with his wide pants, horrible shoes, and the latest catchphrases he's picked up from the Americans.

Anyway, he may be a son of a bitch but what else are bosses supposed to be? He obviously comes under a lot of pressure from those higher up and has to vent it somewhere. His boss, though, the department director, he's the real son of a bitch. Maybe the more of a bitch someone's mother is, the better his chances of rising through the ranks.

It was the habit of this director of ours to postpone vacations as he fancied, on the excuse that the department was in urgent need of the employees during those critical days and all our days in the department were critical. That's why, with the exception of scattered sick-leave days here and there, I had never had a vacation and kept postponing, year after year, my ambitions to travel to Prague or St. Petersburg. But the days when the company really was subjected to cyber attacks were the worst: pressure of work would require us to spend extra hours there, attempting to log every operation each employee had carried out via his account and isolate the machines that were suspected of having been hacked, even if the cause for suspicion was no more than someone having once or twice used the wrong password. These extra work hours weren't subject to any financial compensation: the employee was supposed to work them out of concern for the company's interests. On such occasions, the aforesaid director would make the rounds of the desks on his way out, his beard dangling over his neck,

15

like a turkey's wattles, clapping his hands right and left and repeating to us in encouraging tones, "You are our Unknown Warriors!" before leaving for home. How strange the expression "Unknown Warriors" seemed in relation to working for a petrochemicals company, although somehow it always managed to raise the employees' spirits.

Such things aside, though, it's all right, and a job's a job. One gets used to anything when compelled to engross oneself in it as a part of one's routine, just as one gets used to entering via the side door. And, to be fair, it isn't the worst job in the world. One just has to keep reminding oneself that things could be worse.

For example, when I started at the company and before I was transferred to this department, I was obliged to work in a room that I shared with three other employees, with none of the privacy to read and write that I have now. And those three were terrifying models of commitment, Unknown Warriors in the full sense of the words. Not one arrived after eight and not one left before five, and between those times they scarcely left their desks. After all, you never knew when the director might not pass among the desks and fail to find you, or an email might arrive that you didn't open within a minute! I never once saw them eat and, naturally, I never saw any of them go to the toilet either. Their entire existence was dedicated to work, and in its cause they had, with the discipline of genuine warriors, subjugated their bodily needs to fit their work schedules.

The moment the lunch hour began, they would leave, not returning until it was over, because their absence from their desks during that hour was a part of the rigorous observance of the rules that every true warrior must practice, for if you work during the lunch hour it means you weren't working hard enough before it to deserve to take a rest. Similarly, working after five wasn't necessarily a sign of application; indeed, it might mean that you hadn't been organizing your time efficiently enough to complete your tasks during work hours.

Their professionalism lived up to the expectations of Management, which embraced the most trivial of details, such as the cables under your machine not being tied together, for your own safety, and how well arranged your papers were within the narrow confines of your desk. And even though some of these details were not acknowledged criteria for the employee's performance evaluation, nevertheless, given the large number of employees, they continued to be included among the Management's secret criteria for the responsible employee. No one knew where these secret criteria began or ended, which were taken into account and which not, but these three were always fully prepared for the test, as though some unbiased eye was watching every event that took place there, great and small, and would reward them, some day, as they deserved.

The presence among them of someone as undisciplined as myself could only be considered deplorable. I never stopped eating, for example, mainly because there was nothing else to do. It's a problem I no longer suffer from, now that I've lost my appetite for the limited offerings of the cafeteria, but at that time it was one of my few pleasures and was under threat, since you feel a kind of embarrassment when you are the only person eating somewhere. The moment I entered with the food, they'd show that they could smell it by emitting an annoying kind of sniffing sound, as though the pastries or the sandwiches were spoiling the air for them. Then, the moment a morsel entered your mouth, you'd feel you were being watched and that every sound was echoing off the walls, since they made hardly any noise themselves. Sometimes, if your stomach started to rumble, the atmosphere would become stiff with tension. It would have been less constrained if one of them had made a sarcastic comment or shown amazement at the rumblings but they contented themselves with making strange, pointless movements, such as one of them shaking the mouse in his hand or moving his chair in time to the noises just enough to let you know that he could hear them, that they had ruined his concentration, and that you'd better do something about it. It didn't help to calm their indignation that they knew you'd just eaten. On the contrary, it made things even tenser, since there was nothing about their bodies—so regular in the times at which they ate and shat—that would make any of them understand that sometimes the stomach rumbles just like that, for no reason, so they might think you were deliberately making it rumble simply to annoy them, as though it were an act of pure obscenity directed by you at them. They might even have made observations to Management concerning the matter—"The new employee's stomach rumbles more than it should!"—as my boss in that department once came and stood behind me, laid his hand on my shoulder, and asked, "Are you well?" and because I wasn't suffering from any other accompanying physical symptoms, I replied that I was. He then turned and looked in the direction of the other three for their confirmation that I was the subject of the observation. When their looks confirmed it, he patted me on the shoulder as though to say, "Pull yourself together!"

The only time they displayed open contempt for me was when I asked them something to do with a job I'd been given. It was an unspoken rule that it was shameful to ask questions: knowing how things work is a gift everyone is supposed to possess, and they always made it seem easy; in fact, you ought not to be working in that department at all if you weren't able to find the answers to everything on your own. So when I asked one of those silly new boy's questions that confirmed I was completely out of place in that specialized department, I heard them laugh for the first time, and their guffaws, contrary to my expectation, were boisterous, ringing, and so exultant in their disparagement of what I'd blurted out that one of them couldn't control himself and got up and told the supervisor, to give him a laugh too. Though when he came and heard the story, he didn't share in the laughter.

Instead, his face assumed a rigid expression that cancelled any room there might have been in my question for whimsicality, an expression that implied my ignorance would have serious consequences that one shouldn't belittle with sarcasm.

A while later, that same supervisor of mine informed me that I was being transferred to another department. One morning, his hand suddenly appeared on my shoulder and when I turned to face him, he gestured with his head to the small meeting room. I followed him and we sat down opposite one another. Earlier, he'd given me a task to do, so I thought it was just another ordinary work day for me in the department, which was why, when he led me to the room, I was totally unprepared, and it came out of the blue, in spite of all my earlier expectations.

The reason might have been that question, or the rumblings of my stomach. It might have been to do with the fact that one day I'd left before five, or maybe after five. It made no difference. It wasn't clear that he knew the reason either. He spoke in a roundabout, cryptic manner, placing his hand on the desktop and moving around a sheet of paper that had nothing to do with the matter at hand, as though drawing from it the gravitas, professionalism, and bureaucratic backup called for by the meeting. All the time he was speaking, he used the passive voice, giving one the impression that the decision wasn't his and, furthermore, that one would never be able, no matter how far one followed the thread, to get to the source of the decision within the company's administrative pyramid. The only thing that was clear, and that implicitly, was that it was a demotion, and one with which one would be branded for as long as one worked in that company and no matter how many times one moved from department to department. From now on, one would never be moved up, only down, to lower departments. That was what all his twisting and turning and reticence about revealing anything to do with the grounds was telling me: that there is no way to improve a first impression.

There was nothing personal about the transfer to another department in and of itself. Such adjustments happen all the time, everywhere. They're simply an administrative necessity in order to sift out the productive elite and get the less productive out of the way. What makes the punishment humiliating, however, is the total elimination of choice when it comes to your reactions, even if your preferred option would have been, had you known in advance, not to show any. The decision is communicated in the most discreet, concerned, and abbreviated fashion, as though it was something you just ought to feel embarrassed by, before hiding from sight.

In any case, in my book it was a move for the better. My place here, next to the printer, isn't bad, in comparison. I'm able, every now and then, to steal time for reading and I've begun to write regularly, though I have to be careful that the tapping of my fingers on the keys isn't heard too much as you never know whether this may not, if noticed, be counted against you. Whenever I feel I've attracted too much attention, I print some random piece of paper as camouflage, and stand up and retrieve it, to give the impression that what I'm writing has to do with work. I pretend to glance at the paper, then throw it into the recycling box. Everything that is printed has to be thrown away in the end but people are always printing, which works to my advantage on many occasions, as for example when I exploit the fact that I've stood up and go outside for a smoke.

Downstairs, I remind myself not to hang about too long in the outside courtyard as the glass façade only allows you to see out, and you can't see if there's anyone watching you from the elevator lobby. And there's always the chance you might run into one of the directors in the elevator on your way up or down and he'd fix you with a look that makes you feel your presence between floors is itself a breach of the rules; when no punishment follows, you still go on feeling that it's on its way. Perhaps all it takes is for you to have finally gotten used to its not coming for you to find, at that very moment, a hand on your shoulder, and its owner behind your back with an expression on his face that says, "The time of reckoning is come!"

I sit on the seats in the garden reserved for smokers. One cigarette, but the moment I finish it I feel like I've smoked a whole pack. I brace myself and stand up slowly. I drag myself along, one heavy step after another, like a wounded soldier dragging his injury through the battle—but I'm not fighting anything, so where does all this weakness come from?

In the lobby, I wait, once again, for the elevator. The tall glass façade lets in large quantities of sunlight, and on top of that there are bright interior lighting fixtures that dangle on cords just above head height, as though to dispel any remaining shadows. There are no seats, or even convenient places to stand. Just huge marble columns, regularly polished. The ceiling extends ever upward, into an extravagant distance. One gets the impression, from the terrifying height and from the absence of anything there to stand next to, that the place has been designed to make the individual appear the most insignificant thing in it.

Week 3

I'M TRYING TO GIVE UP smoking, and right now I'm distracting myself by writing, which could be more damaging to my health; my mother says I have to give up books and cigarettes, as though they were the same thing—"How much longer are you going to spend your money on things that harm you?" she asks. I argue with her as though she'd attacked the essence of my being, while secretly admiring her naïve intelligence, for literature and cigarettes really are the same. However, I have no desire to get into lengthy philosophizing, so let's stick to the facts.

I have stopped buying cigarettes and resist, with difficulty, the urge to take one from time to time from whomever. The advantage of the lobby's glass façade is that it lets you observe the outside courtyard, where people stand and smoke, which is its drawback too, if you want to give up. My lungs are no longer in the prime of their youth. I watch the older men going out to smoke throughout the day and say to myself, "How do they do it? Why isn't the scene that follows the finishing of their cigarette that of them dying as they gasp for air?" I've often wondered whether there isn't some secret recipe for keeping one's energy up or some intuitive health habit that everyone sticks to throughout their lives but that for some reason has never gotten through to me.

My capacity for writing, on the other hand, has been reinvigorated recently. I hadn't written for a long time, and I may never have written with the same fluency, but I spent the weekend burning to return and continue what I've begun over the past two weeks. This division of time seems to be easiest if I'm to put an end to long periods of not writing. It reminds me of my old enthusiasm for the weekly composition and expression class at school, which was perhaps the first time I discovered my fondness for writing. My adrenaline level surpassed even that for gym class, and I'd keep writing right up to the moment when the bell rang, then be amazed that the time had passed so quickly and wish that the classes for science, math, and other indigestible subjects could be swapped for more composition, instead of its being scheduled only once a week. It didn't matter what the topic was, or how exciting the story: what mattered was the continuous outpouring of phrases as one gave birth to another. For a child as withdrawn as me, it was one of life's great revelations.

When I moved to middle school, I was deprived of that habit of weekly writing as composition wasn't part of our schedule. From then on, I began writing at home, with greater freedom, and when I showed my mother some of my poems, she appeared happy with them, for in the arena of her competition with my uncles' wives as to which had the most talented son, my clumsy writings seemed like something she could use. Soon, my poems were being passed from hand to hand in the family, and when I greeted my uncles, one would address me as "the Poet," another ask, "Anything new?" and a third start reciting my unmetered verses out loud. Suddenly I found myself a target of embarrassing attention and comments among which it was hard to distinguish between the encouraging and the sarcastic, and right after this I stopped writing for a number of years.

Throughout that period, however, I kept up my reading, a habit that I was able to develop further, thanks to the volumes of the classics and the religious tracts in the library at home. We weren't a religious family but it was a fashion at the time to adorn houses with libraries of this sort, and I applied myself to them because we didn't have anything else; under their influence, I even went through a religious period during my adolescence. When I think of it now, though, my religiosity, in essence, didn't go beyond a kind of rebellion against my family, an objection to their lifestyle and its lack of spirituality. I used to feel jealous of my peers, whose fathers would beat them and tell them off for neglecting their prayers, seeing in such rebukes an expression of interest. And when my mother demonstrated a certain reserve toward my religiosity, even though she knew it wasn't something for which children were usually censured, I became more stubbornly observant, arguing to myself that it was important to "stand firm in the face of impediments" and rejoicing internally at the anxiety that it all caused her, as though it were an opportunity to subject her to a punishment I believed she deserved. In the end, I think, I just got bored. My rebellious inclinations were generally short-lived anyway.

My subsequent turning away from religion was accompanied by an increased interest in Western thought when I reached high school, which is to say when I began to enjoy enough independence to buy books for myself. Despite my random barging about from topic to topic and writer to writer, and my frequent inability to understand what they were talking about, I kept up those readings for a while, though I never managed to stumble across anything that really got through to me. There was this great gap between the life I wanted to lead and the one I was living, and I was desperate to fill it with experience, and that couldn't be done just by thinking. It could only be done by means of something that would break through to me in a tangible way, using words transparent enough to get under my skin. This happened the day I read *Hunger*. It clicked. That was all it took. Immediately, I was seized by a peremptory feeling that a new world had opened up before me.

I remember I finished the entire novel in a single day, during which I was so focused on reading I barely ate. The next day I woke up feeling sick and disturbed, my mind racing from hunger, prey to the same sensations experienced by the hero of the story and which Hamsun had drawn from his own life. Despite this, I found myself longing to undergo hardships more terrible than Hamsun's, if that would bestow on me the ability to write like him. That morning, unable to think about anything else, I prayed to God, with feverish intensity, that He punish me for my neglect of religion with a range of miseries and, in exchange, grant me the ability to give expression to the suffering with which He was about to reward me. It was almost like a vow and perhaps a kind of spiritual compensation, or alternative form of commitment.

I followed that novel with another. Once I learned that the destitute writer in *Hunger* had been influenced by the character of Raskolnikov, I buried myself in *Crime and Punishment* and fell mightily under its sway—the sway of its hero's thinking and his impetuous and passionate desire to immerse himself totally in experience. It even crossed my mind to commit some random murder, just to suffer Raskolnikov's torments and feel his internal conflicts within my own soul. In order, however, for God to grant me a real and not an artificial experience, I concluded, the Cruel Fates would have to throw something or other in my path, without any sinful effort on my part that would violate my vow to God.

Gradually, driven by these influences, the idea took on the form of an obsession for me. Pleasure came to reside in the conversion of everything around me into the lucidity and liveliness of the literary, and my mind began to apply a sort of writing exercise to everything I observed. When, however, I actually took up writing again, the results seemed meager and lame compared to what I was reading, something I attributed to the propitious circumstances and required Cruel Fates not yet having made an appearance. Before me still lay, as I thought, a long life of skills and experiences for me to acquire.

Naturally, my mother took a position against this new orientation, especially when my preoccupation with it increased—for throughout my college years and up to just before I got a job, I continued to spend most of my time at home, glued to books, and she couldn't hide her concern over this, as though, by staying at home like that, I was committing a secret sin, or spoiling something in the family order. At first, she'd caution me in a sarcastic tone that she tried to make as jokey as she could, aware that staying at home wasn't something that was usually disapproved of in sons. She'd point out, for example, that I'd be a great help to her, if I were a girl, following this with an exaggerated laugh to show that she wasn't serious but without losing her mocking look, which she thought would drive me to give up the books and spend more time outside. Her anxiety wasn't very different from what she'd earlier felt over my religiosity. In her eyes, all I'd done was swap one form of extremism for another.

It's not so different, these days, except that she has begun to direct her criticism at important matters and issues that can't be overlooked, such as my not going to visit my grandfather or not considering getting married yet or not making more of an effort to advance myself professionally. For a long time now, my relationship with her has been tainted by a kind of mutual criticism, which is why I try not to show that I care. I even transferred recently to a room at the back that had been my father's office: it's full of sunshine from mid-morning till sunset, which is the period I spend on reading, mostly on weekends as I rarely have enough energy to read during the week. To her, my behavior seems to represent a kind of challenge: instead of beginning to look for other things to do, outside the house, I've reinforced my presence within it, like someone confirming that he intends to stay a long time.

She's taken to coming in suddenly and standing at the door, like someone with an urgent request that requires an immediate answer. She silently rolls her eyes, and I understand that she's simultaneously criticizing the mess and renewing her disquiet at my move. She sees a book in my hand, but she asks me what I'm doing, simply to emphasize that the problem lies precisely in that. Quickly she adds that I'm burying myself in a world of illusions and made-up stories and cutting myself off from reality with foreign ideas. She looks at the bookshelves searching for inspiration and her eyes fall straightaway on a shelf holding a complete set—eighteen volumes with similar covers and different titles. She pulls one out and pronounces the name—*Du-stow-fski*—saying it wrongly but making it sound nice, then looks at me, waiting for a response, as though the name alone was an accusation. "A Russian writer," I say.

"And why do you have to expose yourself to all that misery?" she asks, as if grasping, with her innate intelligence, the nature of his stories and characters; or perhaps she's concluded that I'm exhausting myself by reading him just because his name is difficult.

I tell her he's a well-known writer, and that there's no intrinsic relationship between the difficulty of the name and the contents, as he wouldn't be any less complicated if his name was Sasha and it would probably still have been Dostoevsky if he'd grown up to become a peasant or a shoeshine man. She likes these kinds of discussions by nature and goes on at great length, inventing creative arguments. She's also stubborn enough to try to twist anything I say and starts making a quick examination of his books to find something to support her deduction, then reads out the titles one after another—"*The Idiot! Demons!! Humiliated and Insulted!!! Notes from Underground!!!! The House of the Dead!!!!!*"—and looks up at me with a movement that confirms that these titles are enough to bring her to her main point, which is: "How can you hope to be happy after all that?"

Our discussion now diverges, with me saying I'm happy with the way things are going and her shaking *The Idiot* in her hand and saying I have to wake up. The conversation heats up and is diverted from its original aims because it revolves around Dostoevsky, and I seem to have become one of the miserable Russian characters in his novels.

It could all have been different if she'd pulled out, for example, a book by Hemingway, with his joyous, solid personality, so accepting of life, not to mention his macho nature, always urging him to set off on adventures, win difficult prizes, and hunt things and love them and punch them, and wrestle even with bulls. And even if she disapproved of his long foreign name, I would have stuck out my chest and defended him, and she would have left, her confidence restored by talk of the energetic exuberance of his style, the positive impact of his message, and how for him life never took a wrong turn even when it went bad, and one could always keep up with its twists and turns and go with the flow, given determination and toughness, and I would have proposed she read *The Old Man and the Sea* to prove it. Or if she'd chosen Tanizaki's little book *In Praise of Shadows*, I would have had in it a solid argument against any criticism she might direct at my taste, since even when he's speaking of going to the lavatory, he puts everything into an authentically Japanese poetical context with a discretion devoid of any pretentiousness, vulgarity, or tendency toward misery. These were esthetics toward which no man could feel contempt.

Instead, though, and because her hand happened to fall on Dostoevsky alone, I am left at a loss as to what to say, and the situation turns into a terrible misunderstanding, and we shift into a long debate over "duties," and "family roles," and "personal responsibilities," and "important decisions," and "Look at your brother!" and "When are you going to visit your grandfather?" and "This is a mess," and the house and the room and "How much longer, son?" Then she goes, leaving the door ajar, and I feel that everything around me is at variance with my very nature.

There was never any way we could get along. Her idea of motherhood was tied to her feeling of guilt regarding her responsibility for me, as though I would one day hold her to account for failing to push me to higher levels of performance. She would often bring up my talent when I was young and how she used to boast of it in front of my uncles' wives, to use it against me as an argument for my buried ability to become something outstanding if I'd just stop being lazy, meaning really if I'd do anything other than become a writer. When I was rude to her, she'd pretend to understand and retreat a little before my short-lived fierceness. She'd calm down and turn aside, though only to return to the attack with greater fury and begin repeating, irritably, that there were some things she couldn't simply ignore, and ask me to get out of the house more, on this or that crrand, like a vulture kicking one of its young out of the nest for its own good.

Her concern that I visit my grandfather, specifically, was one of the things she could not give up on. When my father died, his brothers had supported us for a while by covering some of our expenses, and when relations broke down, even among themselves, my grandfather took it on himself to support us financially until my brother and I got jobs and my sister married. Thereafter, though, even though he went on giving my mother money voluntarily, even insisting when she refused, he still reproached me, every time I visited him, for not having made her independent of him, and it may be that he went on giving her money just so he could have something to blame me for. Anyway, this wasn't new, as he was always inventing new reasons to rebuke. My mother, on the other hand, still maintained the same esteem for my grandfather, which was reciprocated, and was always reminding me to visit him. In some way, he constituted for her a sort of compensation for the absence of my father, his son, and perhaps for the death of her own parents too.

Money was, in any case, the perennial problem. Even though we live relatively comfortably, anxiety over the future has always been there, especially now that the topic of my brother's getting married has come up. The latest plan requires that my mother move in with him afterward; the house will be sold and handed over to its new owner next winter, as soon as the wedding has taken place. This was planned with everybody's agreement, but our assent wasn't spontaneous: it had required the deployment of my sister's witchery.

Break. Yesterday I suddenly felt nauseous again the moment I got on to dealing with said sister. I would have avoided talking about her now if she hadn't come to see us again yesterday evening. Recently, she's taken to visiting us continually, to make sure the plan is working the way it's supposed to.

You can always tell she's coming from the way her heels rap on the stairs. When she enters, she'll have her headscarf, which she's just taken off, in her hand, her hair will be carefully coiffed, and her perfume will waft in with the air coming through the door. We only ever see her resplendently elegant, as though she's trying to prove something; often, she even wears large pearl earrings, one of which she has to take off when she talks on the telephone and put back when she replaces the receiver. She keeps her shiny legs crossed all the time she's talking on the telephone or to my mother, and will rush to wipe off her two-year-old daughter's snot, speak to her angrily, then go back to the sofa, next to my mother, and, crossing her legs again, continue her conversation but in a tone that makes you think she's still speaking to her daughter.

You can tell simply from a person's voice, and without regard to what it may be that he's chattering about, that he's just begun a new life, and her voice was confident, firm, and full of plans—the voice of a woman who has recently assumed a life of ease, her husband being a bank director and from a well-known and influential family.

At the beginning of the month, she pulled off, through her own efforts, my brother's engagement, having persuaded him of the suitability of the daughters of one of her husband's rich acquaintances and them of my brother's. To see the plan through, she comes and talks to him and to my mother about the arrangements for the wedding, her voice acquiring, when she does so, a certain loudness that is the result of her awareness of her responsibility as the official coordinator between the two families. The moment I enter the picture, though, that domineering voice falls to a lower register, guarded, equivocal, and almost cautious, and that's only when she's talking to others in my presence; when we're on our own, she and I, a certain tense, monotonous quiet comes over her—the special reserve you impose on yourself when you're with someone with whom you feel ill at ease.

In any case, her wariness was nothing new to me. When she gave birth to her daughter, for instance, she was afraid even to let me hold her, as though I might do so because I wanted to try it out and might drop her on her head just to see what would happen. The truth is, I held her because propriety requires that when you visit someone who's just given birth in the hospital you hold what they've produced, even if she will grow up to be a mass of snot, and I kissed the child out of good manners, simply because I couldn't find appropriate petting words to say. All the same, I'm sure I looked to her like King Kong, the giant gorilla who gazes with curiosity at a beautiful young girl settled heedlessly on his palm, then runs off with her. My sister stretched out her arms from the bed for me to give the child back to her in what seemed a supplication, even though she tried to appear natural and affectionate; perhaps it had in fact occurred to her that I might at any moment open the door, run away with her daughter, and climb to the roof of the hospital the way King Kong climbs to the roof of the Empire State Building at the end of the movie.

Even before she got married, my sister was extremely careful to make sure our paths crossed as infrequently as possible. If we woke at the same time, she would go back to sleep, and if I came out of one bathroom, she had to use the other, and if I sat on the couch, she would sit on a chair, and if I sneezed, she wouldn't say, "Bless you," and if I entered after her, she wouldn't hold the door for me, and if I went out in front of her, she'd hang back so that I couldn't hold the door for her. She never once came knocking on the door of my bedroom and I doubt if she knows what it looks like on the inside. On evenings when we were the only ones at home, we'd communicate by phone. Do you want something for dinner? Yes. No. And that was the end of the conversation. Only rarely would she be the one to feel hungry, if I was the only person she had to share a meal with. One day I proposed to her that we eat at a restaurant and she asked doubtfully, "Why? And how? And what would we do?" and refused categorically, as though the invitation were a cunning trick of mine to kidnap her. When I happened to drive her somewhere, we'd say nothing while we were in the car, and even while she was saying nothing, I'd feel that she had reservations about my taste in music, or my driving, or the mess on the floor. She'd express this by frowning or staring continuously out of the window or kicking at things on the floor throughout the drive.

The floor of my car was clear proof that I wasn't dating any girls, not because I didn't want to but because the whole act of getting to know one didn't suit my personality. You are required to be charming, attentive, and full of sensitivity when you're with them, to convince them that you're trustworthy, and this without the girl doing anything in return. In fact, just by the power invested in her as a female, she enjoys an innate right to have you acknowledge her presence with amusing sallies and by opening interesting topics for discussion, keeping the conversation flowing and easy, making your cultivated ideas and principles clear, throwing out words with a perfect American accent, and proving that you're accustomed to spontaneously talking to women; otherwise, she'll either turn her eyes away from you toward the wall or the window, giving you the opportunity to remove yourself with your dignity intact, or bury her face in her smart phone in the hope that by the time she raises it again you'll have gone away. Sometimes one of them will suddenly close her abaya while talking to you, or suddenly pull up the upper part of her dress to cover her cleavage, even if it wasn't visible to start with, even though you rarely break your habit of avoiding staring into others' eyes when you speak. I also think that if I was entirely innocent, they'd find something nice about my awkwardness and perhaps be so charmed by my embarrassment that they'd be driven to get beyond it, maybe embrace it and take it by the hand. But it's obvious that behind this same embarrassment I harbor a kind of viciousness, a wicked mind, a greedy curiosity, and a readiness to plunge headlong into strange fantasies. So, yes, it would be easier for one of them to date King Kong, if she were given the choice.

Anyway, to get back to my sister. Why, I wonder, do I always wander off into other subjects when I write about her?

My sister was always one of those girls whose beauty imposes itself on everyone, so people find themselves seeking to please her. It didn't matter, from this perspective, whether it was her father or her two brothers; in fact, it may be that the closer one was to her by birth, the stronger the effect of her domination. Naturally, it wasn't like that when we were small, and I didn't really notice till the day she got engaged.

I was twenty-two at the time, and she was two years younger. I was sitting playing host, with my brother, to her fiancé, in our cramped little reception room and the fiancé was sitting waiting, with a conceited smile, confident that he would get what he'd come for. He began asking me about my forthcoming graduation and employment ambitions, questioning me with the kind of artificial kindness that exposes a lack of interest. I, for my part, wasn't interested in his type either. I'd heard his name and position earlier, and that an alliance with his family wasn't something to be passed up. My sister had agreed immediately to see him.

When she entered, her figure was more curvaceous and full, her movements more delicate, and her glances more diffident than I was used to; indeed, there was an extra beauty that she had, perhaps, spent her life carefully concealing just so that she could cause astonishment when she finally revealed it on just such an occasion. At that moment I didn't feel I was any less a stranger to her than the other, who was seeing her for the first time. In fact, I felt she was such a stranger to me that I might have been watching an advertisement on the television. The whole situation was disturbing and I sat there with my head bowed and gaze averted, seized by a mixture of bedazzlement at her beauty and estrangement at its unexpected appearance. No more than a minute had passed before I removed myself from the room, as though I no longer had anything to do with any of it.

Sometimes, under her domination, my own understanding of myself becomes confused, and, without being aware of it, I suddenly start seeing myself as she sees me. I am therefore compelled to expatiate a little here to explain my position and clarify what was going on in my head that day, despite my earlier determination not to get bogged down in philosophizing.

Our warring goes back to the days of our childhood for the very reason that it was a natural concomitant of our bond of blood. There was nothing to indicate we were siblings beyond this constant and ugly quarreling, which also made our dealings with one another more spontaneous and candid. That day, when she came in, presenting that picture to both us and her fiancé, all of that was threatened. There was nothing left in her appearance that gave any indication of the screaming, the exchanges of insults, and sometimes even the kicking, hair-pulling, throwing of stuff, scrapping, and all the other things through which I'd become used to viewing her. Everything about her had begun to contradict the image that had made her my sister and not some girl no different from any other in whose presence I could feel awkward.

I tried to maintain my old way of treating her, but it was clear that there was something artificial in my aggressiveness toward her, something that drove me to be pleasanter, less fierce, and more decorous with her, as befits a gentleman dealing with a young lady. Our confrontations decreased little by little, but that didn't bring with it any greater affection. On the contrary, a vast gap imposed itself between us in place of the quarrels, to the point that our lives barely intersected anymore. She was aware of this difference in how I treated her and grasped that it was a product of that sudden change in her appearance, and this only made the situation more embarrassing, because she, whose interpretations always tended to assume things that would increase her distaste for me, discovered in my new way of treating her something sick on my part. And when I tried to prove to her that things were not as she thought, I went overboard in creating distance between us to convince her of how wrong was her interpretation of my intentions, which resulted only in further failure of communication. Then she got married, and it became reasonable to accept, given that she'd moved to another house, that estrangement was the way we naturally behaved toward one another, each pretending that all that had happened was that we'd become too old for clashes of that sort. All the same, as soon as we were obliged for some reason or other to communicate at close quarters, something unsavory rose to the surface.

During her repeated recent visits, as my brother's wedding draws closer, she has had frequent opportunities to be on her own with my mother. The moment I enter, she abruptly stops talking to her. She continues to interpret my consent to the plan with her usual suspicion, especially given that I haven't made any serious effort to find a new place to live, though this is, from my perspective, simply a matter of procrastination. And over everything, there is my mother's strange feelings of guilt toward me for having sold the house, as though, as soon as they move and I leave, I will be without a roof over my head, and this arouses in my sister the suspicion that I, specifically, am the one who's going to ruin everything.

Yesterday I overheard her, from somewhere she couldn't see me, talking in the loud voice she's developed in her big house. "I chose her myself," she was saying. "A well-bred girl. She'll look after you very nicely." Referring to me, she said, "He isn't a young man any longer. He should be left to sort himself out on his own. If he doesn't want to get married, that's his decision, and he'll have to put up with the inconveniences of that on his own. You've put up with him long enough." My mother was nodding and crying. "You can't take care of him more than you have done. God knows, you've put up with him long enough!" my sister repeated, while my mother wept and wailed, saying, "God knows, I've put up with him long enough!"

After my sister left, my mother threw herself into my path with those brimming eyes of hers. She began blaming me for being negligent and putting things off, as though all I wanted to do was punish her by throwing her failures in her face. There was no possibility of mutual understanding. She expressed her worries about me through contempt, and I gave her back disdain, for the same reason. Both of us were wanting in gentleness.

Week 5

I WAKE IN A SWEAT. Nausea, headache, blood on the pillow, pains in the joints—as though I'd fought a battle in my sleep. Nothing new, nothing serious. I piss, take a shower, clean my teeth, get dressed with the usual haste but without enough energy to gain any time. I stumble while putting my pants on, fall, stand up, catch my breath, and hurry out.

I arrive at the office later than usual. I find two stickers on my screen: maybe he's trying to tell me I've gone too far this time. I crumple them in my hand and leave them on the desktop. I get a bottle of mineral water and gulp it down in one go. This is my only prescription against exhaustion—lots of water to energize the circulation. It's a technique I learned as a child so I could rally my forces after nosebleeds and get back to playing before my nose could start bleeding again. When I was nine, I underwent a painful operation to cauterize the vein inside my nose and seal it, and every time I asked the doctor when it would be over, his answer was never less than "Five minutes."

It's the only operation I've ever had. Maybe I need to repeat it, because the nosebleeds have come back again lately.

I get another bottle and drink some more, watering a neglected cactus on the desk with the last drops. I like to think that the reason it's turned yellow is that it, like me, doesn't belong in this place. Maybe I even forget to water it regularly just to fit this idea of mine: that the wretched cactus is, is it not, a perfect embodiment of the link between literature and reality?

I can hardly take anything but water: my appetite doesn't tolerate eating early, these days. I am indebted to the Old Man next to me for paying no attention to the noises produced by my empty stomach. When I turn to look at him, I don't know if he notices that I'm scrutinizing him: there is just the same gaze, fixed on his screen, and his gentle moving of the mouse, without any clear indication that he is actually working on anything. Sometimes it occurs to me to have a conversation with him, to find out more about him. Where do you live? How do you spend your day? Tell me about your family. Things of that sort. But I prefer not to disturb the silent harmony between us. Once two people who are sitting next to one another start talking, it's difficult for them to go back to not talking with the same degree of comfort.

I open a novel on the screen, choosing it arbitrarily from a list I've downloaded from the internet. I immerse myself in reading, while keeping my hand on the mouse. Whenever anyone goes past to retrieve his papers from the printer, I immediately change the screen to the news page, which I scan absentmindedly, feeling far from everything that is going on— nuclear threats, terrorist attacks, a prisoner strike, greenhouse gases, gasoline prices, El Clásico. This kind of reading doesn't require the same degree of discretion. I've long believed that the reading of literature, specifically, ought to take place in secret, maybe because it's associated in the popular imagination with heightened feeling, burning emotions, and impressionability, even though, in fact, these have never been obvious qualities of mine.

I remember that one day someone rushed past behind me to retrieve his papers, and before I'd succeeded in changing the page on my screen, he'd caught sight of it and realized from the way the lines were arranged that I was reading a poem. To show his admiration for this activity, he exclaimed, in melodramatic fashion, "All hail the readers! All hail the poets!"

His voice was sufficiently audible to attract the attention of the employees sitting in the row in front of me, and they immediately turned around. They were two dolts of approximately my age who seemed always to be waiting to talk to me, should the opportunity arise, so I had no choice but to turn to the histrionic character standing behind me with a mocking expression indicative of my contempt for his rhetorical exclamation. "How highfalutin!" I murmured, turning my eyes back to the screen and attempting, with this sarcasm, to distance myself from presumptuous people of his sort and join the clan of those who affect indifference, or even hostility, toward literary concerns, as though my reading of the poem had involved nothing more than the sort of quick glance one gives an invoice one finds in one's pocket. The dolts smiled as they turned back to look straight ahead once more, but I couldn't make out if it was a mocking or a complicit smile. I felt as though something in my expression must have betrayed me and shown them that, in my attempt to ward off suspicion, I was no less inauthentic than he.

Finally I go through my work mail. I discover that one of the two yellow stickers my supervisor left me this morning contains a notice that I have to attend some meeting. It's supposed to be something important as they're going to invite more than one Outstanding Employee to tell his success story. Only new employees of my generation are invited and attendance is obligatory.

The conference hall contained approximately two types of person—the successful and the would-be successful. And then there was me. Given that I was a relatively new employee, it was no coincidence that I'd been put in the would-be-successful category, as Management always assumes that the employee seeks to achieve self-realization through service to it. The would-be-successful were excitedly taking their seats a quarter of an hour before the meeting, reinforcing this assumption.

Their eyes shone as they awaited the success stories that would change their lives, and might even have already started changing them before they heard them, as the stories all resembled one another and it was easy to work out their endings, because all of them—surprise! surprise!—ended in success.

One of them asked if he might sit next to me, and the smell of his perfume began to penetrate my nose, my eyes, my brain, the desk, the girl sitting next to him on the other side, and the jinn in their distant abode beyond the veil. As soon as he'd sat down, he took a deep breath and said, in perfect English, "Isn't it refreshing to find oneself surrounded by young people?" as though urging us to inhale more of his perfume. After he'd asked his question, he went on gazing at me for a while, and I realized that it was addressed to me. I didn't know how to answer. Was he looking to me to embody his idea of young people? When he received no response, he directed his conversation to the girl. I've always been a bad conversationalist, especially when I don't say anything, and I wondered whether the girl had left an empty seat between us deliberately because she could read that trait in my face. I wasn't the ideal choice for whiling away the time with a side conversation before the meeting.

I began looking around me at the hall. The table was oval in design, allowing me to take in at a glance all the participants. I deduced that I was the only one who hadn't had enough sleep the night before. This was clear from their countenances. It was also clear that I was the only who'd had trouble putting his pants on that morning. Every male was smartly dressed, brightly polished, exceptionally well turned out, and wore his clothes with style. The only explanation for how they could maintain this degree of care for detail was that all they did after returning from work was prepare for the coming day; in fact, they looked as though they'd been preparing for this appearance their whole lives. The tabletop was supported on legs that allowed the shining shoes and matching socks beneath it to be seen, and these, the moment I saw them, convinced me that their underpants too must be smart and of colors that went with the rest of their look. I couldn't actually see their underpants but the look on their faces showed me that they were happy with them and prepared for anything, so that if I were to ask one to show them to me, he'd get up straight away and say, "Of course! Observe how well-matched my underpants are! I have nothing to hide."

The girls looked as though they'd just walked out of an advertisement for washing powder, with their ironed multicolored abayas, their head coverings precisely adjusted at their temples, and their hair that projected just enough to show that it was carefully arranged under the scarf. Their faces glowed brightly under the influence of the secrets of modern cosmetics, at which one can only guess. They were distributed among the men in such a way as to give the impression that they were no fewer in number than their male counterparts, as though they had planned this distribution together before entering. There was a kind of affectionate collusion among them from the moment they entered the hall, even if they had never met, and when one observed the kindness, gaiety, and diffidence in their conversations, their spontaneity and lack of restraint as they introduced themselves to one another, so gently and harmoniously, one failed to understand all those wild stories about girls' jealousy and underhandedness, their malicious setting of traps for one another. At this moment, their communication seemed to belong, at first glance, to a world of peace and intuitive concord whose intimacy nothing could disturb. As I listened more, however, to the side conversations, I managed to work out that their distribution through the hall had not come about as randomly as I had first believed. Nor was it restricted to the girls. It appeared that everyone knew he would find himself in that hall alongside his opponents, the people with whom he would one day contend for promotion, and that, at the same time, this meeting was seen as an opportunity by some to build up a network of relationships he might use in the future to arrive at his goal. Maybe it was the topic of this particular meeting that had sharpened such forward thinking, since merely seeing the speakers standing in front of them incited people to parade the successes that set them apart from their peers and set to work immediately on achieving the same level of distinction.

When the speeches began, and everyone was absorbed in listening, I let my mind wander to other things. I began amusing myself by composing a short story in my mind and plunged headlong into the shaping of its events, characters, and dialogs, determined to write it down as soon as I got back to my desk. The story, in brief, dealt with an employee who suddenly finds himself in some meeting, without knowing how, as though he had been hypnotized and led to the hall, where he wakes to find that the doors have been locked. When the employee decides to protest against being there, he can't find an acceptable point at which to interrupt the proceedings, because it's a respectable, well-organized meeting and anyone who wants to leave can do so only in accordance with the preset agenda and the rules that everyone has undertaken to observe. When he stares at the others, he finds that they too are bound, just like him, by those same rules, the difference being that they seem happy to be forced to be there, in the hall with the grand doors that anyone might be pleased to find locked against him.

A storm of laughter pierced my ears and brought me back to the present, and I immediately thought I should include this detail in the story: that the laughter stopped and started to a rhythm that seemed to have been agreed on by all. I thought too that I might call the employee K, if Kafka didn't mind. I thought of calling the story "The Conspiracy Hall," as a play on "the conference hall" or something stupid like that.

I listened in a little to what was going on. The speakers who were telling their success stories were professionals, and eloquent, and used their hands in ways that showed they had taken intensive courses in public speaking, while their Western accents gave the impression that they had studied abroad for at least seven years, a fact also to be divined from their repeated references to their academic qualifications. They chose their words, and their pauses, with precision and skill; even most of their spontaneous jokes seemed calculated, as though they had prepared them ahead of time. Everyone was aware that there was a time for fun and a time to be serious, and it rarely happened that one of them would say something funny at an inappropriate moment, or laugh at a serious one, or even fail to chuckle at some quip, for to do so would be no less serious a mistake than to laugh at something serious. I also noticed that one of them kept looking at me with a doubtful expression because I remained despondent during things that everyone else thought worthy of a cheerful response.

I felt short of breath and in need of air, plus I needed to urinate after drinking all that water—sufficient reason for me to consider it an emergency requiring permission to leave. It's good that I've stopped smoking or I don't know what state my lungs would be in now.

In the bathroom, I urinated at length. I rolled up my sleeves and washed my hands and face. A bruise had formed on my arm as a result of my fall that morning. I'd fallen on my forearm, but the bruise extended to part of my wrist as well. It was a contused red color, though it didn't hurt enough to mention. I took a deep breath and gazed inquiringly into the mirror, as though I hadn't looked at myself in years.

Apart from a certain pallor, the result of too little sleep and bad nutrition, I didn't look too bad, generally speaking—not completely Bohemian. At least I've always managed to stay clean without having to advertise that fact by sharing my perfume with everyone in the same zip code. All the same, I don't see the need to shave every day, often leave my fly open, and sometimes dress like a bum. Each morning, I look in the drawer for a matching pair of socks, then lower the bar to trying to find two of the same color, then submit to wearing one navy with one black, or one brown and one blue, or other similar colors like that. My shoes I haven't changed for two years and the dirt on them has perhaps imparted to them a classically elegant look; that, at least, is what I hope. I've often attributed why I postpone buying a new pair to the high cost of good shoes and the difficulty of finding any, these days; I'm responsible for the expenditures of a family, partially at least, and I don't possess the means to squander my money on such luxuries. Another part of me is aware that it all has something to do with a feeling that new shoes would alter my appearance and perhaps lead to comment.

I urinated once more to make sure I wouldn't have to leave and go to the bathroom yet again; once was the maximum number of times that one could acceptably leave a two-hour meeting. I buttoned my cuffs, made sure I'd closed my fly, and stared again into the mirror, as though I hadn't just done the same. For a while, after resuming my seat, I made a show of following the flow of the conversation with interest. I imagined that people were still watching me after I returned, and that some might have thought, given how long I'd stayed in the bathroom, that I'd had a bowel movement. Immediately, this idea made me blush with a silly kind of embarrassment, which I then couldn't get rid of, even though I realized how childish it was, and eventually I felt it reflect itself in my features to such an extent that it would be difficult thereafter to repudiate the charge. Sometimes I wish I could just control my facial expressions so that they reflect what I want them to in any situation; after that, everything would go well on its own.

The microphone began to circulate among the audience so that they could ask questions and give their opinions following the speeches. There was still half an hour set aside for discussion, which was enough time for everyone to speak, if it was divided evenly. Some, however, used the segment as a golden opportunity to push themselves forward, impress the speakers, and attract the attention of the rest. When my turn came, I passed the microphone to the perfume bottle sitting next to me, who took a deep breath, released it into the microphone, and said, "Isn't it wonderful to find oneself surrounded by young people?"

He said this in a tone that gave the impression he'd just thought of it, and everyone nodded appreciatively, smiling in agreement. Then he spoke briefly of his personal experience of success, even though no one had asked him to do so, just to show how appropriate it would be if he were to be among the speakers next year. After him, the girl next to him gripped the microphone with fingers covered in rings and meted out lots of praise for the speakers, appearing so smitten you'd think she'd never heard a success story before. This made them very happy; they always became more cheerful and attentive when the microphone passed to a girl.

In any case, I was no better than them: it looked to me as though she was gripping the microphone like a hard black phallus in her beringed fingers. Her excited and optimistic speech, however, with its insistence on the word "inspiration," drove the thought from my mind.

Anyway, let's get back to the story, I thought, as there was still some time left. If it could have a good ending, it might be the only worthwhile thing to come out of the meeting.

So K finds himself obliged to follow the rules of the hall in order to find a way to leave. It follows that he, like the rest, has to wait for his turn to speak so as to be permitted to protest his presence there. The dilemma is that he is not, at the same time, allowed to take part. This doesn't happen in an explicit, open fashion: rather, when his turn comes, he is waylaid by sudden interruptions that prevent him from speaking. The man next to him, for instance, keeps inhaling though his nose and the sound is so loud it blocks K's ability to hear or follow the proceedings. Also, when the man inhales, he draws in through his huge nostrils all the oxygen surrounding K, leaving the latter in a state of nausea, exhaustion, and shortness of breath, further disturbing his concentration so that he misses his turn at the microphone and has to wait for a new round. These rounds take a long, long time before they start over. As a result, as soon as a round begins, everyone is in a hurry for his turn to come, and is in fact happy when someone else misses his and with each successive turn the microphone passes among them faster and faster so that some can prevent others from getting it, and in the end its passing lasts only an instant. The only way to stop it is to be in a state of perfect readiness and have something prepared with which to open one's comments, even before it's one's turn.

The moment the meeting broke up, I moved fast to exit before everyone else. Hurrying out was the only form of protest I allowed myself. It occurred to me that if I'd attended a meeting of this sort when at the peak of my intellectual zeal a few years ago, I'd have felt a desire to ruin it. When my turn came to speak, I would have thought nothing of smiling sarcastically throughout. I might even have prepared in my head an oration that would undermine those success stories of theirs, imagining at the same time the multiplying reactions and the admiring silence that would fall over the place—plus perhaps some of the inevitable objections and expressions of annoyance from the girl with the rings and her like, though these would only confirm the truth of what I was saying. Probably, though, I wouldn't have put any of these fantasies into action or made any orations. I'd have left, privately ecstatic at the perfect statement I'd imagined in my mind, as though I'd been wrestling with an enemy made of wind.

I return to my desk and find the Old Man absorbed in work, as usual, as though he weren't going to retire at the end of the month. I say hello, he returns the greeting in his familiar wan voice, perhaps unaware that I've already greeted him once that morning. Only occasionally does he follow his greeting with a small nod, perhaps in acknowledgment of the fact that I don't distract him with conversations. Our possibilities for communication go no further than this but in an unspeaking and simple way I feel that the alienation of the one mirrors that of the other. I think of asking him what he's going to do when he retires but prefer to let that go too.

I consider getting down to work too but once more distract myself by writing down the story that I'd amused myself making up during the meeting. I find it impossible to arrive at a convincing ending, so sentence it to oblivion. It lacked originality, in any case, like most of my conscious attempts to make use of what goes on around me. What do I lack? Inspiration? And how does one grasp something as evanescent as that?

I've always found serious writing hard work, and it may be the most difficult profession in the world, as says Hemingway, who fought wars, moved around the world, hunted, boxed, performed various harsh, demanding feats of endurance, and was never at a loss to describe anything, or so he claims. I'd cut off my right arm to write like him, but how can I? I've traversed a little more than a quarter of a century without a single important thing happening in my life or in the lives of those around me or in any city I've lived in, and I've only traveled in the immediate vicinity, so to what personal experience can I turn, and how am I to get to that fertile ground where writers find something to say? When I'm older and try to write about this period of my life, what will I remember? My endless personal absence from my own memory! The void in it will be filled by the long days of work, without any clear remembrance of their details, just that feeling of wasting time, of exhaustion, sleeplessness, and endless clicking on the mouse.

When the thought of all other writers depresses me, Kafka is my sole consolation. I imagine him working busily all day in his office and his supervisor coming up behind him and placing his hand on his shoulder, when all he wants is a holiday in which he can be free to write his novels, even though he was incapable of finishing them even when he did have free time. His diaries were the final refuge in which he could transcend his extreme self-criticism and perfectionism; in them, he maintains a sober style worthy of the literary status that he will one day acquire, when everything of his is published. In the end, though, he's Kafka, and he brought great stories, letters, and novels to consummation, even if they were unfinished. But what have I achieved till now?

From the time I became conscious of myself, I was consumed by a special feeling that I was older than my age and that I'd acquired a maturity my peers hadn't found time to. I felt I possessed the will to become something great, to change the world, or some crap like that. I even wanted to grow up fast, so that I could become worthy of my ambitions. Little by little, however, I ceased to be convinced that I could bring about any effective change in the world around me. Indeed, any efforts I made became restricted to turning in on myself so as to prevent the world from exercising any effective change on me. When I heard an old person talking about how age was just a number and how he felt as if he was still in his twenties, and repeating expressions like "You're only as old as you feel," it seemed to me sad and embarrassing, and I'd think about the multiple levels of self-deception he'd had to master weaving to believe such claims were true. Inwardly, I used to say, "I'll never let that happen to me. The passing of time will never delude me as it does others." And I kept adding to my supply of knowledge so that I could get a head start on what others only found out after it was too late.

I went through my school years clinging to the following idea: that I could spring the snares of advancing age and protect myself from its subsequent sorrows. Even when I found myself on the battlefield of university education, acting in a way that didn't resemble my own idea of myself, I continued to keep alive inside me the voice that said I wasn't made for this and that ahead lay some turning that would take me back to the road I ought be on. I was so certain that this idea would be fulfilled that I didn't take seriously any obstacle that might lead me away from my path, and even when I was forced to take this job, with all the evidence of failure it implied, I continued to treat it as a necessary evil, just an obligatory preparatory step toward my waiting destiny. This gave me the ability to put up with any situation and to overcome it by analyzing it mentally when on my own. In fact, I was prepared to bear the cruelest forms of misery and frustration, and all the dips in the road, because they would form a fertile experience from which I could later benefit.

Three years in this place were enough to provide me with, and then embed within me, repeated instances of the true nature of these pretensions. I finally realized that I was among the most backward and least mature of my contemporaries and that I'd let life pass me by while preoccupied with not being taken in by its outward forms or, rather, by belittling its practical demands and responsibilities.

I saw others performing their jobs, integrating into this fabric, and taking their first steps on the paths on which they saw their future selves, while I couldn't stop thinking, How did I end up here, and how can I protest without being crushed, and how can I find a way out? All the same, part of me still believed that I'd be leaving soon and that the only thing stopping me was that I hadn't yet found my excuse. I didn't even stick a card with my name on it on my desk, because not doing so continued to reinforce my feeling that my presence in the department was temporary, even though this did elicit some comment from Management.

I get agitated when I have a bad day, but at least this one is drawing to a close. And perhaps my goal in writing shouldn't go further than this: to make time pass as quickly as possible. But I wonder how much longer I can maintain this routine.

I stand up to take a little exercise and, as soon as I do so, feel dizzy. I make for the bathroom and it occurs to me to take another look at my arm. When I pull up my sleeve, I wince at the sight. The bruise, which has spread up the rest of my arm, is dark, bluish, and loathsome, as though I were sick with something more than just this job.

Week 7

I SCROLL THROUGH THE NEWS on my laptop, read a bit, then write, as though still at the office.

The fever began last week. I bore it, as usual, using painkillers, but my temperature continued to rise. Then, a few days ago, I woke to find I'd completely lost my voice. My brother took me to the emergency room at dawn and my mother came with us. They said I was burning up. I received a tranquilizer shot and some tests were carried out. They said the doctor would see me in the morning but I insisted on going home. I began to feel better and my voice came back somewhat, but I was forced to take another week off work. I didn't go back to the hospital to get a sick-leave permit, so the days will be deducted from the balance of my annual leave, if the director agrees.

I haven't used up much of my vacation time so far, thanks to the habit of the aforementioned bewattled director of refusing long holidays. All the same, I still harbor fantasies of saving up the balance for a long journey abroad one day. From time to time, I search the internet for tourist spots in Prague or St. Petersburg or wherever some other writer who has influenced me was born. I often recall, avidly, the endings in which the hero determines to leave suddenly to liberate himself from the ties that bind him, like at the end of *Hunger* or *Portrait of the Artist as a Young Man*, whose last paragraph I remember well: "Welcome, O Life! I go to encounter for the millionth time the reality of experience." This is what the young Joyce wrote before roaming Europe and ending up with Heming-way in Paris, which is perhaps why I'm considering that as one possibility. Thanks to Tanizaki, I think too of Japan, but the distance and cost are obstacles to its inclusion in my plans. Every time it crosses my mind, I think of something I read in some story: "Everyone should have in his life a place he thinks about, learns about, and maybe longs for, but will never visit."

When dreams of travel seem unattainable, I take refuge in another kind of fantasy—imagining that a terrible disaster befalls me and denies me any hope of a happy life. This idea is usually accompanied by a degree of masochism, as I find myself taking pleasure in the particulars of my adaptation to the disaster and how it will eventually bear fruit in my life. For example, after my temporary dumbness during the last few days, it seemed to me that it wouldn't be such a bad idea to remain dumb forever. First, the company would be obliged to dispense with my services and to compensate me, in addition, with a pension because they'd have to dismiss me on the grounds of disability. Second, I'd be excused the visits and social duties, where I'd always felt I was betraying myself. And if this communicative atrophy had its negative aspects, I could take advantage of it by expending all my expressive energies on writing, and perhaps new powers over the written word would be born of my inability to utter it. Furthermore, dumbness specifically, compared to deafness, blindness, and other afflictions, would leave me still able to enjoy to the full books, films, and music, and would not rob me of any of the receptive senses those require, so I'd never be left with nothing to entertain myself with throughout the day. That would provide me with justification for sinking into a comfortable, quiet isolation, which was the most beautiful thing about the idea—the possibility of using circumstances as an excuse against the voices that demand one rise to meet their expectations. And if some imbecile were to say, "It's not a great loss. We didn't use to hear much from you anyway," I could always kick him in the testicles or give him the finger, since such things would be excusable now that I'd been deprived of other means of expression with which to defend myself.

This wasn't the only childish idea to keep me company during my illness. Last week, I put to the test various forms of the saying "A mother's favorite child is her sick child." My mother had devoted a great deal of attention to me in the hospital, sitting sadly at the end of the bed and constantly placing the back of her hand against my forehead to measure my temperature. As soon as I opened my eyes, though, I'd find her teary, mournful look reproaching me: "Why are you sick? Why did you wake your brother at three in the morning? Why weren't you a girl?" Memory quickly brings before my eyes a scene from my early adolescence, when my body had begun to develop and she was holding my arm and saying, "What strong boy's arms!" though I could see the grief in her eyes. I remember it well because we'd stopped touching one another sometime before that, even if her touch, that day, was affectionate.

My older brother had always been her favorite son. I didn't feel there was any injustice in that, as her bias had its justifications; I even encouraged it in some fashion as it distracted her from concentrating her observation on me and her insistence on evaluating every step I took. I wanted to be noticed in some special way, but I didn't want at all to be the one who attracted the most attention. It was an instinct that was part of my character: I was always embarrassed when I was obliged to be at the forefront in any of life's arenas. This reminds me of a study that says that the second-born in the family always strives instinctively to marginalize himself. Or could it be that, by so doing, he strives to distinguish himself?

In any case, I owe my brother a lot for arriving before me. It would be difficult to imagine the extent of the pressures I'd be obliged to withstand if I were the eldest of my siblings. The fact is, I'm not the sort who wakes up at dawn to take someone to some wretched hospital. He, though, being the head of the family following my father's death, has been in a permanent state of following up on things, heightened alertness, and pursuit of the common good. In addition to his duties to the household, his responsibilities in his new role as the head of a family include, for example, the building of social relations, to preserve what standing is left to us now that our uncles have parted ways. Even when my sister proposed his fiancée to him, he showed more enthusiasm for her family, because of its standing, reputation, and wealth, than he did for the girl herself.

I share in the material responsibilities insofar as I can. We spend our two salaries almost equally on the requirements of the household, over and above my father's pension. Yet even while that's enough from his side, from mine it's always characterized as insufficient. There is a simple explanation for this: my setting aside of professional ambition reduces the value of my participation, even if I offer most of what I earn. My brother, on the other hand, is forever taking training courses, studies for his master's degree after work, and expends all his energy on acquiring certificates, salary increases, and promotions. Even though he has yet to get to where he wants to be, his persistent striving to improve himself has always made him the object of support and respect, especially from my sister: he meets the criteria of her social circle, which links an individual's highest value to his professional success.

I confess this makes me a little jealous sometimes, but I go on treating the matter the way I do my mother's preference for him, that is, as the natural equilibrium by which our roles have to be distributed in keeping with the differences in our natures. In particular, his calm, peaceable nature has often helped me not to take my jealousy more seriously, and it is thanks to this that my relationship with him has remained, since infancy, free of the competitiveness, the attempts at domination, and the provocations that usually occur between brothers. The age difference between us is only two years and there is nothing, on the surface, to indicate any fundamental differences. Our childhood was largely shared: we slept in the same room, went to the same school, practiced the same activities after school. Together we learned to ride a bicycle and play soccer, and I would always imitate him at social events and dinners, so that I could learn how somebody my age was supposed to behave. Taken as a whole, one could say that my childhood was less miserable and confused thanks to his presence in it, as we complemented one another comfortably. Later, however, that all changed. It's strange to track what different paths two quiet persons may take, however closely they may resemble one another in their quietness.

These days, he's taken to entering my room suddenly, just to reassure himself that everything is as it should be. All it takes him is one glance before his discomfort at being there becomes obvious. The moment he opens the door, he's taken aback by the huge number of boxes, randomly distributed, most of which are still where I put them when I moved in. To progress through the room, you have to walk carefully through the boxes, as though you might just step on a basket of eggs. Usually, therefore, he contents himself with rolling his eyes in distaste, perplexed at such a way of living. It's a look he's managed to keep intact from the time when he found out, during our adolescence, that I'd started smoking.

I seem weird to him, a person with no scruples about breaking taboos, just because I can't see what would prevent me; indeed, he's so sure that I perform forbidden acts in total secrecy, he thinks that if he looks more closely at the stuff around me he'll discover confirmation for his fears and his wariness. When he can't think of anything to say to me, he'll start asking about anything he can see in my proximity—"What's this glass of milk?"—and stare at me with an expression that implies that the strangeness lies in the glass, not in the question. When I answer that it's just a glass of milk, he keeps on staring, the suspicious look on his face never fading, as though I haven't fully answered the question. Some-times we laugh at the strangeness of the tension between us in such situations, but this only leads to more discomfort, perhaps because we remember how we used to laugh before. Things are very different from how they were when we were young.

Obviously, he's trying to play surrogate father, only even he can't take the part seriously. In spite of my sympathy for his good intentions, my outward acceptance of his advice, and his feelings of responsibility, he's intelligent enough to notice my aversion and contempt for this artificial fatherliness of his. Sometimes I feel as though I'm the one who is playing the role of father to him, with my neutral critique of everything that emanates from him. To be fair, though, my father was a hard act to follow, and anyone else is likely to look artificial in comparison. Maybe tomorrow I'll complete the family por-trait and write about him, hard as that task appears—which is perhaps why, so far, I've avoided it.

It was like gazing at a mask: always, there was a distance sep-arating him from everything else. That's what draws me to his image and that's also what makes it now so resistant to anal-ysis. He wasn't the most complicated of men, but he had an ability to get to the heart of things. With one word, he could cut you to the quick. I hated that, but I didn't hate him. After he died, I even learned to admire him, but the way some peo-ple admire Hitler—simply because there was no one else like him— with no desire to see him return.

I don't feel that he, for his part, hated me, but it was never clear that he particularly loved me either. He was neither a tyrant nor a scold and he wasn't concerned about how fathers should teach sons lessons. He'd just tell you, quietly, not to exaggerate, and that was enough to put you in your place. There was no criticism in this directed at you personally: if a baby cried next to him while he was reading the newspaper or watching television, he'd tell it, quietly, not to exaggerate.

What was supposed to happen next was that the baby would understand and shut up, not that he would stoop to the level of understanding the baby.

"Don't exaggerate." That was his favorite expression; in fact it was the only expression he used to set things to rights. If he were to read this now, even, it would be his response, and perhaps he'd be right. It's one of those expressions that can never be wrong, or which he never used to anything but good effect. He had his own special quiet way of uttering it, so that it never had the same effect when it came from someone else. There was no cruelty, or kindness, from his side in the way he used it, just a natural tendency to strip things of inessentials. Perhaps that was what made it so effective—its complete absence of compromise.

I remember once that I'd brought him my grades from school. I was in elementary and I entered the house running and full of joy, shouting that I'd gotten perfect grades. All he did was to say quietly, "Don't exaggerate," and my voice dried up on the spot. But how did he know? He hadn't looked at my grades yet and he didn't possess any evidence that would refute my claim. On what basis could he doubt me? When he noticed the look of protest on my face, he took the list from me and glanced at it. Then he simply pointed to a minus sign, against handwriting. But was handwriting really an academic subject? It was something trivial, not to be taken into account. Did I have to say that I hadn't got perfect grades because the bastard Arabic teacher didn't like the way I wrote the letter *K*? But it wasn't that. Perhaps he'd found me out from my voice, or the way I'd entered the house.

Sometimes I wouldn't do anything. I wouldn't shout or run or say anything, but he'd find a way to show that I was exaggerating—exaggerating doing nothing. He'd come home from work exhausted, in the late afternoon—precisely when I was most engrossed in my games and activities—and throw himself down on the couch in the living room. I'd sense that he needed rest and quiet, so I'd keep quiet and motionless. I'd sit like a statue, confident, concentrating on showing that I wasn't disturbing him, and he'd suddenly look at me and say, "Don't exaggerate!" as though to say, "Enough pretending!"

I was a shy boy, biddable, but his eagle eye could always expose my stratagems and the intricate means I used to attract attention. It was obvious to him that the excessive good manners I deployed to please him and others didn't spring from any purity of intention toward them but from a weakness in my nature: I desired to be accepted by others even when I couldn't stomach them. I wasn't without pride, either, as sometimes I'd make up my mind to be contrary and stubborn to prove that I didn't care what anyone thought, and in this too it wasn't beyond him to discover a measure of exaggeration.

When I reached high school, I began to give my rebellious tendencies full rein. Reading had increased my confidence and sense of freedom and individuality. I'd started serious reading, about Western schools of thought in particular. From time to time, my father would cast a glance at the books I was reading; he was the one who gave me the money to acquire them, so long as I asked his permission for what I bought. He didn't seem to object to this new habit—it wasn't the worst thing a boy might do at that age—but it wasn't clear that he approved either. All I could conjecture was that he'd noted some change was taking place within me as a result of these readings. I'd begun to contradict my elders at get-togethers and had dared to throw doubt on their assumptions; in fact, in one discussion, I announced my refusal to adhere to social convention, on the argument that I refused to be one of the herd (thus giving the impression that my introverted nature was in origin a matter of choice).

Then one day I happened to need money to buy a book by Nietzsche. I'd read *Beyond Good and Evil* and it had made a profound impression on me, so I wanted to acquire everything else that that lunatic had written. My father was sitting down, his eyes fixed on the television, following a talk show, but with

the same look with which he would "gaze into the abyss."
When I asked his permission to buy the book, he remained
silent, so I supposed he was waiting for further clarification. I
told him the title—*Ecce Homo*—and he stayed silent for a little
longer. Then he said it, without raising his head to look at me
and without warning. But why did he say it at that moment?
How could I have known? And what disturbed me more was
that he still gave me the money, which I took from him doubly
confused. I didn't understand at all but at the same time I
understood. It was the kind of expression that goes right to the
heart of things and doesn't call for any explanation.

I could relate an infinite number of memories, from my
childhood to my mature years, in which his only role was to
show me up with that expression. It was the standing expression that shaped me from childhood on and infused much of
my confusion and doubt regarding what I did and thought.
When I think about it now, it seems to me his influence on the
foundations of how I think was tangible, and more effective
than that of any philosopher. I refrained from any spontaneous
acts in his presence just so that none would seem artificial, and
even, in fact, did so when he wasn't around, using his sharp
eye to expose exaggerations. This taught me to be honest with
myself, or to be more skillful at hiding my stratagems, there
being no difference between these two lies.

As I grew older, I developed a feeling that there was some
hidden motive behind everything I did. I kept, therefore, strip-
ping away layer after layer in an attempt to get to the bottom
of my motivations, like a child with a leaning toward analysis
entertaining itself, except that I did this totally seriously, to the
point that I'd strip my actions of any positive meaning, and
perhaps of any negative meaning too.

I wasn't, however, the only one in the house to be affected
by this paternal criticism, because I was so sensitive or something like that: my elder brother was the same, and he may have
received more than his fair share of it because he was older.

My little sister transcended it, in some magical way, as did my mother, maybe because the female always follows her instincts, so she can't exaggerate, even when she's exaggerating. I well remember the sight of her in the hospital room, collapsed on the chair, her tears running night and day as he lay next to her stretched out on the bed, conscious and consoling, never scolding. I was sitting far off, at the other end of the room, on the black leather sofa, as though extraneous to the scene.

I always wondered how his marriage to her could keep going without conflicts. Where did they come up with all that harmony? My mother was the human embodiment of the idea of exaggeration. In fact, when I think about my early distaste for everything sentimental and emotional, I can trace its roots to my mother's hysterical outbursts, which would sometimes so completely overwhelm her reactions that she'd lose all control. Despite all this, something about her inclined him to indulgence; I didn't know what it was, but I knew I didn't have it.

Those were his last days. Only two weeks before his death, no one knew he was unwell; maybe he didn't know it himself. He suddenly fell ill with a fever, and it would have been exaggerating, of course, to go to the hospital. When he got worse, and we took him, the doctor was astonished. "Why didn't you come earlier? The liver enzymes are appallingly high!"

"Don't exaggerate," he responded quietly. The enzymes continued to climb without changing his attitude.

"If you've inherited anything from your father, it's the obstinacy," my mother keeps telling me, during our arguments, and it's a moment of contentment and reconciliation for us both.

Then his organs began to fail, one after another, and he went into a coma, at which he was moved to the intensive care unit. The doctor informed us that the chances of his surviving were slim, though he didn't know that yet. He woke the next day, with an oxygen mask over his face, to find himself surrounded by huge pieces of medical equipment and screens buzzing on every side. He awoke in distress, shouting indistinct words from behind the mask, and for a moment I thought he was asking us angrily to do away with all these exaggerations. We were taking turns to stay with him in intensive care and it was my shift when this happened. His bulging eyes were looking at me, almost popping from their sockets, and the oxygen mask was filling with the condensation from his breath and his muffled cries. For a while, I remained rooted to the spot, terrified, then realized he was asking me to fetch the doctor. I rushed off, a newly kindled zeal at work inside me; at that moment, I was determined to help him, to do anything he asked of me, even if it were to remove from him all those instruments so that he could die in peace.

When I returned with the doctor, his eyes were shifting from right to left, his lids were fluttering at terrifying speed, and his breaths were growing louder as they tried to catch any oxygen there might be in the room. His voice had turned into a moaning that was neither human nor bestial. What terrified me then wasn't that I was witnessing his death, it was finding him in such a state of panic. None of the routine measures the doctor took could lessen his awareness that his time had come; in fact, they made him more conscious of it, although he continued to ask to be rescued. When his heart stopped beating, the ventilator was still pumping oxygen into his lungs so his chest was still rising and falling.

That bizarre image of a dead man breathing remains fixed in my mind even now. Only when they removed the ventilator and he finally subsided, a slack, silent corpse, did he take on something closer to his normal appearance. A moment later, a vivid sensation, difficult to recall exactly now, assailed me. Something seemed to be saying that life was all just exaggeration.

Week 8

THE FIRST THING TO CATCH my eye on my return to work was an email from the bewattled director:

> Permanence is God's alone. Our former employee [name given], who served the company so well for the past thirty years, has died.
>
> Condolences will be received by his brother by telephone [an unfamiliar number appears at the end of the message]. We are God's and to God we return.

I contacted the number given in the message and when someone answered, I immediately tensed. It was his brother, no doubt about it, but his voice resembled that of the Old Man to an uncanny degree—the same pallor that accumulates in the throats of those who go for long periods without speaking. I couldn't prevent myself from thinking, in some naïve way, that I was offering my condolences to the Old Man himself.

His death was a surprise, but a surprised reaction would have seemed unnatural. Everyone knew the Old Man, but no one knew him well enough to claim the right not to have suspected that the moment of his death was close, and the fact that that moment occurred precisely one week after his retirement gave the impression that this sequence of events was logical: as soon as he retired, everyone accepted that his presence in their lives was over and that they probably would never see him again; his death was merely the confirmation of that conviction. In addition, a new employee had taken his place next to me, appointed just before the Old Man's death and immediately after his retirement, or in other words, during the two weeks when I was absent and all this happened. Because no vacuum ensued immediately after his death as far as his chair was concerned, it felt as though there had never been a gap. Everyone went on with their work as usual, to the point that one might have thought the new employee had been sitting there for ages.

Death didn't generally affect me. I didn't shed a tear even at my father's, and all that came of it was a short story, whose flippancy, inauthenticity, and lack of specific detail derived from real experience displeased me. I didn't feel as though my father's death was something that concerned me; it was as though he'd isolated himself even after death behind that mask with which he distanced himself from everyone. That that particular old man, who'd sat next to me for nine hours a day, should die, though, and within a week of his retirement, was something I could not but take personally. For some reason, I felt as though it was my responsibility to preserve his death as a felt presence in that place. As usual, however, it was just a feeling and never progressed to the stage of protest. At what, precisely, was one supposed to protest anyway?

It may be that learning the news so soon after my return from sick leave placed me in a different stage of mourning from that of the rest, whose time for being moved by the event had, it seemed, expired. In the end, he was a former employee, and it wasn't even a rule of the company's that it should announce the death of its retirees; if the company were to start making an announcement every time a retiree died, our mailboxes wouldn't have gone a month without a funeral, since it seemed that all that these retirees did after they left was die. Despite this, our director had deemed it appropriate to announce the news of the Old Man's death within our department, in a humane initiative that might be expected to win the approval of all. By so doing, he was confirming the solicitude with which he surrounded his employees and his eagerness to maintain, by announcing the fact whenever one of them quit this life, the special treatment and recognition that was his Unknown Warriors' due.

What made my annoyance even greater was that the new employee sitting next to me didn't look like someone who'd just taken the place of a dead man. There isn't any special way for one to show that, but this particular person looked as though he was ready to walk over the graves of others if that was the only path to a better position. He talked the whole time about having new ideas for developing the department and put them forward with a tone of contempt toward all old blood that confirmed how natural it was that everyone who went before him should die. In fact, in everything he does, he seems to be saying, "Look at me! I care for nothing that isn't practical and of the future." Maybe he hopes to become head of the department one day, even if he doesn't say so openly, for he always turns up in a proper suit, with jacket, necktie, and everything—and if anyone praises his elegance, he always says the same thing: "Dress for the job you want, not for the one you already have."

This philosophy of his is designed exclusively to bewitch the others, for as soon as they find that he's more ambitious than them and more likely to move ahead, they make way for him and try to win him to their cause. It has taken him only two weeks to achieve this assimilation into the department, while more than two years in the same department haven't seen me advance one step in my relations with any employee. The two employees who sit in front of us have taken to turning around and chatting with Necktie next to me. They ask him about this or that, or to settle some issue with his pedantic views and confident beliefs. This happens every day at nine, during the breakfast period, as conversation at other times provokes comments from Management. During this period, one of the two will turn toward me to give me the chance to join in while he consumes mouthful after mouthful, a white residue of food ringing his mouth, which is enough to make me lose my appetite for the rest of the day.

I've noticed that the mere departure of the Old Man has made it easy for them to fasten on me as a conversational partner, and this is the first manifestation of his absence. Before, his presence acted as an impediment to the magnanimity they now reveal toward me and which they suppose I will accept simply because we are of approximately the same age. And why shouldn't one want to join in their conversations? There are always thrilling matches that took place the night before, and if you don't follow soccer, you can talk about the upcoming Olympic Games. Then there's cars, cell phones, real estate, the stock market, and the various religious, political, and social debates with which Twitter abounds. And if there's nothing there that interests you, you're bound to have ideas about work, developments in the different departments, the low level of the salaries, the battles among the directors, your prognostications for the future of the company, and your aspirations for advancement up its ladder, since none of these topics requires that a person be personally drawn to them: he is compelled to be interested in them by their very nature. If, on the other hand, you refuse to take part in any of these discussions as well, it can only be an act of unabashed rudeness on your part, and there may be something suspicious about you, something perhaps to do with being a spy, or being willing to snitch.

The new dandy next to me looked on my lack of interaction with them in these conversations with excessive wariness. He sensed my indifference toward his personality, knowledge, and sparkling ideas, and this inspired in him a kind of reciprocal hatred. Within two days of my return, he had begun making funny comments about me, with a malicious skill that made his rudeness seem somehow friendly, saying, for example, that the ones who didn't talk were always the ones concealing the worst secrets, keeping a smiling gaze trained on me as though expecting me to confess. Given my lack of quick-wittedness and inability to come up with suitable responses, I'd always counter by appearing inattentive and ignoring him. Without any intention on my part, this would succeed in provoking him further, mobilizing his suspicions and his desire to uncover whatever I was hiding, and I suddenly found that he was monitoring my most trivial actions and directing more comments toward them.

That was the second manifestation of the Old Man's absence: without him, I feel exposed, without shade. The days of secrecy and privacy are over now and it's only possible to write on those rare occasions when the pedant has left to attend some meeting or other crap, and when he comes back to his desk, and I quickly hide on the screen whatever I was writing, he asks me if I was composing a snitch report to Management, in a tone that implies he's caught me red-handed. The other two turn around to scold him laughingly, without entirely disagreeing with him, and gaze at me with an affection that attempts to involve me in the merriment, sounds of chewing and speaking blending in their gaping mouths. This always ends with my being overtaken by nausea.

Sometimes I look to my side to see if he's noticed my obvious exhaustion, and I find him staring at me arrogantly and challengingly, casting looks whose purport is that his good health is well earned, not some gift of life's: he is sound and healthy due to all the choices he's made over the course of his life and which have proved, so far, to be the right ones for him.

The hospital is still trying to contact me even now to show me the test results, as is to be expected. My fever, on the other hand, has gone away completely, leaving behind it only a certain weakness and lack of appetite, which is perfectly natural, given my lack of sleep, my malnourishment, and my mood, which has been up and down these last few weeks. All I need is a time to convalesce and be taken care of, so that I can recalibrate my body. If you're going to start imagining things every time you feel strange, you'll end up making yourself sick just by thinking. It's enough that the social media sites, these days, and the chat groups on the various apps on your phone are overflowing with an extraordinary number of illnesses and maladies, which they pump out to their subscribers on a daily basis "to raise awareness and reduce the number of sufferers by 51 percent worldwide." It follows that, looking at it from a statistical standpoint, you're bound to find that you're suffering from something or other. I remember that recently I found in the news a medical report about a sickness called "chronic fatigue syndrome," which is one of those diseases you feel you must be suffering from the moment you hear of it. The symptoms were familiar enough—headache, lassitude, difficulty in sleeping, pains in the joints and muscles—and it was usually associated with work-related stress. The report advises you to get rid of such stress by walking around the workplace, or doing exercises in front of an open window— idyllic solutions, but impractical here, since the tower is designed to make walking around it something like driving a garbage truck down a narrow street, and the windows don't open at all in case the design drives someone to suicide. Anyway, the report says there is no definitive cure and you're going to have to live with the fact that you're chronically tired, though it would be a good idea if you could come up with some sonorous name by which to refer to this imperfection in your makeup.

It is important that you follow some uplifting, positive principle: this hasn't happened to them, so it won't happen to me. After all, no one gets enough sleep but they still get through their day, everyone smokes and lives for years and years, everyone gets headaches and feels exhausted but still keeps up their activities, so what I'm suffering from isn't any more serious. And when I lose my appetite, I think of the poverty-stricken writer in the novel *Hunger*, or children in Africa who survive famines, or prisoners who spend years eating bad food and still emerge in reasonable health and may go on to live to old age, so why shouldn't I stay in comparatively good condition even if I make do with only a little food?

Similarly, for ages now I've been an expert at self-diagnosis, a skill I've gradually developed to the point that I now avoid going to doctors. I imagine I could have been an outstanding physician, if Fate had led me to that profession. I remember that, as a child, when a grown-up asked me, "What would you like to be when you grow up?" I'd always answer, "A doctor." I'd say it straightaway without thinking. I'd say it not because of any enthusiasm on my part but simply because I'd worked out that this choice went down well with adults since they inferred that you were a good, polite boy, and they wouldn't push on into further interrogations or tests of your good conduct. In reality, though, I had no leaning toward that profession; quite the contrary, I had a prior aversion to its requirements—to the smell of hospitals and the stitches, to the idea of touching the bodies of strangers, especially sick ones, to pressing on their stomachs, putting stethoscopes on their bare chests, and inserting thermometers into their armpits and under their tongues.

There was another thing that made me averse to this profession, which boils down to the fact that one has to spend more years than anyone else studying to become a doctor. I hated school as much as anybody and wanted to be done with it as soon as possible, which is why I was such a good student. I looked with curiosity and astonishment at the slow students who would repeat years without caring or feeling any prick of conscience, and some of whom may even have harbored feelings of pride and achievement at spending more time on one educational stage than anyone else. Some grew so old at school that they had beards and mustaches resembling our teachers' and huge, fully-developed physiques, so that their mere presence behind one at the back of the class was disturbing. I usually sat in the second row; the only thing that stopped me sitting in the front was my usual embarrassment if I ever found myself there. I had lots of questions for the ones sitting in the last row. Sometimes I even considered turning toward them in the midst of their uproar and din and confronting them with them, and I would perhaps have done so if it weren't for their constant tendency to bully and make a joke of everything, and especially of disciplined people like me. One might have picked up the cane and hit me ironically, or slapped me on the back of my neck and pelted me with chalk like any teacher. All the same, I continued to follow what they did, with fear, curiosity, and maybe also admiration, while in my mind I was turning over the following questions: how, and why, did they act like that? Didn't they understand? A whole year of a person's life wasted on a repetition from which one got nothing. A whole year that could have been erased with a little seriousness and study. Didn't another additional year between the walls of this school make them feel depressed?

For me, a year was a big number, a whole lifetime, as it is to everyone when they are young. So I kept up my efforts throughout the various academic stages and graduated with a single goal in mind—to start work and leave at the end of the work day to do whatever I pleased. Starting life as an employee meant in my mind being done with tests, rules, homework, and all the other forms of attack mounted by the teachers on your private time. No other burden could be bad in comparison. I had been confident for so long in the knowledge that simply to go home was to be left alone to do whatever I wanted that anything that happened during work hours would be bearable. This—getting a well-paid, secure job—was, on its own, an attractive motive for continuing to do well at school. Yes, indeed: starting work meant to me setting off down the road to freedom—until I actually started working.

I now realize that work means spending the best half of the day working relentlessly to swell the pockets of the company's stockholders and strengthen your director's chances of promotion while submitting to systems and laws stranger than you'd find in the silliest dystopian novel. At the end of the day, you leave the office exhausted, burned out, and sluggish, emptied of resolve, your mind and body finished. If any feeling of anger at this situation should seize you, at the end of a long, hard day of work, all you need to do is look, on your way home, at the laborers crammed into buses, none of them with the energy left to hold up their heads, their necks still red from the burning sun that has been roasting them all day, their heads swaying in the open windows of the vehicles, which are themselves worn out and which distribute themselves through the streets in numbers large enough to remind you that you are better off than their passengers and should thank God.

Thus pass your days, in lockstep with the work regime during working hours and the struggle to restore balance to your sleep regime once you get home. All weeks suddenly seem the same. You scud around, your eyes set on the salary at the end of the month and the exiguous bonuses after every six, and on hopes of change with a switch of directors and departments. Each year passes like the one before it and the one before that and the one before that—just a long period of time with a predetermined end, and it's too late for you to go back and start all over again. Then you direct your efforts toward distant plans, you get used, employing various pretexts, to being patient in the hope that one day you may be free of all this and do what you want. You surprise yourself with your capacity for patience, your capacity to pass long years, even entire decades, in the same temporary situation, the same uncomfortable posture, only to discover at the end that you free yourself from that situation only to die. But what else can you do?

Week 10

WHEN I GOT TO MY desk this morning, I found a letter from the hospital requesting my presence and mentioning that they'd booked me a morning appointment. This means, of course, that I can skip work for the rest of the day, as the hospital's appointments system is coordinated with the company's online system. In other words, I can ask for leave without this involving me in any breach of discipline. Nevertheless, the Turkey began scratching his wattles in front of me, as a way of showing his displeasure, and hinting that it was one of the qualities of an Unknown Warrior to ignore his medical appointments when these clashed with work hours, especially as I'd been absent for two weeks at the start of the month because of my illness. In the end, he had no choice but to agree, though a dubious expression sketched itself on his face, implying that he'd be keeping an eye on me and that my tricks, whatever they were, couldn't fool him.

Management's strict habits regarding leave complemented my own habit of procrastinating whenever I came down with something, especially as the insurance policy required I be treated only at the company-specified hospital, which was always stuffed with patients of every description, so that one was rarely lucky enough to get an appointment within a week, or even a month, of falling sick. In addition, I'd heard that some doctors were refusing to give you a medical pass when you visited them, making do with a letter of proof that you'd visited them, which Management did not regard in and of itself as an official sick leave permit. Emergency rooms weren't any easier as the wait there could be so long that, with the passage of the hours, one came to believe that one was sicker than one had been before. And, who knows, the wait might lead to your catching other diseases from those waiting with you.

This morning, in the waiting room, there was a number of people, aged and adolescent, and the place was full of the smell of foulness and decay, as though it would make them sicker if they took a shower. They were sitting squashed up against one another, one with a broken leg, some in their nightwear, and many with masks over their faces. In the corridor that opens directly off the room, a large board had been put up calling attention to the symptoms of corona virus and set out next to it were leaflets raising awareness of how to prevent the disease and avoid infection. The outbreak of the virus was now contained, but fear of it hovered over the place like a vulture. The moment anyone coughed, all eyes turned toward him. Even the man with the broken leg appeared more scared of the virus than of what had happened to his leg.

I was sitting among them, in clean office pants, a formal shirt, and old but not shabby shoes that might even pass as classic; when you placed them like that, next to the shoes of the patients in that room, they didn't look too bad. I got up and began walking in the passage, as though to leave my seat for a patient who really needed it. I was in a cheerful mood, thanks to being out of the office at that time of day; it reminded me of test days, when they would let us out of school early. I stood next to the closed door to the ward and started observing every passerby approaching or trying to leave, and after a while I started opening the door for anyone who needed help, whether it was a man in a wheelchair or a pregnant woman or a man carrying a sleeping child in his arms. Then I began imagining that I was a doorman who'd been doing this job for years and discovered that it was a pleasant occupation that encourages good feelings and began secretly practicing my part and smiling: "Please, sir, this way! Please, madam, this way! Quiet now, children! Don't run like that, you little rascals, haha! A tip? No no no! That won't do, we're put on this earth to help one another, and I'm only doing my duty. Oh, very well then, just to make you happy, hahaha! Please! Please, everyone, this way!" Wouldn't being a first-rate old doorman be a perfect fit for me?

Some of those waiting gazed at me doubtfully, imagining perhaps, from my appearance and playful mood, that I'd turned up at the hospital just for the fun of it, and when the nurse called my name, even though they'd been waiting for longer than I, I could feel their envious looks following me. They were thinking perhaps that I'd deliberately done something irregular to get in before them, and in fact even the nurse's face failed to register any pleasure when she saw that I was the one who answered.

I followed her to a small side room to update my data. She took my weight and height as she was supposed to and made a sound out of the side of her mouth that indicated she wasn't happy with the number ranges. She inflated a blood-pressure measuring sleeve on my skinny arm, muttering and sighing in her mother tongue, and while she did so would raise her eyes and fix them on my face, even though the distance between us was so small. I asked her where she was from, to lighten the atmosphere. She mentioned a country in West Africa—Ghana, I think, or Guinea—and began sighing deeply as she stared at me, as though I'd reminded her of some tragedy taking place there. I asked her if she knew anything about why I'd been called in, and she said it was to do with the blood test I'd done when I'd gone to the emergency room the time before. So what was the result of the test? She said she'd seen it in my file but didn't have the right to tell me anything. But what was the worst that could come out of a blood test anyway? She told me to go back to the waiting room till she called me again.

I went back to my seat and sat there, thinking. Here, the phobia about corona virus strengthened my feeling that my condition, whatever it was, couldn't be really serious in comparison. But what if I'd contracted some other virus, one even more deadly, a virus of the blood? That had always been a worry of mine, perhaps because of the sermons against fornication that I'd listened to so often as a child. I was terrified by the frequently repeated stories of people who'd gone for an ordinary test, or to give blood, and discovered that they had AIDS. I well remember my nervousness when I went once to give blood during my father's illness. It was the first and last time I did so. I started following the movements of the West African nurse with my eyes, examining her looks for anything that might point to misgiving and imagining that the doctor might come at any moment and say that the test results were positive. I even imagined all my possible reactions—first denial, then laughter, and then anger, with me striking the desktop and shouting at the doctor, "How dare you?" Then I'd tell him I'd never in all my life had sex with a woman, or a man, or an ape for that matter. There must be a mistake—I'd hardly done anything yet. Then I'd return to my senses and affect a degree of calm and ask him, impassively, "How much longer do I have?" and when he said "A year and a half," I'd collapse in bitter tears.

I was entertaining, and scaring, myself with these old stupidities and waiting for the nurse to call me again, when the doctor himself came out and called my name. From where I sat, I could see him standing, with his stout, spherical body, in front of his room on the corridor, holding the handle of the open door, his foot against its bottom so that it wouldn't close. He was standing quietly and calmly, but that didn't stop me immediately imagining that the moment we went in and he examined me, he'd start making irritable movements with his hands and shouting, "If every man started coming to the clinic just because he thinks he might have AIDS, the clinics would be full and they'd distract us from the important cases!"

If I'd had to choose, at that moment, between being sick and being well, I might well have chosen to be sick, just to avoid the embarrassment of appearing before him for no good reason.

While I was walking toward him, he summoned the tea boy and asked me if I wanted a cup. I nodded, so he ordered two. We went into the room, and the nurse went out. She remained standing anxiously in the corridor following me with that tragic look of hers while the door closed itself.

The doctor went behind the desk and sat down in the chair with the low back, its wheels turning and squeaking under his weight. He gestured to me to sit while he propelled himself on his chair toward his side of the desktop till its edge was pressing against his large belly. I felt it only needed him to press against it a little more for his body to explode like a balloon. His hands were plump and he joined them together in front of him, solemnly interlocking his fingers above the surface of his desk. On the other side of the desk were two facing chairs, on one of which I sat, while the other remained empty, and I drew my feet closer to me, as though someone unseen was occupying the opposite seat. He asked me how I was, and I shrugged my shoulders without replying. The moment the conversation began, my mind immediately began to wander, his preoccupation with the preliminaries granting me an opportunity to relax and rid my mind of my old forebodings and my desire to flee.

When he got to the point, I tried to adopt a serious expression, as though I was listening carefully to what he was saying. I nodded at scattered phrases in his speech but was unable to join them together well: the results were as expected, the blood count was far below normal levels, we need more tests to be sure, a sample of bone marrow, it was usually painful but there was a hospital in the capital, he knew the doctor there personally, he'd make me an appointment for next week and in the meantime there'd have to be regular blood transfusions, three bags at least.

He talked without interruption, analyzing and explaining and allowing me no chance to react, and all the time his hands were in motion, in keeping with the practical nature of what he was saying. A certain tension had taken hold of them, resulting from his desire not to scare me despite the need to convey to me how important the matter was. There wasn't a trace of artificiality in his movements, or any feeling that they were calculated based on his having faced innumerable patients before. This stirred up inside me a certain curiosity and confusion. It would have been more normal if he'd been grave and morose, given how accustomed he must have been to dealing with situations such as this.

The tea boy knocked and entered. He put the two paper cups on the desk and left, without giving us time to thank him. A few moments of silence passed, while the door leisurely closed itself. Then the doctor told me I ought to give serious consideration to chemotherapy, in the same tone someone might use to tell me it was time for me to buy a new pair of shoes.

I was quiet, the doctor was quiet, the room was quiet, the temperature inside it was properly adjusted, and steam rose from the paper cups of tea in front of us. I carried the cup to my lap and looked down at it in silence. Low sounds reached me from the corridor via the crack under the door, along with the cries of patients and sounds of nurses moving light-footedly in pairs of white shoes, each step sticking to the tiles. From an area a little further away, the piercing crying of a baby began repeating itself; probably it had had an injection. When the doctor began speaking again, I was still holding the cup, which now felt even hotter in my hands. I continued to scrutinize the tea with interest, as though the doctor's voice was coming from there.

He ended by saying that the biopsy would confirm if the disease was present, its subtype, and the stage it had reached, which was why it had to be done as soon as possible. When he finished, I noted that this was the right time for me to come up with a reaction. I searched for something suitable to say. I took a sip from the cup to gain time and returned it carefully to my lap. The only thing I could think of was that the tea needed another spoonful of sugar. Finally, I told him that I'd have the tests done in the capital and put the cup back on the desktop, as though that held the solution to the problem. He nodded encouragingly and informed me that he'd be in touch. The nurse came in right away, as though she could tell from his tone alone that the appointment was at an end.

When I left, the rest of the patients were still waiting in their seats, and the same nurse came out behind me with another file and called someone else's name. I remembered I'd left the cup of tea where it was on the desk but it seemed ridiculous, after the news I'd just received, to go back, pick it up, apologize, and go out again. At the same time, I felt nothing inside that was at odds with such behavior. I even held the door open for two people while I was leaving the ward. A part of me felt I was still healthy because I didn't have AIDS.

I went home and passed the day as though everything was normal. I read, I scrolled through the news, I watched a documentary on the television, and I bought more books from a website, like someone who is sure that one day he'll read everything he hasn't yet had time for. Perhaps I should spend these days drawing up some kind of backup plan, go over things in my mind, decide on my priorities and what I should do in case that which was to be feared should happen. I say "that which was to be feared" as though I'm not the one doing the fearing. I haven't made up my mind yet. More of the procrastination, more of the heedlessness, more of the nonchalance that doubt provides, for as long as it remains possible.

Two

Week 11

I TOLD MY FAMILY I was going on a business trip, took a number of my many annual leave days, and booked a seat on the train. The doctor had advised me not to drive if I was going alone. "No one knows what state you'll be in," he told me, "if the news is confirmed." I wasn't convinced of anything he said, but it was just a precautionary measure in any case. It's better to dismiss such preoccupations quickly, before they can grow, so that I can get back to my ordinary life as soon as possible. The day of my journey, I went to the station early, perhaps too early, like anyone who takes a form of transport for the first time. I sat next to the window, took out *The Magic Mountain*, and started reading.

Quiet reigned inside the car. Then they got on, with noticeable sprightliness, like people who rode the train every week. This showed itself in the nonchalant way they treated the storage lockers and the way they sat down right away, each in his seat, in an arrangement they appeared to have practiced many times. They had tickets for five seats, and I was the sixth. The youth sat next to me. The girl, who was a few years older than him, sat facing me, and to her left was the maid, the four of us sharing a single large tabletop. On the other side of the aisle sat the little girl and the veiled woman, who was catty-corner to me. Between them was a smaller tabletop.

I was keeping my eye on them, waiting for some signal, or some turn of the head, to be directed toward me that would give me to understand that my presence would detract some-how from the pleasure they took in feeling so at home. The girl opposite wiped the window before settling in her place, confirming that that was the reason she'd chosen that seat. As soon as she sat down, she began looking out in delight, even though we hadn't yet left the station. Then she called sedately to her mother, spoke affectionately to the maid, and played with her little sister, making childlike petting sounds, after which she'd laugh quickly, cover her mouth, and make new facial expressions and additional hand movements that, it was plain, weren't a part of her before she boarded the train. Her brother, though, she frowned at and issued didactic advice to, giving the impression that she was well-versed in etiquette, telling him, for example, not to disturb the others with the loud noise from his phone; he answered her with derision and told her to eat shit, without looking up, his nascent mustache gleaming in the phone's shiny rays. She told him he was rude and began complaining about him to the mother, who wasn't paying attention to anything and had kept talking throughout the boarding process, as though she were getting on a plane where use of the network was forbidden after takeoff. Her voice, behind her face veil, gave the impression that it was just transitional, a temporary excitement after which it would return to its original state, but she kept on talking in the same tone throughout the call and her voice never shifted into a different range. Based on the signs of strict adherence to the rules of religion that were apparent on her, I guessed that, as soon as she finished her call, she'd summon her elder daughter to leave her place facing me and switch with her. In fact, no such thing occurred. Rather, the moment she finished her call, she began texting enthusiastically, her eyes smiling at what she was writing in a way that had nothing to do with her age, while the little girl opposite her began calling to her too, asking her for the phone to play with and screaming and kicking her feet. The maid was the quietest among them, though she was noticeably tense, which made me think she wasn't a long-established part of the family. From time to time, she directed anxious glances at me and she may have been the only one to notice that I was a foreign element within the group. The others didn't seem to have any reservations about a strange man sharing the row with them; on the contrary, they seemed somehow delighted to be breaking that customary reserve. I concluded that they permitted themselves additional freedom in the absence of the father; in fact, one might say that the sprightliness with which they'd boarded derived its liveliness precisely from that absence.

The last person to enter the car was an elderly foreigner whose robe showed that he was of some African nationality. He was unmistakably ailing and accompanied by his wife, who held his arm; the colors of her scarf showed that she too was African. Like him she was old, but more active, perhaps deriving her energy from his need of her to serve him, or from her need to serve him. Their belongings were old as well, so that the suitcases seemed to creep along with bowed backs instead of walking smartly. The couple sat down in the second row, on the left, so I could see them: he was facing in my direction; she was in the opposite seat. The little girl in our row turned around and smiled at the man, but nothing in his exhausted face changed. He wasn't in a fit enough condition even to think of smiling.

As soon as the train set off, everyone in my row relaxed completely, except for the maid, who looked even tenser than before, as though, with the departure of the train, any hope she might have had of returning to her own country was lost. The mother gave her phone to the younger girl and pulled out a box containing sandwiches, which she didn't intend to hand out to her children yet, but rather to demonstrate to the stewards on the train that someone wasn't going to eat their terrible food. I soon noticed the curiosity of the older girl, who was sitting facing me and darting sideways looks at the book in front of me; when I caught her eye, she turned away quickly and looked out of the window. Then she started correcting her brother, in an attempt to recover her poise, before turning back to me again in embarrassment. She was too young for me to find her presence disturbing and too old for me to indulge her attempt to create some kind of interaction. I raised the book to make a barrier between our eyes and went back to reading.

I don't know how long it was before I felt nauseous. It wasn't clear whether it was a result of my immersing myself in the book, or of the motion of the train, or of the stifling air that remained unchanged inside the car, but it got to some place deep inside me. On the car's shared screen, a documentary film about sharks was being shown. I fixed my eyes on it in an attempt to lose myself in the deep blue of the sea, and suddenly my heart started to beat faster. I felt that if I were to stand up, or open my mouth to speak, something catastrophic would happen. I opened the book to read again but felt the nausea increase in severity every time I laid my eyes on a line of type. I shut my eyes, trying to keep my insides in place, and then the mother started distributing the sandwiches. I was on the verge of asking her not to do that now, but said nothing. They took them joyfully. The maid alone looked at the sandwiches in alarm, so the daughter turned toward her and encouraged her to eat, telling her their contents, which the maid didn't know the language well enough to understand, making the girl laugh, covering her mouth, in embarrassment at the maid's ignorance. She turned to her brother and ordered him harshly to wipe the traces of food from the side of his mouth, then stole another glance at me. I looked beyond her to the old African man in the next row: he had spilled coffee on his chest, which his wife was wiping at with a wrinkled handkerchief, as though massaging his heart. He seemed to tell her to stop but she didn't hear him, all of which made me feel extremely annoyed, as though his heart was hurting me, or it was my heart that was being massaged.

I was puffing audibly, as though in an attempt to expel the strange pain from my heart, focusing all my mental forces on the idea of returning to my normal state, when suddenly the train entered a mountain pass, the window filled entirely with the mountain's sharp, stony strata, and the air, compressed between the mountain and the train, rose in a sound like a long scream.

I stood up in a hurry and looked for the bathroom. My legs were shaking and I felt I might faint at each step. As soon as I'd closed the bolt on the door, I tried to vomit but my throat was too tight for me to do so. I washed my face in front of the mirror and remained staring at my wet features. I could feel every movement around me. The yellow mirror light gave off a nauseating buzz, above the throttled hum of the train's wheels. I begged the train to stop, for any miraculous reason, or to reduce speed, as though that would convince my palpitating heart to calm down. Nothing changed, and someone began knocking on the door. The moment I came out, I realized that that was a terrible mistake. I still had two hours to go until we arrived. I would have to sit the whole time. I stiffened my resolve, as though getting through this turbulence depended on my staying seated.

I went back to the car and found the place in a state of chaos—crowded and humid and rancid with the smell of food, breath, and bodies sweaty from sitting too long. They raised their heads again, surprised at my desire to sit among them, as though they'd forgotten that anyone had been sitting there from the beginning. Between me and my seat was the youth's awkward body, which was changing and growing by the minute, impinging little by little on ever more of life's spaces. I pushed past him without waiting for him to make room for me, the sister watching me in astonished disapproval at such boorishness, and the moment I sat down, my pulse started to race again, or my heart to palpitate more strongly, I don't know which. I picked up the book again, opened it, and closed it, while a cold sweat oozed from my body. The mother was texting, fast and with irritation, while the little girl cried in front of her, and she wrote and wrote, and the child cried and kicked and screamed, and the youth raised and lowered his voice on the phone, and the maid looked on anxiously, heading toward something she didn't understand, and the girl spoke to her and laughed, petting her and saying poor thing and laughing, and the maid didn't understand but sensed that she was a poor thing, and the old woman held a pill to her husband and her hand was shaking and his hand was shaking and the pill was shaking and he swallowed the pill as though it wasn't medicine, as though the yellow spot on his chest hurt him and there was no medicine left to help him, and he gazed at his wife to say something and realized that she couldn't hear him, so closed his eyes in exhaustion.

I went on sitting with my eyes shut, then tried keeping them on some spot or other, then shut them again, then stared out of the window. Outside, the weather was dusty, as though turbid with my own misgivings. And there, in the middle of the bare, dusty desert, a herd of camels was moving, slowly and sluggishly, without any sense of resolve. I leaned my head against the window and sighed deeply, so that my breath clouded the glass. For a moment I thought how terrifying, how terrifying, how terrifying it is that one must exist.

I don't know if I fell asleep or briefly passed out. By the time our arrival was announced, my stomach had settled but my body was weak, and a current of hot air was blowing. The asphalt platform alongside the train disposed me to calm. I decided to take my time getting down. Only the old man and his wife remained behind in the car. She was helping him up, holding his arm, her face bearing a fixed, patient expression. He seemed annoyed at the way in which she was helping him to rise, as though she was the cause of his decrepitude, on his face the same expression, which seemed to draw its patience from hers. Together they descended from the car, the steward behind them helping them to lower their suitcases. The suitcases also seemed to be trying to hang on, though with great effort, so that it seemed that at any moment they might fall apart, scattering their contents. The old woman adjusted her thin shawl over her head and shoulders, then asked the steward if it would be possible for him to find them a cab. He gestured to her to enter the station and ask. A lost expression drew itself on her face, as though she was living in an age she didn't understand, and immediately the same expression appeared on her husband's. She took his arm and they set off together in the direction of the gate with twin expressions, it being unclear which of them had lent his expression to the other. The suitcases rolled along after them, two puzzled children following their parents in silence.

I overtook them and proceeded to the gate of the station. My body had regained its calm, but inside a desire to return to where I'd come from was eating away at me, and though I kept moving forward, this was more the result of weakness and a desire to be done with all this than of courage. In front of the gate a man was waiting, blocking the entrance with his broad body, a stern expression and thick mustache on his face, whose features resembled what would be the youth's in the coming years. Just from seeing him you knew you'd reached the capital. I was in a daze but of this I had no doubt: this man was the capital. The family made its way toward him sluggishly, in an exhausted mass, as though not one had enjoyed the journey.

In the hotel, I kept to my room, to avoid any complications with the biopsy as the results were supposed to come out at the end of the week. In any case, I felt no desire to go out. I'd chosen Thomas Mann's novel, which ran to a thousand pages, thinking I'd keep myself busy reading throughout the days of waiting, but now I could barely finish a third of it. I kept myself entertained with my laptop, writing down everything that had happened on the journey, going over what I'd written time after time without capturing the truth of what I'd felt. I began searching the internet in my usual self-diagnostic mode. I discovered that the symptoms that had assailed me in the train matched those of a panic attack.

I changed the search topic to the reason for my being there. I compared what the doctor thought was likely with what was said on the medical websites and advice pages. No sooner had one question brought me hope than the next made that hope seem silly. There were other disorders that were superficially similar and I leaned automatically to those, even if they were rarer than what I was suspected of having. In fact, I was prepared to adopt additional symptoms, no matter how disturbing, so long as they kept doubt alive—anything but this nightmare. Nevertheless, the more I read, the more bewildered I became and I wished that a kind hand would reach out and change the list of symptoms that were beginning to repeat themselves before me, making all other possibilities more and more unlikely. I immediately felt sorry that I'd set about the search on my own instead of waiting for the results. I even wished I could somehow be afflicted with memory loss and forget the reason for my presence there, then go back and continue my life from where it had stopped.

I'd noticed some of these symptoms often in my body in recent months without drawing any conclusions from them as a whole. My body was always complaining and extremely sensitive to any disruptions. If it had told me I was suffering from something important, any such alarm would have been lost among its myriad other complaints. There was no way to work it out, unless you were to take seriously every rare possibility and unlikely danger, in which case you would end up obsessed and insane.

However, the thing that would most prevent you from realizing from the beginning what was going on was the disease's refusal to manifest itself in any clear, explicit form, especially its liquid variety, which multiplies unseen in the blood. Isn't such the nature of things that lead one to death? The more covert the pain at the beginning, the more likely it is to be one of those things that develop till they have a deadly effect on you. On that basis, how many things would you have to be wary of? No, such a thing couldn't happen to me, so marginal and so given to hiding from sight: it would be too ironic a paradox.

I sat in my room blundering from doubt to doubt and thought to thought, switching without a pause from the furthest reaches of despair to the furthest reaches of joy. At one moment, I'd think this really was the end, my heart would start to pound, and I'd pace the length and breadth of the room, go into the bathroom, and almost vomit from panic. When I got back to my bed, I'd review all the stories of patients who'd been diagnosed with serious illnesses and then, when they consulted another hospital, it had become clear that things were much simpler. That made me remember all my old worries, which had turned out later to be trivial issues, and I sat there roaring with laughter at my exaggerated reaction. Then a fast-moving drop of blood suddenly ran down from my nose, made a turn around my mustache, and dropped.

I felt the wetness with trembling fingers, and when my eye fell on the scarlet spot, my whole body shook. That brief moment of panic was the decisive moment, the moment after which there is no return to safety. It wasn't, I realized, just a nosebleed. It wasn't just a passing twinge of fear that could be dispelled from the mind because its source was unclear. I was confused and apprehensive, but I didn't have the energy to doubt any more. Every bout of nausea, every hemorrhage, every headache, every new bruise, every minor symptom, whatever it might be, would henceforth acquire, in the light of the latest data, a more threatening character and would be linked directly to its malign origin. It wasn't any longer only a matter of a suspicion in the mind but of a firm, heartfelt knowledge that this was, indeed, happening.

It's like a colony of bedbugs, growing beneath you in the bed: all that separates you from them is one layer and you sleep on top of them each night, unaware of the voracious filth bedded down beneath you. You may see insignificant bites on your body and pay them no attention because there isn't any pain yet. A little malaise, perhaps, but nothing you can't put up with. Then the red dots on your skin multiply and begin to raise doubts and fear. And one day you decide to lift up the mattress, just in case, and that's the moment when the pain begins—the moment when you see that huge ugly black colony, squirming with thousands of insects, and their eggs, which have hatched hundreds of times just while you've been gazing at them. The pain begins at the moment you discover these greedy tiny creatures have been feeding on you and have grown up quenching their thirst with your blood, and they have set up a base inside you that you can no longer fight against because even if you treat it you will still be weak; because you will still be a likely site for invasion and reinvasion; because even if you survive to the furthest possible point, you will never be able to patch over the panic that burst open inside you at the instant of your discovery.

Week 12

THE MOMENT I RECEIVED THE results, I put them into my suitcase and made for the airport. Even though the weather remained unstable because of the change of seasons, I wasn't prepared to repeat my experience with the train. I had decided to isolate myself from anything that could return me to the fragility I'd felt during the past few days. I prepared for the journey by drinking liquids all day long to stimulate my circulation and make up for the blood I'd lost, and as soon as I boarded the plane, I felt an urgent desire to urinate.

As soon as I got up from my seat, the stewardess hurried toward me repeating that I had to wait until the plane had completed takeoff. She raised her voice, in an attempt to warn off everyone else from doing the same. I sat back down, thinking it wouldn't take long. The moment the captain's voice, announcing the completion of takeoff, was heard, I rose, without listening to the rest of the announcement, and there was the stewardess hurrying over to me again repeating that the seat-belt sign was still lit, because of the bad weather and air turbulence, and that everyone should stay seated until further notice. The rest of the passengers turned toward me, and I realized that from now on the fullness of my bladder would be a matter of collective concern.

I was sitting in the middle seat between two men. The man to my right, next to the window, had a mocking expression that gave the impression he was ready and able to make fun, to himself, of anything that might cross his path. From time to time, he'd let out a laugh for everyone else to hear as he stared at the entertainment screen, and, although he appeared to be absorbed in the stand-up comedy routine, he turned around every time I got up, as though keeping count of the number of times I needed the bathroom. The man to my left, next to the aisle, opened his buckle every time I got up, preparing himself to move so I could get by. He was fat enough to overflow his seat a little, which made the process of undoing the belt, getting up, and sitting down again more of an effort than it should have been, despite which each time his face wore an artificial smile, indicating his cooperativeness and understanding for things of this sort.

An announcement informing us that we were now beyond the area of turbulence was heard over the sound system, but I didn't hurry to get up. That way I could pretend I didn't have to empty my bladder now, which might give the others the impression I'd forgotten the whole thing and hadn't been in that much need of relieving myself from the beginning. When, I ask myself, will this habit of mine of monitoring myself through others' eyes come to an end? Why this unceasing sense of shame?

Minutes passed. Then I got up from my place, like someone doing so for the first time since the flight began. I was certain no one would stop me this time because the seat-belt sign was off and the plane was moving forward smoothly. I made my way from my seat down the aisle to the bathroom at the back, but when I got there, the sign on the door said that it was occupied. To make it worse, a man suddenly appeared from the narrow space between the bathroom and the storage area to inform me that he was there first. Avoiding the eyes of the others, I walked back toward my seat, a smile on my face indicating my bad luck, and I shrugged my shoulders in a self-deprecating way, to make my situation appear as funny and random as possible to anyone who might be watching.

Before I could make it back, I found that the steward-ess had begun passing with the food trolley, thus blocking the aisle. She had already passed my seat and had begun handing out the food to the rows behind it, so I couldn't go back and sit down without passing her. She had her back toward me, and the steward who was standing on the other side of the trol-ley was busy asking the passengers who had taken their meal whether they wanted coffee or a soft drink. I didn't seem to have caught the attention of either. I opened my mouth to say, "Excuse me," and I think I must have involuntarily raised my voice more than the situation called for in an attempt to make it immediately audible. The stewardess jumped, then turned in annoyance, informing me that the aisle was too narrow for me to get by. The steward, for his part, asked me, in a calm but commanding voice, like one who had no other possibilities at his disposal, to retreat and wait by the wing, which was the only place where there was enough space for the trolley to get past me. Even though, practically speaking, it would have been possible for him to pull it back, the steward's tone and his look, so conversant with airplane etiquette, indicated that this wasn't an option.

I went back to the empty space next to the wing and stood waiting, while the eyes of those in the neighboring rows who hadn't yet received their food bored into me inquisitively. In one of the front seats there was a little boy, who stood and turned toward me with large, anxious eyes, his apprehensive look unable to hide that what was happening to me embodied his worst fears.

In my mind, I recalled a situation I'd found myself in a long time ago, maybe fourth grade. It was during a math class, as I well remember. I was copying from the blackboard along with the other students in the class. We weren't talking at all, or when we did so, we did it in whispers, because the teacher, who was well known for his bad temper, was quite capable of flinging the chalk in any direction from which a sound might reach him. If the sound came again from the same direction, he would tell the pupil who had made it to come forward and stand in front of him next to the blackboard, where everyone could see him, and tell him to hold out his hands, while he raised his ruler (the same thick wooden ruler he used to draw acute angles) to shoulder height. The student would stand there, tiny, shrunken, his trembling hands opened in front of him, cringing, and the moment he heard the teacher move, he'd pull his hands back, while the ruler gave out a terrifying sound as it cleaved through the air. Then the teacher, made even angrier and more bent on punishment, would yell at him and raise the ruler higher even than the top edge of the black-board, and as soon as the student held out his hands again, would bring it down on them with a stroke that cleaved the air even faster and more violently than the first, to be followed by the resounding smack of the blow breaking against the hand of the student, who would run, doubled-up, back to his place.

My eyes would wince involuntarily the moment the ruler descended and my head retract between my shoulders, like a turtle's, as though the blow had fallen on me, and then I'd watch, with great terror and perplexity, as the student returned, hugging his reddened hands, which now trembled more than ever, while the hot tears fell from his eyes as he howled, but in silence, for fear of making a sound by crying and getting beaten again.

I never experienced that sensation, not so much because I was afraid of the beating as because I was afraid that the teacher would rebuke me out loud in the hearing of the rest of the students. I was always extremely well mannered and hardworking, copying down every word and diagram that was written on the board. One day, I began drawing something with the compass—at that level, we had just started using the geometry set—when I let it slip by mistake and the sharp end pricked the tip of my finger. I exclaimed softly at the pain, holding in my voice, and nobody noticed except the boy who sat next to me and wore a permanently apprehensive expression that implied that some as yet unknown danger lay in everything.

He examined my finger, which I had wiped with a tissue, with that same look, and whispered that I ought to go and wash it in cold water. I didn't dare discuss the matter because I didn't want to risk our voices reaching the teacher. It was just a trivial little wound that had already stopped bleeding, and I knew that the pain would go away soon, but his anxious look, his serious tone, and his whispering made me believe there was a greater likelihood of the teacher getting mad at me if I didn't stand up and ask permission to leave the classroom.

I plucked up the courage to stand in front of the teacher and asked his permission to go out and wash my hands, as I'd pricked myself with the compass. I provided him with this detail so that he wouldn't think I didn't have a genuine reason for asking for permission. When he asked me to show it to him, I held out my hand and indicated the prick, which, now that the bleeding had stopped, was barely visible, then pointed with the other hand, in which I held the tissue so that the small spot of blood on it would confirm that my claim was correct. All he did was give me a contemptuous look and then begin imitating my voice, repeating everything I'd said, saying the word "compass" again and again in a loud, mocking, whiny voice, drawing the letters out as much as possible till the whole class exploded in laughter.

I stood where I was, confused, furious at his dishonest imitation and at the same time terrified of any further reaction from him. He extricated me from my quandary by ordering me to go back to my seat before he could doctor me with a stroke of his ruler on my hands that would teach me the true meaning of pain, at which the students' voices again erupted in laughter, as though they were urging him to do so. The worried boy next to me joined in, with a loud, affected laugh that failed to erase the anxiety from his face and in fact increased it, as though he was trying hard to distance himself from me by making as much fun of me as possible.

Finally, the trolley passed and I returned to my row, where the fat man was still eating, his tray, on which he'd arranged the various dishes in eager anticipation, open over his belly. When I interrupted him with my desire to sit down, he exhaled, displeased, as he picked up his tray and stood. The number of people waiting in front of the bathroom had increased now that they'd had their food, and I was angry with myself for not having been content to wait and letting my embarrassment at standing there for a long time make me go back to my seat.

After that incident at the school, the rest of the students in the class ganged up to make fun of me and started imitating everything I said in a whiny voice, then laughing and calling, "*Com*pass! *Com*pass!" with the letters drawn out. It had been officially determined, with the blessing of the math teacher, that I needed to be made fun of. I'd get furious, the blood would rise to my face, and one day my nose started to bleed, so all I did was let the blood run and drip onto my clothes for them all to see. Everyone was terrified. Some ran away so that they wouldn't be punished and someone told the principal and the teachers.

"It's nothing," I said. "It happens to me all the time. All you need to do is press with two fingers from the outside so that the vein closes on the inside," and I held the upper part of my nose to show them how. I was speaking through my nose and the blood was dripping through the fingers that were holding it and it was running down onto my arms without my batting an eyelid, while they watched me, amazed at all the scarlet blood, which took on a darker color where it fell on my clothes.

After that, rarely did any of them make fun of my wussiness: my calm and composure in front of all that blood proved my ability to withstand things they couldn't. Nevertheless, by one means or another, and in everything I did, I continued to avoid anything that would make me seem spoiled or a butt for mockery in front of others. I hardly ever asked for permission to go to the bathroom and if I did so, out of extreme necessity, I'd feel the eyes of all turn toward me. Sometimes it amazes me to imagine the amount of trouble I'll go to so that I don't find myself in an embarrassing situation, only to end up embarrassing myself even more.

I felt my bladder had reached a point of fullness that could no longer be glossed over, so I got up, determined to get into the bathroom at any cost. The ironic man on my right turned immediately so that he could record this in his accounting of the number of times I'd gotten up. The fat man on my left obviously had to move sluggishly, now that he'd filled his belly with food. He undid his seat belt and made do with pushing his feet out into the aisle without standing; the space looked narrow but it was enough for me to pass without disturbance, so long as I apologized for treading on his feet.

The bathroom at the back was still in high demand but I noticed, through the half-drawn curtain at the beginning of the aisle, a sign indicating that there was an empty toilet at the front of the aircraft. Straightaway, with a hurried motion, I pushed past the curtain, afraid that someone else might get to it before me. It was only when I had almost reached it that the tall body of a stewardess blocked my path as she informed me that that bathroom was reserved for first-class passengers only.

I stopped and looked around, at a loss. It was then I noticed that the seats, which formed two rows there, were indeed larger, that the countenances of the passengers who occupied them seemed the sort of countenances that would travel first class, and that their heads were tilted a little to the rear on their head rests, in their comfortable seats, which could be pushed back freely without inconveniencing the passengers behind. Quickly, I returned my gaze to the stewardess, whom I now saw to be taller and more beautiful than the other and who had a Western-looking face, for which precise reason she had perhaps been chosen to be the stewardess for first class. When I opened my mouth to try to convince her that the other bathroom was occupied, and before I could explain to her how much I needed to go in, she cut me off by saying she understood but that the airline's rules prohibited passengers in economy class from using this bathroom and there was nothing she could do about it. She spoke in a hurried, hard way, as though making an announcement about the seat-belt sign, and I guessed, from her insistence and the speed with which she uttered the words, that she was used to passengers' protests over the matter and nothing would persuade her to change her mind. The people seated around me were watching the situation curiously and in comfort in their quiet cabin, as though I'd been provided expressly to entertain them with this post-prandial encounter.

My full bladder gave me sufficient courage to inform her that I understood what she was saying, but it couldn't do any harm as no one else was using the bathroom at present. Again, the stewardess hurried to repeat that she was well aware of that but I should have booked first class if I wanted to use this bathroom, and she nodded toward the passengers who had paid an additional amount for this class, as though they had paid specifically so that this bathroom would be available for them whenever they wanted it, even if none of them actually intended to use it. They didn't appear to disagree with this point; on the contrary, they merely stared and followed developments with hard eyes. The faces of some took on expressions indicating that I'd used up the time allocated to me for discussion and that I should immediately put an end to the situation and go back and piss on myself at the rear, as my arguing was disturbing their rest.

For a moment, I thought that that was what I was actually going to do, and I may even have started to turn around, but then, without my thinking, the words "But I have cancer," came out of my mouth. And for a while silence reigned.

In the moment that followed, someone could simply have asked what that had to do with getting into the first-class bathroom, and if they'd done so I wouldn't have had an answer and would have had to retrace my steps, defeated, but nothing of the sort happened. A tense, anxious look came over the stewardess's face: there was nothing in the users' manual she could use to refute that argument. A few "*There-is-no-power-or-strength-but-in-God*"'s resounded from the neighboring seats, which was enough to prevent her from any attempt at a riposte. A dignified woman raised her voice in a pitying tone to ask, "What type?" and I quickly answered, "AML, monocytic." More "*There-is-no-power-or-strength-but-in-God*"'s arose. I don't think they'd heard of this type before but the name alone was enough to make them feel the gravity of the situation. "It's a kind of leukemia," I added, in confirmation, in case any of them didn't yet appreciate how serious things were. I was even prepared to take the medical report out of my case, if necessary, though in fact my answer was so detailed it left no one in doubt as to my credibility. The stewardess retreated in confusion, leaving the way open to me, while I walked up the aisle in a slow, dignified manner befitting one as sick as I, the whispered prayers of the passengers for my good health, along with a few impressed murmurs, following behind me. The effect was magical. If I'd pulled out my penis and pissed in front of them, in the middle of the stupid first-class aisle, they might have found it tolerable, coming from someone in my condition.

In the bathroom, I urinated at length, slowly and peacefully, absorbed by the transparent gush and the strong, pulsing whizz, which trailed off until it came to a complete stop. It was the most beautiful piss I'd had in my life. I washed my hands well with soap, and then my face, and if there had been a shower, I would have had no objection to taking one, just to wallow in the luxury of spending as much time as I wanted without anyone saying no.

When I came out, the other passengers' sad expressions followed me, as though they were blaming themselves for delaying my access to the bathroom. I went past them, a sensation of intoxicating lightness in my limbs and my bladder. It crossed my mind as I left their compartment to go back and say it had just been a joke, I wasn't suffering from anything, and began imagining their reactions and laughing to myself at the idea. I returned to my seat and, without wiping the smile from my face, asked the fat man, in a stern tone that implied I would accept no less, to stand so that I could get past, then sat down, full of confidence in my conduct.

What had happened was so strange that it astonished me, and I began to feel so refreshed and in such great form that, if anyone had asked me the secret of my happiness, I would have replied, "It has been confirmed that I have cancer!" My stifled laughter provoked the displeasure of the man sitting to my right and he looked at me indignantly, as though it wasn't proper for a person to laugh on their own. What an idiot! The expression on his face had given me cancer! I think I shall use that phrase more often in the future. Whenever I'm confronted by extraordinary stupidity, I'll be able to turn to the perpetrator and say, "Look here! You've given me cancer!" And I'll always have that right. I'll say it whenever anyone jumps a line I'm standing in, or belches next to me, or scratches his privates in public, and I'll have the right to say it every time I have to chase after some government service, or a traffic cop stops me, or my order takes too long in a restaurant. I'll have the same right too when I watch a bad movie, but only if it's bad enough to give me cancer. And when my mother asks me to drive her to the market, I'll reply, "Mom, you're giving me cancer!" The market too gives me cancer, likewise bright lighting. Finally, I shall announce to my supervisor, "Your Skechers have given me cancer!" And if a girl says no to me, I'll say, "How come? I've got cancer!" and if she goes on refusing me, her rudeness alone will be enough to give me cancer and I shall be sure to inform her of that.

My heart was pounding to the point of collapse, either from the illness or perhaps because I was so excited—it came to the same thing. I kept repeating to myself the technical expression I'd used—AML. I even got the report out of my bag under the seat and started examining it proudly, absorbed in the fact that I was suffering from something serious. Immediately I was seized by an overwhelming desire to meet that doctor who'd examined me when I was a teenager, rub the test results into his face, and say, "Is this serious enough for you?"

I felt very solid—that I could face everyone, anyone could challenge me in a debate and I'd silence him, and that whatever might come along, I'd be fully prepared for it. I was determined to vanquish something, but it wasn't the disease. The disease might reign over me, and I'd be happy to let it do so, as long as it continued to grant me the power to reign over something else.

As soon as I got back, I went to see the doctor, who received me graciously. He was as sturdy, if not sturdier, and as fat and sound of body as the last time. His belly was still stuck to the desktop, as it had been when I left him, the test results were open in front of him, his hands open above them, perhaps in lieu of an embrace, and he seemed to be saying, "There was nothing we could do!" His body language seemed to be apologizing, on behalf of medicine and of all doctors, as though they were the ones who had manufactured or, more accurately, invented the disease. I felt I could have gone so far as to hold him guilty for my having fallen sick because he had diagnosed my sickness, and not the other way around, and that he would have accepted such frivolity from me and gone to great lengths to apologize. And why not? If one has to put up with the hardships of illness, one should also make the most of whatever privileges it offers. The seat opposite me was empty, so I stretched out my legs and relaxed, and

I felt that if I were to lift them and place one on top of the other on the empty seat, it wouldn't seem like a breach of good manners.

As he was just a general physician, he transferred me to another doctor, a specialist. This other doctor, by contrast, was lean and tall and wore a coat whose sleeves didn't cover his wrists. To hide this, he would put his hands into his pockets, then take them out for no obvious reason. This made him seem like a magician who might at any moment produce a rabbit, or a colored handkerchief, or a whole, well person. Each time, though, his hands emerged empty.

Sharp-featured, he was bald and serious, his seriousness seemingly springing from the seriousness of his specialization, diseases of the blood. He quickly adopted an energetic, practical mien, like a businessman accustomed to making deals in a hurry, and began talking in long, connected sentences that left me at a loss as to which part of them I wanted to have explained. He said he'd prefer to begin the treatment immediately as the case wasn't in its early stages (this could be considered sufficient justification for his speaking so fast). During his speech, he would suddenly mention, without pauses or breaks, chemical treatments the pronunciation of just one of whose names would turn one into a foreigner straightaway; it may be that they choose such terms just to make you believe they know more about the matter than you do, since they have the effect of submerging you from the start in a sense of your own ignorance, thus persuading you to leave the decision to the doctor.

"Chemotherapy is the only solution," he said, "so let's not waste time discussing the other options. We will be forced to do radiation if the primary cancer has spread to other parts of the body, so they'll run tests to be sure. There'll be a heart exam to make sure it's capable of withstanding the chemotherapy, and weekly tests of the blood count and MRA test for . . ." I know not what.

Suddenly I lost my ability to follow and asked him to do whatever he thought appropriate. I felt he had a clear plan. My agreement to it pleased him, so he moved on to what had to be done.

He presented me with papers and asked for my signature. One contained a long list of the risks and complications of the treatment, which I was required to accept. Above and beyond the usual side effects, the long-term risks included disorders of the liver, kidney failure, heart palpitations, impotence, sterility (isn't that encouraging?), and weakness of memory, comprehension, hearing, and sight, but the largest piece of the cake was reserved for the following—the possibility of contracting another type of cancer, most likely another blood cancer, as a result of the toxic effect of the chemicals.

So, the way things are done is to poison you in the hope that this poison will kill the cancerous cells before they kill you. And if this "treatment" cures you of your current cancer, there is the possibility that it will result, by virtue of its toxic-therapeutic effect, in making you sick with cancer again. Excellent. I signed without reading the rest and he kept handing me paper after paper, one giving him the right to act as he saw fit in cases of emergency during which I was incapable of taking a decision, and another releasing him from any responsibility for such decisions; pink papers and then yellow papers and then blue papers. Each time I signed one, he handed me another related to this or that test or to possible emergency operations; he told me their contents and I signed them directly, to get it over with quickly, as though that way I was getting done with the test or the operation itself.

Anyway, the most important step as far as I was concerned was connected to the certification from the medical insurance company that it would assume responsibility for all stages of the treatment. This filled me with a sense of triumph, as I'd be forcing my company to squander its wealth on treating me, a thought that gave me comfort throughout the signing of all those papers. Take this operation, you bastards, and these medicines, and pay for this room at the hospital, and agree to bear the costs of these tests! Go on, pay for your employee! He deserves it.

When the papers were finished, we still had a few administrative procedures ahead of us and he had to go by the office of the head physician to get them endorsed. It is astonishing that bureaucracy has found its way to this institution too. Maybe you can never be liberated from it, no matter where you go, for even your death can only be made complete via signed papers establishing your demise.

We went back to the doctor's office, and he asked me some questions about my medical history and that of the family and whether any of my relatives had suffered from the same disease. I mentioned to him my grandmother and felt strange because my own case had only now reminded me of hers. I don't remember many details of her struggle with the disease and it may be that I hadn't observed any evidence of it. All I know about the circumstances of her death I heard afterward from others, who said, for example, that, as she lay dying, she would try to get up to give my grandfather his medication, as she used to do every day. For some reason, this was what came most often to my mind, out of all the other details.

At the wake, I was sitting following the grown-ups' conversation about her when one of the adults came over, patted me on the head, and told me I should pray that she should find God's mercy, as though the fact that I was holding myself aloof from the other children was the result of the depth of my mourning for her. In fact, I always held myself aloof from my peers and found great difficulty in fitting in with them, and if one spoke to me or tried to involve me in their play, I rarely responded or would quickly withdraw from the group, giving the impression that I had something to attend to.

At the time, I didn't feel embarrassed by my aloofness per se, only perhaps by there being nothing to justify it. I would withdraw into myself and become yet more deeply reserved. It was the only thing I did to attract their attention, though there was nothing in that, in and of itself, that would attract attention. I probably didn't want anyone to come near me in the first place, just that their interest in me should be aroused, at a distance.

When my grandmother died, and I received all that sympathy from strangers, I realized in my childish way that what I lacked was the brand of misfortune—an external event that would attract the interest of others without any direct involvement from me in its creation and that would bestow on me the natural right to be so uncommunicative and distant.

I remember that I was in sixth grade at the time or, to be more precise, in the summer vacation before I moved to that level, because I couldn't wait for school to begin so I could tell the others. On the first day of school, while the students were gathered around one another's desks telling about their vacation trips and the classroom was alive with the excitement of meeting again after separation, I threw the news out to them completely without emotion, as though a grandmother of mine died every vacation. It was the same kind of pride as that with which a rich child might inform us that he had spent the vacation in Europe and create more astonishment with his nonchalance than if he had displayed enthusiasm.

This produced precisely the desired effect. Some of them gathered around me and questioned me curiously. "Cancer," I replied, and I shrugged my shoulders as though that were the least of what happened in my family. I even told them about her trying to get out of bed at the moment of her death so that she could give my grandfather his medication, in a way that implied that her death wasn't anything out of the ordinary even to her. I thus created the impression that death was routine in my milieu and demonstrated I had inherited the same blood line, in which disasters were commonplace. An idea of that sort gave me the right to appear, alone among the others, like one who was constantly going through things that were difficult to talk of openly.

I recalled those stories as I was leaving the hospital, intoxicated to be in possession of a new piece of information, as though I had just been informed that I was pregnant.

I thought I'd let them know like that, with an ironic smile, a chuckle perhaps escaping me before I began to talk, as though I was about to tell a joke. Then, be my guests—cancer! In fact, I ought to say it in English, which is scarier, has a stranger ring to it, and is more likely to cause confusion. No nitpicker would have the gall to say, "Why are you using English? You should be proud of your own language! Say 'I have cancer.' Don't say, 'Ay haf kansar'!" That would be a first if it happened; I'd even let the speaker get away with it. But none of them would. They'd all stick to decorum, pity, respect, and embarrassment at not having been stricken along with me. Their faces would fuse from the effort of adopting an appropriate reaction, and each would say to himself, "Thank God Fate chose him, not me!" I would smile at all this, with total control over my expression, and maybe take pity on them because they were still at the stage of being wary about using the microwave. All the same, the smile mustn't be understood as a smile of strength, like the ones borne by the brave patients, the ones on whose faces stupid, optimistic expressions that speak of patience and resistance are drawn. No, you mustn't be one of those fairies who provide a source of inspiration for others. It had to be a smile that said, "My day of reckoning with you has arrived, accursed world!"

Of course, I was not without fear. The fear is always there, but is retreating now beneath waves of heightened feeling, the feeling I sensed when my grandmother died. Something is happening to me now, me alone among the others, and none of them has what it takes to compete with me in it. Oh, yes! Certainty bestows such happiness!

Week 13

My mother is sitting with me, to make sure I tell everyone: "Have you contacted your uncles? You have to phone each one personally to tell them"— as though I was giving them Eid greetings—"your oldest uncle at least. Are you, a young man, going to sit there and wait for your elders to phone you?" She picks up the phone, places it against her ear, and moves her fingers over the numbers while still directing her words at me: "They're your uncles and it's their duty to support you at such times, even if we never hear a good word from any of them, and if your father were here none of them would dare ignore us like this. In fact, it was his death that put them up to this disgraceful treatment. They were disrespectful to their own father and had nothing more to do with us or even with one another so now they've each gone their separate ways, but bad cess to us if we're going to be like them. Do you want people to think we're going to deal with this as though we don't have family? Hello, greetings, how are you, what's your news, how are the children? And the grandchildren? We're all fine, here's my son. My son's with me and he wants to tell you something, here you are . . ."

"Hello, Uncle. How are you? I just wanted to tell you that I have a touch of cancer . . . Oh, so you heard? Sorry. I don't want to take up your time. Keep us in your prayers. Goodbye."

"See? It doesn't take any time at all. Now phone the rest."

She takes the receiver and dials another number. "Auntie, how are you? How's your health? . . . Oh, I'm sorry to hear that. Don't let it get you down. I hope you feel better soon. Health and strength! . . . I'm fine, just leukemia, nothing serious . . . Yes indeed, that's life." I don't think she got it. "Amen. And how's my dear uncle? . . . Oh, poor guy. I'll pray for him. For both of you. . . . Right, for all three of us! And for every sick Muslim, indeed! Amen. . . . No, I won't speak to him. . . . No, let him rest. . . . No, I don't want to disturb him, I just wanted to give him my . . . Hello, greetings, yes, amen, and everyone else, yes, yes. And is your son well? . . . Excellent. At least one of us is well. . . . Nothing, I just thought I'd send him my greetings, God preserve him for you, amen. And preserve you and preserve my aunt and, right, my mother and my brother and sister, and all the Muslims, of course. I won't keep you . . . Hello again, Auntie. Amen, amen, I won't keep . . . Amen, Auntie, amen. Good . . . Bye bye."

"See? It takes no time. Who's next?"

It wasn't the way I'd imagined it, of course. There's always the heavy feeling that you're hurting someone when you tell them. "I'm sorry you have to listen to this," I say, when someone is incapable of coming up with a reaction, or "Right, it's terrible, we shall take patience as our adornment," when they go overboard to show how moved they are. Everyone behaves in the way they think you need and you are obliged, of course, to respect their attempts and make them feel good about their efforts. As a result, you find yourself forced to perform social duties more than at any time in the past. But all these are just passing, bearable trifles compared to what goes on at home.

My duty to her was the most difficult of all—my mother, I mean. Everything I imagined about the sickness being an excuse for quiet retreat fell apart at her hands. When I told her, at the beginning, she fainted. She suddenly fell down, the way they do in bad soap operas, and we took her to the hospital. However, after a few days, this ceased to be novel. Such breakdowns repeated themselves in diverse forms, so as not to lose the element of surprise. She'd cry in the house, in the car, at the hospital, in other people's houses, and once she cried at the market, when she bought an herb that the vendor said was good against cancer. My response was that it was all nonsense, and she began to wail, screaming, "What are we going to do now?" as though all the disasters in the world had suddenly fallen upon us. With her, I feel as though I were walking in the middle of a minefield: anything could go off anywhere.

Soon, however, her passionate emotions merged with her practical energy into an amazing mix, and she plunged into a flurry of activity such as I had only seen from her when my father was sick—the same sense of responsibility that makes her erupt in all directions. She began contacting relatives in every city, as well as acquaintances who might be able to help us with this or that. She consulted doctors, clinics, and television programs, the importance of whose counsels were for her on a par with the instructions of her female neighbors and the mediums of expired internet forums. Each new datum got added immediately to her plan, any old how, and fashioned another network of treatments that I was supposed to follow. It was a bit like having a director at work who takes all the decisions away from you, even though you're the one who will have to put them into effect and bear their consequences.

She was completely convinced that it was a collective matter. "You mustn't be selfish," she'd respond, when I resorted to my own personal ways of facing the situation—as though the sickness was a bequest I was refusing to share with them. The question of money, especially, was a source of worry for her: the hospital charges, which she saw as exorbitant, would have us thrown out onto the street. When I brought my health insurance and the leftovers of my salary that I'd saved into the argument, she'd wave her hand dismissively, as though all my savings together were no more than chaff, which wouldn't spare us anything. I'd get angry and swear mighty oaths that no one but I would spend a penny on the treatment, and she'd quickly get hysterical and appeal to my brother for help and call my sister, complaining to them in my hearing, which would make me cling with greater determination to my stubbornness, and we'd argue and argue till she took us by surprise with a new breakdown. The others would try to calm both parties down. They'd talk to her in private, saying, "He's sick, you have to make allowances." They'd talk to me in private, saying, "She's your mother, you have to make allowances." As a result, in the end, I'd make allowances.

Part of me felt guilty, since it occurred to me that this condition of mine was reviving her memories of my father's final sickness. Sometimes I'd see her looking at me in silence with an expression that said, "Why are you doing this?" while shedding copious tears, whose source I was wrong to think might have dried up.

The night he died, I went into their bedroom at a late hour. Her tears were streaming onto his pillow and she was sobbing quietly. The bed seemed wider than usual in proportion to her body, which was occupying the left, which until a few days ago had been my father's side of the bed. When she noticed I'd come in, she quickly raised her head and looked in the direction of the door, hoping perhaps that it might somehow be my father who'd entered. I was eighteen at the time and had recently reached his height. She stared in silence for a while, her eyes full of tears that gleamed in the dark. When she made out that it was I who'd come in, she buried her head in the pillow and began sobbing again. I asked her how she was but she didn't reply, just went on wailing, in a louder voice, as though to tell me that my question was pointless, and that I wasn't my father.

It occurred to me to lie down next to her in the bed and I continued to stand for a while, hesitating, while I thought about whether that would comfort her. I lay down on the right side of the bed without saying anything. I did, however, lie down with a loud sigh, to make clear that I would be with her for that night only. After a moment, she stopped sobbing, but she didn't utter a word. She just extended to me my half of the covers, turning her back to me, and after that didn't move. I pulled the covers up to my neck and lay absolutely still. I kept staring at the back of her head, while the scent of her hair came to me from her old pillow, where I had laid mine, and her tears dried on my father's pillow as she fell into a deep sleep. I resisted the desire to move closer to her so that I could breathe in the smell of her hair directly from her head; the distance between us was wide and our physical communication hadn't been comfortable for at least ten years. There is an estrangement between a man and his mother that has to come about at some point during his boyhood, and it takes the form of the utmost reserve, without either grasping why, or which of the two initiated it.

In my childhood, I'd be with her in many of her activities, but without getting in her way; I'd just move along in the warm aura that surrounded her as she swept the floor or cooked or hung out the wash. I preferred to be to the side, watching her without requiring her attention, marveling at the skill with which she did everything. She'd notice my admiration, find comfort in it, and yet more warmth and energy would emanate from her, and from time to time she'd smile without looking in my direction, knowing that if she took too much notice of me she'd scare me away. She didn't talk to me on such occasions except to ask me to do something, like helping her carry the wash, even though she was perfectly capable of carrying it all herself. It was as though with these small tasks she was rewarding me for being around her.

The image of her from those days most firmly fixed in my memory is that of her scattering flour over the kitchen table, her naked brown hands sprinkled with the white powder to halfway up her arm, while the specks flew around like fine dust floating in a diaphanous veil formed by a thread of sunlight that descended at a sharp angle through the high windows. She would put the butter and sugar together into a bowl, blend them well into a yellow mixture, add more flour and blend them again, then break an egg and drop it in, raising, with a delicate movement and in the opposite direction to the rest, just her little finger, which was thus kept separate, in a gesture to something far away. She would beat the mixture, her brow gleaming with beads of sweat to which a lock of the hair from her temple had become stuck. At the back, her hair was gathered carelessly so that the tresses that were supposed to go behind her ear drooped down and dangled toward places closer to the side of her neck, which revealed, under the same thread of light, a small white smudge of flour the size of a finger, evidence of her attempt to push a stray lock back into place.

This was my favorite pastry, and before making it, she'd call me to keep her company by watching her, so I'd sit on the kitchen table, holding myself still, watching every step she took and not even swinging my fidgety legs. My memory doesn't now provide any evidence for the presence of either my brother or my sister in such scenes; maybe they were playing and racing one another someplace in back. This world in which my mother and I intersected rested on intimate, unspoken rules that no one else could be a part of. Both of us were aware of this world, kept it by common consent as it was, and allowed ourselves to indulge in it with total spontaneity. It was like a secret that, it seemed, would never cease to grow.

The mixture in the bowl ended up each time as a soft, cohesive dough from which she would take small pieces that she shaped with precise, deft fingers, one after the other, and made into smooth, soft balls, then arranged on the tray that later would be placed in the oven. On days when the tray was larger than normal, I knew we would have guests. One day, the tray was new and large, and she warned us all, without exception, to stay in our rooms when they arrived. I understood that they were old school friends whom she hadn't met with for a long time, perhaps even since their marriages.

In the evening, their voices reached me from below. I tried for a while to remind myself of her command, then somehow reached the conclusion that it was meant for my brother and sister but not for me. I therefore left my room and hid at the top of the stairs leading to the living room and started watching them. From that angle, it was hard to make out where among the rest of the bodies she was sitting. Then I traced her voice, which had its back to me and which, despite its familiarity, sounded strange. I was about eight at the time and I felt as though I had never seen her before with other women.

She was laughing for no reason, talking a lot, moving her hands in all directions, interrupting the others to blame them for not eating enough of the pastries, assuring them that she had made them with her own hands that day and that they were delicious, devouring a piece and making seductive sighing noises while it melted in her mouth, then laughing crazily, while everyone laughed along with her and talked, screamed, and ate at the same time. She was the gathering's leader and her voice was the loudest, which I didn't like because I'd never imagined her as a leader and I didn't like to see her raucous and excited and agitated, bereft of calm and dignity, as though the silent aureole that we shared meant nothing to her. Even her hairdo was strange, like a wig, similar in its crafting to those of the others. She seemed happy, I cannot doubt that now, but nothing in that happiness had anything to do with me, as though she was happy precisely because she'd forgotten about me. I was seized by a desire to spoil that happiness, which, at that moment, I decided was not real.

I called to her but she didn't turn to me in the midst of the racket, or perhaps she heard but pretended not to, and this made me more determined and more convinced that she needed to be saved. I descended the stairs and began calling to her in my loudest voice but she didn't answer. I was certain that through the sheer force of my presence I would bring her to her senses and show her friends that they could never keep her occupied for long or corrupt her nature by imposing their merriment. The third time, I went close and screamed at her, and she abruptly stopped laughing and turned toward me, her face having become totally transformed—even before her eyes fell on me and at the very moment when she realized the small, discordant, piercing voice crying "Mommy!" was calling her—into a scowl. She fixed her gaze on me in silence, the voices around her fell quiet, and they all turned around. I had imagined that when I achieved that degree of notice, I would have won, even if I wasn't ready for what I would have to say after my triumphant achievement of that reaction.

In a loud, scolding voice, she said, "What do you want?" She had read all my intentions at a single glance and deduced from my pleading expression that all I desired was this interruption. I realized that I had immediately to appear convincing, miserable, sufficiently distressed to justify my spoiling the gathering's joyful atmosphere, and my face took on the lying expression that she could always distinguish when I made up excuses for myself. Before I could utter a word, however, she cut me off with an incisive formula that bore no repetition: "Go to your room!" I, though, had decided, again, not to believe that she meant what she said. I began walking toward her, in the hope that some pitiful lie would flash across my mind before I reached her. She didn't let me take a step before following her order with a roaring scream: "Now!" I stood, rooted to the spot in terror, while she, without even checking to see whether I had obeyed, turned her whole body toward them with a motion that implied I was no longer of any consequence and began talking to them again, and the bursts of laughter rose again around her, goading her on to further merriment, some of them even beginning to stare at where I still stood, their mouths open in laughter. I could tell that she was talking about me and had begun sarcastically bemoaning her luck and striking her naked throat with loud, fast, continual blows as though she were saying, "This is what I've brought on myself—this childish creature that hovers around me. See? This is what I have to put up with every day—this thing that stands there helplessly, like an idiot." Then she turned around again and found me still standing there, stunned and stupid, and brought her hand down on her thigh with a loud, violent smack, the sound exploding in my ears, and I was jerked out of my stupor, as though her hand had landed on my face. She began talking to them again, waving her hands and making movements that hadn't been part of her nature before they arrived, the sound of her accusations growing louder, encouraged by the others' screams as they tried to interrupt her, sharing in her complaint, and then they laughed as they moved on with her to something else.

I left them and went to my room, slamming the door behind me hard, to echo that smack of hers on her thigh and hoping that she'd hear it and get mad. I passed the night tossing and turning in my bed and reached a firm decision not to answer her the next time she spoke to me, and that in fact I would never speak to her again as long as I lived. But I fell asleep waiting for her to come in and see me.

During the next few days, she showed no sign of regret and, thanks to my being habitually taciturn, she might not even have noticed that I'd become a little more so. Then I went back to talking to her, with reserve, when needed, and little by little need became the main reason for us to talk to one another. The number of words we exchanged wasn't that much different from before; what was different was the nature of the silence. It had come to lack that intimate shared aura, and all that was left in its place was disobedience on my side and agitated reaction on hers. The tension lasted until I lost the desire to be around her when there was no reason to talk. It was clear that some kind of break had to happen, and it started with that incident. Nothing, not even something of the magnitude of this illness, could bridge that gap, or prevent it from widening.

Week 14

"LISTEN TO ME CAREFULLY!" SHE barged angrily into my room, as though expecting opposition. "You can't exploit this so you can accuse me of not being understanding or violating your privacy and all the nonsense you've learned from books. I'm not putting pressure on you about anyone else, but when it comes to your grandfather it's different. You can't tell him by telephone like the others. He's as important as your father. In fact, he's your father's father and asking for his blessing is like asking for your father's. You have to go and—"

"Fine. I'll visit him today," I said. She was standing by the door, waiting for the expected objection, and when I said nothing more, she departed, leaving the door open.

But what was I suppose to object to (apart, of course, from the open door)? The idea had come to me before she talked to me about it. As much as I wanted to avoid telling him in person, putting it off was no longer possible: the longer the wait, the harder the task became. He has this amazing ability to remember how long it is since each grandchild has come to see him, which doesn't mean he'd be pleased to see you even if you visited him once a week. The best one can hope for from him is that his displeasure is at its lowest level, though it is also the case that his displeasure rises to its highest levels, for no clear reason, the moment you enter his reception room.

When we—my cousins and I—were young, we used to call him, among ourselves, the Sphinx. I don't remember where we got the name from but I do remember that, whenever we went in to see him, we'd find him sitting with his legs folded underneath him and his hands extended, like two animalian claws, on the arms of his sand-colored armchair. Giving him your greetings was the hardest part, since a single look from him was enough to inform you that you'd done so incorrectly, and when that happened, you felt lucky if that was all he did, and on the next occasion you'd have to take special care to avoid some mistake of which you were unaware. If, on the other hand, he took to berating you, then the whole room would fall silent, out of respect, and it was as though the fury of Heaven had fallen upon you, and your father and everyone else would disown you since, because of you, the anger fell on them too. Later, you'd find out the reason was that you'd entered wearing your shoes, for example, or you'd tripped on the carpet as you walked toward him, or you hadn't pressed your lips close together as you were supposed to when you kissed him and you'd left a trace of moisture on his hand or his head. Any of the above was enough to unleash his displeasure at your whole generation, at the way your parents had brought you up, and at the barber who'd given you that haircut. And then you'd find him cursing you randomly, with the harshest things, for as long as he cared to, without anyone daring even to think that he was going on a bit.

This feeling wasn't restricted to us children. The adults too greeted him with extreme submissiveness, a submissiveness I couldn't understand, as though each of them owed him a private debt. They'd wait at doors for him to go through first and they'd go up to him and, as they kissed his head and hand, remind him of their names. They performed these duties happily and with total acceptance of all the gruffness that was to be expected from him, such as his shooing them away with a bad-tempered gesture of his hand, to which they would always insist on exposing themselves since it would be worse if they didn't establish the fact of their visit. Even if he suddenly shouted at someone for making too much of a fuss in greeting him, or doing so at the wrong time, and even if that person was the most respected and looked up to among them, you'd find him cringing and retreating while laughing in a servile manner as if to tell everyone how much he loved and honored this grandfather and how right he was to shout at him.

He was unique, and if he hadn't been my grandfather, it would in no way have divested him of his right to behave like that, given the air of natural entitlement to respect and awe that he possessed. And there was more to that entitlement than his having reached a certain age, though how exactly he acquired it and at what stage in his life he assumed that image I never knew. I often felt he'd been a grandfather since the day he was born and perhaps, like the prophets, he'd discovered, through some form of inspiration and without any special joy or pride, that he was destined to become this grandfather and had accepted the role as his unavoidable fate.

I was thinking of all this as I entered the old neighborhood in the middle of which stands his house—a kind of Kaaba, around which the other houses have grown up. It's so ancient in appearance that it's impossible to imagine any other building existed there before it—as though he'd come to this vacant land and said, "Here I shall build a house!" after which he'd built next to it a mosque, a grocery store, and a few other residential buildings that he'd begun renting to the families who had made their way there little by little. As a result, people had accumulated in the neighborhood and his wealth had accumulated with them, and despite all the attempts of his children and grandchildren over the years to persuade him to move to a more upscale area and invest his commercial activity in other ways after the quarter had grown old and shabby, and the only ones to live there were workers, he continued to insist on staying there to the end, without even renovating his apartment. He used to speak of the building as though it were entitled to the status of a sixth son—the way a real Bedouin speaks of his camel, which forms the source of his livelihood, his food, and his drink, and which is dearer to him than his children. Even when his business stagnated, his health declined, and he became chair-bound and lost a portion of his prestige, it all just made him rougher and harsher. His children dispersed to more upmarket quarters and he remained, stubbornly alone, despite their visits; in fact, a visit from one of them represented to him an opportunity for revenge, when he could tell them that they were good for nothing and that they and the generation that came after them were a burden on the land. For him, time came to a halt with his generation and nothing lay ahead but a slackness that could lead only to collapse.

I knocked on the door well aware what species of dinosaur was waiting for me inside and that I had to communicate to him something specific to me that would benefit him nothing, something that was just a trivial piece of news about a trivial grandson who he thought deserved to die anyway. I could almost see him saying, "A young man of your age and suffering from cancer? Aren't you ashamed of yourself?"

No sooner do I knock, using the rusty iron doorknocker, than the door suddenly opens. I immediately recall those terrifying scenes in animated movies when someone knocks on the door of a haunted castle and it swings open of its own accord. From this opening, however, doubting eyes peer out at me with the suspicion of those unused to visitors, though her suspicion may have been made worse in that she had somehow been expecting me and perhaps had been standing behind the door all day long. She was the servant, nurse, and cook all in one, all these things ground into an old, blank face, a face that looked as though it received a thousand insults each day. She opens the door with a slow movement, her expressionless visage staring at me like that of an exhausted Asian ghost. She has lived her wasted life in this house year after year and perhaps, with the passage of time, has forgotten what she had come for; in fact, it's obvious that there is nothing left for her in her country of origin. I realize that she knows who I am, even though it has been so long since I've seen her, and she opens the door wide so that I can go in, but without a word, then suddenly disappears in the manner of a ghost, as befits her life, this house, and her sudden appearance behind the door.

I have barely taken one step inside before I remember to take off my shoes. I heave a sigh of relief for having thought of it before it was too late. A reel runs before my eyes showing all the times when he'd shouted at me for entering with my shoes on, as though we were defiling the Earth, not the apartment's disgusting carpet. I make my way to his room barefoot, my footsteps muffled, feeling the ancient floor covering against the soles of my feet. The apartment seems smaller than I remember from my last visit but has the same smell—a mixture of incense, dust, old wood, and other, obscure, scents. In every corner of the apartment, there are memories of things I've been scolded about, with or without cause, as though my presence was cause enough on its own.

The lighting is dim in the corridor that leads to the room but light steals in through the crack of the open door. I look through the crack and see him—the Sphinx, seated on the same ancient seat, firm and immobile. It's hard to tell if he is awake, despite which a shudder still runs through my body. There is no response when I knock on the door. I go in cautiously, as though there is a wrong way to do so, and the door creaks, confirming my fear.

His eyes are open but he doesn't turn his head in my direction. I thought that my mother had called him and told him I was coming. I kiss his head twice, then his hand once. Have I forgotten to kiss something? I sit in front of him on the edge of the bed. He stares at me as though I *have* forgotten to kiss something. Maybe I'm not supposed to sit on the bed. Big deal.

"How are you?" No answer. The idol-like face is the same, despite the further advance in age, and though the eyes are glassier than usual. He isn't wearing his spectacles and perhaps hasn't seen me yet. How often he'd terrified me with his naked eyes when he wasn't hiding them behind their thick lenses.

"God grant you good health!" Why do I say that? I don't know. Fine. So let's get down to it. "I have bad news."

"And what else can I expect of you but bad news?"

Excellent. At least I've confirmed that he can hear me. I have to stay silent for a few seconds so that he feels I've accepted his rebuke.

"They've discovered that I have cancer." Who are "they"? I don't know but I have to avoid saying *I* have discovered so that the whole thing doesn't become my fault again.

"I know. I got the news."

Excellent. He knows. What now? One, two, three: "It's at an advanced stage. They said it's hard to catch this type early. God's will." He doesn't reply. I list a few additional details for him, keeping them practical and reassuring and as far away as possible from anything that might incur reproach.

"Next week I start in on the treatment. I've done all the required tests and now I begin a six-month round of chemo-therapy, one session per month." He remains silent. I go on with the explanation so as to appear like someone who's in control of his situation: "A session is three consecutive days in a month, with a period of convalescence in between so that the body can recover its strength before the next session, and if that doesn't work, I have a second round."

All the while I'm talking, I'm waiting for the look that will say, "And what about your mother and your brother and sister? What about their needs and responsibilities? Isn't it enough for them that your father died? Aren't you ashamed of yourself? And at your young age?" but he doesn't even glance at me. He remains silent as an idol. "So God grant you good health!" I don't know why I keep saying that. We remain silent. Two minutes and I'll leave, using my need for rest as an excuse. The cockroaches that pour out of the drain in his bathroom are more welcome here than I am.

I run my eyes over the contents of the shabby room, which in its own way seems more elderly than he. The first thing to catch my eye is the iron safe next to the window. It's of the ancient kind that even a nuclear explosion couldn't open. It is protected, in addition, by eerie green curtains, made of some terrifying fungal fabric, the only logical reason for his having chosen such a cloth being that it would scare off the thieves. What a suspicious, mean old man! The safe is even located right next to the bed because some plot may be hatched against him and he has to keep his eye on it while he's asleep.

His wide bed bears the traces of a second body on the other side of the mattress, as though the ghost of my grandmother still slept at his side every night. There's a bedside table, which in appearance, size, and weight seems no less massive than the iron safe. Over it is a patterned white waxed cloth of the kind it is impossible to remove because over the years it has stuck and stuck, and continues to stick, to the table so hard. The radio set still manages to work, by some miracle; it may date back to the First World War, or a century before that, since when it has been transmitting news from a scratchy station that must have gone off the air years ago, leaving the announcer's ghost pointlessly repeating his words over the airwaves. The radio, likewise, has stuck to the bedside table, on top of which, aimlessly, cups and an infinite array of medication boxes is also set out; he may well be taking the tablets after their expiry date and without any effect on his body, which is stiff as an ancient tree.

Next to the bedside table is an empty space where the floor is covered with a green mat, of the same shade as the curtains and no less welcoming to its embrace of fungi and stains. The remaining walls are filled by a huge, wide closet with peeling paint, which I surmise forms the cornerstone that allows this tottering room to remain on its feet. If the closet were removed, the walls might collapse on top of one another, spreading a vast cloud of dust over the neighborhood. In fact, the whole neighborhood might collapse as well, the way dominoes do, one on top of another, after the first falls. Only the iron safe would remain in one piece above the rubble, to bear witness that here there was once a quarter.

Everything here takes its bearing from the closet, which stands in lonely splendor before me like a wise ghost. We—my cousins and I—used to gather before it on each festival and family occasion, so that my grandmother could take out the ancient metal sewing box in which she kept different kinds of candy; it was always from this closet, which before used to carry the smell of the Feast. Sometimes when neither of them was there, we'd sneak in and help one another climb up to the upper shelf to steal the candy. How disappointed we would be when we opened the box and discovered that it held nothing but sewing utensils! We would put it back and ask one another where the new hiding place for the candy might be. When my grandmother returned, we'd ask her, in all innocence, for some candy, as though we'd just been waiting for her to ask for permission. And then she'd open the closet, stretch her shrunken frame, and pull out the very same box from the very same shelf and open it under our eyes and we'd behold—and how strange this was!—the shiny packages of candy twinkling from inside the box. We could find no explanation for this other than that the closet, in its mysterious ghostly way, exchanged the candy during my grandmother's absence for needles, reels, buttons, and threads, and only when she extended her short, wrinkled fingers would the box with its contents suddenly regain its magical nature, regain it solely at the merciful motion of that wrinkled hand, which looked as though it had been left to steep for hours in water.

Suddenly, a sound from by my side reaches my ears, as though in response to the same memory. When I turn toward him, his shoulders are shaking and tears are running from his narrowed eyes but unable to fall because his lids are so full of wrinkles; they can only distribute themselves among the deep lines of his lower lids and remain hanging there. I remain silent, while he cries and jerks, like a coffeepot boiling over, and mumbles prayers of entreaty that only God could decipher. All I can get out of them is that he is pleading with God to be kind, to be kind to us, to be kind to my father in his grave, to be kind to my grandmother, and to be kind to him.

After a few moments, he stopped and resumed his stony stillness, his face suddenly returning to its original state, as though it hadn't just now been weeping tears. I rose and asked his permission to leave, and he paid me no attention. Simply out of habit, I kissed his head and then left. The moment I closed the door, I could no longer hold back my excitement. I thought, Amazing! The Sphinx has a heart. Who would have thought it? Wasn't this more exciting than the realization by Orientalist travelers that there was another part of the statue beneath the sand, although the face had been visible for centuries? And then, when they dug beneath it, their discovery—and how strange this was!—that it was nothing less than the body of a lion?

Week 15

I REREAD *THE OLD MAN AND THE SEA*, for the strength I needed to face the day, and got up feeling full of energy, like a fisherman setting off with the expectation of a good catch. I took a shower, ate a light breakfast, and dressed at a leisurely pace. In the car, Queen's "I Want To Break Free" was playing off the disc I'd made of my favorite band. When "Bohemian Rhapsody" began, I turned the volume up as far as it would go and began singing along tunelessly to Freddy Mercury's highest register.

I arrived at the hospital early and parked the car opposite the entrance. The long, low building rose in front of me, and something about it seemed to bestow on me special status because I was a patient. I climbed the outside steps lightly; they're evenly spaced, close to one another, and so conducive to agility that as soon as you've climbed them, you want to go down again and climb back up. But the door opens in front of you unexpectedly and of its own accord and sucks you in, so you surrender yourself joyfully to the flow of air and traverse the public areas, and even though you may want to ask Reception this or that, you roam around wherever you feel like going, with no goal other than to maintain your progress over the tightly fitted flagstones of this strong, ancient building, this marvellous, solidly built structure. Verily, I love it like a dog and want to pat its head!

I had done enough tests in this hospital in recent days, taken into my body enough of its blood supply, for a sort of familiarity to have developed between us, and the lean, serious doctor who is in charge of my case had made an appointment for me in the Oncology department, which is an independent department located inside the hospital but separated from it by a long corridor so as to isolate it as much as possible from the others. Having found my way to the latter, I saw it to be cheery and pleasing to the eye, well suited to leading a person wherever he might want to go. It looked out, on one glass-walled side, onto an open-air playground, while on the other, the wall was smooth and bright, the sun thrown down the length of its floor in squares, like a sunny carpet over the marble. "Oh, my! What a long, thrilling corridor!" I said, as I walked down it on my own. Then, halfway down, I raised my voice and said, "O Corridor, I walk down you for the first time, and I shall walk down you I know not how many more times, but I'd like to say—on behalf of all the times to come when I shall perhaps be too exhausted to tell you—I'd like to say now that I love you and that you are a cheery, exciting corridor. Your lighting is marvelous and your floor warm to those who indulge their feet in the luxury of walking upon it, as well as being pleasing to those who lay their eyes on it! Verily, everyone who sees you loves you, O Corridor, and all who walk down you think, What a nice corridor! What an excellent corridor! The worker who built you loved you, as did the engineer who designed you and the architect who, even before these two, drew you and said, 'Here shall be the corridor, one side of it by a wall enclosed, the other to daylight exposed!' The patients love you, O Corridor, and take a deep breath every time they walk down you, without realizing that you are the reason they do so. In you the doctors loiter and find rest without, unusually for them, coming up with a reason. Likewise the nurses, other medical staff, visitors, and cleaners— how happy, time after time each day, your shininess (attributable to the radiance of the sun beaming up off your marble) makes them! Verily, would it not be natural for a person, on seeing a corridor like you, to want to become a cleaner?"

I kept going until the corridor brought me, at its end, to a wide lobby, as an excellent corridor of its kind should. I notified Reception there of my arrival and sat down in the waiting area. I waited like someone with all the time in the world. I even looked challengingly at the people seated around me. None of them had as much time as I did. I stretched my legs out, proud of this knowledge.

The nurse called me and performed her various duties. She ran tests to make sure that my blood count was good enough to begin the treatment, then asked me to wait again. She had a cheerful look, with a round, shining face, like a loaf of bread, and cheeks flushed with red, indicating good health. She came back and said that everything was fine and my blood count excellent. For the first time in my life I felt proud of my blood and I began the session in the best of spirits. My morale was high and the nurse was careful and understanding and explained to me everything she was going to do and how the intravenous injection would be made via something called a "cannula," which would be stuck into the back of my hand. I looked up the translation of the word immediately and found that it was "a small channel" and felt a desire to use it when writing. I even began saying it out loud so as not to forget it later.

And, indeed, the liquid began slowly to drip, just as she had said, making its way into the small channel via a slim tube, the tube extending from a bag full of the transparent chemical substance, the bag suspended by a curved hook, like a fishhook, the hook forming the upper part of a long metal pole, the pole mounted on wheels that helped you lead it along behind you wherever you went and having an analyzer halfway down that offered a continuous, measured flow of data, numbers, and sounds, and whose job was to regulate the average number of drops dripping into your vein per minute. Verily, a marvelous, judicious invention.

The seat was hidden from the corridor by a cloth curtain that could be drawn aside. The chairs were divided from one another by curtains too, and the wide leather chair was comfortable and could be inclined backward so that you felt that the liquid pouring into your vein was nothing but an anesthetic. I thought I was in excellent health and that the liquid was simply an illusion, just a cool current flowing through the veins. I began staring at my hand, and addressing it out loud—"How are you feeling now, dear hand? Or is it too soon for you to know?"—the way the Old Man does in Hemingway's novel, and my hand just kept looking back and drinking up the liquid without saying a word with that silence that some members of the body have that makes it difficult to tell what they're thinking. That good old hand. The nurse had confirmed that it was an excellent hand and could be relied on; that was when she found no difficulty in bringing up a vein. Afterward, after she'd stuck in the needle, she'd patted it and left, through the curtain.

After a while I too emerged from behind the curtain. I wasn't sure yet how comfortable I'd find it to move or what directions I was allowed to roam in, so I stopped at the door to the ward, cast a comprehensive look around the place, and began observing, so as to find out how people behaved. There weren't many patients; it was the middle of the week anyway, and the ward seemed empty, the nurses relaxed. I watched them as they moved slowly about, passed through the hanging curtains or parted them as they emerged. Some smiled at me, encouraging me to move around. I thought it wouldn't be long before I attracted people's looks, as I was, all the same, new here, and the nurses might begin to feel uncomfortable at my standing so long like that next to the door. I began walking slowly, with short steps, holding the pole, which was almost as tall as me, close. I must have looked like an old man who'd had a catheter inserted for urine.

I found rooms and amused myself by opening their doors. There was a room set aside for white sheets, where the notice outside said Clean Linens. The sheets there really are objects of great admiration: not only do they have a room of their own, they call them "linens"! I contemplated this approvingly, then continued my progress. I found another door, which said Recreation Room, and when I opened it, I found nurses sitting inside, their mouths moving as they ate or spoke, and I thought, This must be them taking their recreation!

They turned toward me and their mouths stopped chewing and speaking. I immediately closed the door, but not before one had cried out, "Do you need help?" as though throwing something through the crack before it closed. From outside, I said, "No. Thank you!" and hurried away, pushing the pole. Once again I found myself in the middle of the nurses who weren't on their break, and suddenly there was my nurse with the round face coming out of the linens room, a clean white sheet folded carefully and respectfully over her arm. I followed her to a new corridor, where she headed with the sheet toward one of the beds. When she went in to see the patient and turned to pull the curtain aside before closing it on them, her face bore that same radiant, warm smile, as though she was about to offer them the elixir of life.

I smiled, approving of all that I saw, and continued my walk, having by now learned how to drive the pole skillfully, as though I'd been driving one all my life. In the corridors, some patients had left the curtains open, some had closed theirs, some were lying on their beds, and some, like me, were walking around with their poles. There was a girl sitting with her head lowered over her lap, and when I walked past her, I slowed my steps, reducing, in a measured way, the speed of the wheels. Shock! Surprise! She was reading! I found myself yelling at her without preliminaries, "What are you reading?" or something stupid like that. She raised her head and looked at me, then contented herself with tipping the book upward while still keeping it in her lap, as though she wasn't strong enough to pronounce its title or lift it all the way up. The title became visible and I read it out loud: "Susan Sontag, *Illness As Metaphor*." I deduced that she was

135

one of those people who like to read serious, useful things, or things that have some direct link to reality, or things in English. She smiled at my terrible English accent, sat up straight, and energy began to course through her limbs, an energy clearly only released when the talk was of books.

"Sontag wrote it after she got cancer. Have you read it?"

I shook my head.

"It's worth looking at. Read it. You won't regret it."

I nodded.

"So are you reading anything these days?"

"*The Old Man and the Sea*."

"And what's it about?"

"The Old Man and the sea!"

"What about them?"

"At the beginning, the Old Man has caught a fish. Then he gets to respect it. Then he loves it. Then he feels it's his sister. Then he wishes it had lived and he had died."

"A novel?"

"Yes. By Hemingway."

"I don't like novels. I read one once, by Murakami, after I'd heard about his bestselling novels, and I don't want to repeat the experience."

"I understand entirely. If the only literature I'd read was Murakami, I'd prefer to change course too and read about fatal diseases, or botany."

She liked that idea, and seemed more willing to read Hemingway.

"Did you bring the novel with you?"

"I didn't bring anything with me."

"You have to bring something, if you want the time to go quickly."

We went on exchanging ideas, and the exchange was all good, and I was standing there absorbing my liquid and she was sitting there absorbing hers, and I was holding on to my pole and she wasn't holding on to hers, as she'd grown out of having a pole. It was clear from the way I looked that this was my first session and clear from the way she looked that she had plenty of experience of such things. Talk turned to the hospital and our cancer cases and treatment details, and then her session was almost over, so I suggested that I send a copy of the novel to her email address. She recoiled and said it was a trick so I could stay in touch with her but as soon as she observed how serious I was and how embarrassed, and how I rushed to exonerate myself, she smiled and stuck out her tongue, so I realized she was joking. Despite the cute way she tried to pull it off, her exhausted smile and lusterless features, and even the color of her tongue, were so far from the effect she intended as to break one's heart. She wrote me her email address on a piece of blank paper she tore from the end of the book, and while she was doing so, I observed her for a while in the suspicious way I always have of analyzing girls visually when they're too preoccupied to be staring me down.

Her head was shaved and she may have had no breasts. Other than that, she looked relatively well. Her features were calm, with a serene expression, and her gestures delicate, so she didn't look bad for a girl who'd undergone two rounds of treatment. She also had an attractive speech defect, the result of her cancer having spread to her brain; she mentioned that she had a tumor in her head the size of an egg, which I thought was a nice figure of speech. As soon as her twelfth session was over, she was going to have the egg removed. If, however, she chose not to have that done, the tumor might develop to cause blindness or near-total paralysis; even if the operation was successful, the possibility remained of some impact on her mental faculties in the future. It was only from her tone that one could guess at how little that agreed with her plans. Despite this, her voice was captivating, tranquilizing; perhaps, at the worst moments of her illness, she would open her mouth and talk, to calm herself, and be charmed by her own words and regain her confidence and feel better, or perhaps it was enough simply to possess a voice like that for her to feel she had lived a full, wonderful life.

When I said goodbye, her face left a prickling sensation inside me, like a cactus in the heart, and I thought that from then on I would be in love with her. By the time I finally returned to my seat, however, I had become more rational about my feelings. I watched her from where I was as she departed down the corridor, in the company of her elder sister, who had taken hold of her arm while the girl's free hand carried a crutch of the kind that supports the wrist. It was clear from the way she shrugged off her sister's assistance that that didn't agree with her plans either. I drew my curtain and closed my eyes, so that I could find peace.

A low moaning, neither the age nor the sex of the source of which, or even if it was human, could I determine, interrupted me from behind the curtain next to mine. I would have liked to look in on it and ask it, for God's sake, to suffer with a slightly lower voice.

I don't know how much time passed. The nurse woke me to tell me it was finished. I raised my head and found that the transparent bag had emptied itself; the liquid was now all distributed inside me. It was no different in its colorlessness and liquidity from water, but the nurse's movements imparted an awareness of its toxicity. She had put a plastic apron over her clothes, protective glasses over her eyes, and was wearing rubber gloves, whose stiff violet touch I could feel on my arm as she pulled out the needle. Then she took the needle, along with the cannula, the tube, and the transparent bag, and threw them all into a container, which she shut tight. The container was yellow and bore a warning sign that indicated there were chemicals inside and looked like a creature from outer space, as though just leaving a container like that open could give you cancer. I wondered what effect the liquid would have on the inside of my body, if she had to take all those precautions to avoid a single speck of its residues touching her outside.

I left the hospital under a sunny sky, the temperature reaching 120 degrees, and it felt as though the burning noon-time sun was actually erupting from my insides, even though the side effects of the treatment hadn't begun yet and wouldn't for at least twelve hours. Tomorrow there would be another round of medication, which would be repeated the day after, and this would continue for three consecutive days each month for at the very least six months. Then, if no cure had occurred, the round would be repeated. By the end of the day, I would have moved from the kingdom of the well to the kingdom of the sick, and all that within just one month of my learning that I was ill. If this shift feels too fast when I write it down here, it's because that's how it is in reality too.

Week 18

I THOUGHT I'D HAVE LOTS of things to write about, but here I am, having completed almost a month without writing a word. The days pass monotonously, each like the last, and short. Nausea is a daily visitor, but I'm used to its appearance. Some days, it's a lot worse, but I'd expected the very worst. Sometimes I'll be lying down and settled and I'll feel that the sickness is kind, because it allows these intermittent states of ease after suffering.

During the first week, I could hardly leave the bed. Something inside me was burning, leaving me dehydrated. I drank a lot of water, especially during the three days of the session; it might have been the only thing I took, or was able to keep down. By the time the end of the week came, there'd be ulcerations in my mouth and I'd find it hard to breathe. My skin would become a bit itchy and there was a slight loss of muscle mass. Sometimes my bones hurt, as though I'd spent a long time sitting on a wooden chair, but with the difference that the pain would last for a long time and spread all over my body.

I spent as much time as I could, or as my headache would allow, reading. When reading became too difficult, I'd doze off for a little, and when I woke, I'd be able to try again. I tried to keep going with Thomas Mann's long novel that I'd begun on the train but I couldn't get beyond a few pages. There was no difficulty with the storytelling: the sluggishness was in my mind. I came to prefer to read three or four books at the same time, moving from one to the next according to my mood. That way, I could prolong my attention span.

Sometimes, I'd just lie there until sleepiness overcame me. I'd keep the air conditioner at its warmest as I got cold quickly, but never turn it off completely because I loved how the air passed over my body. Its sound, too, disposed one to relax, and the total silence would bring strange thoughts to the soul. When I slept, I often had nightmares. I knew they were an effect of the medications, but that in no way reduced their evil impact.

Before, I had rarely dreamed, which had made me feel inadequate. It happened once in my childhood that I told my brother a dream and he told me that it was his dream and that he'd told it to me some months before, even though I was certain I'd dreamed it myself. Maybe I'd been jealous of him and stolen his experience. I often called to mind the story of Tartini, to whom the devil played a composition in a nightmare, which Tartini wrote down as soon as he woke and which became his masterpiece. I hoped I'd be struck by a similar inspiration and that my writings would find their origins in dreams like Tartini's—in surrealistic worlds rich with visions and phantasms. For the time being, though, all I could do after I woke up was forget them as quickly as possible. I'd immediately busy myself with stillness, with repose, with stiff, routine movements, in an attempt to erase from my soul all the disturbing preoccupations resulting from those nightmares. In that state, my body would engage only with momentary concerns: now I have to pull the bedclothes over me; now I have to push the coverlet aside; now I have to turn onto this side; now I have to rest the other. It paid attention only to the pared-down biological impulses that make an animal feel it's hungry or wants to have sex, though without either of those two urges.

Sometimes my mother comes and asks me if I need anything. After she's repeated the question, I answer, as she'll never go away until I do. When she comes, she always opens the door to its widest before entering. The air leaves the room and the temperature changes. She puts down a plate of food and says I have to eat. She picks up the plate from before, which I have barely touched, and begins arranging the things around me. "How do you expect to get better when you're surrounded by filth?"—as though I was deliberately preventing myself from getting better or stretching out my illness to get even with her. I don't blame her, because reproach is her way of saying she wants to help. Sometimes, in the past, this hasn't stopped me arguing with her but recently I've been too exhausted even to lift a finger.

One time, my silence encourages my mother to feel she's my mother and exercise wider powers.

"Give the air conditioner a rest for a bit. It can't have stopped working for days."

Before I can summon the strength to object, she's turned it off. Simply with the cessation of its hum, I lose an additional line of defense. She gives a last look around, her hand resting on the door handle, then exits, without closing the door behind her. The reverberation of the metal handle being released fills the room. Just a few drops falling from the air conditioner onto the tiles, less and less frequently, then complete silence. The pale lights coming through the window form colored patches on my uncovered body. Total silence. I swallow my saliva slowly, listening to the sound of it squirting into my belly and mixing with the juices there, after which their interaction produces a new sound. One of the millions of interlocking biological processes in a strange body that doesn't feel as though it belongs to me in any way. How can this composite, lacking in any homogeneity, function? Intestines, humors, glands, sinews, tissues, corpuscles, cells—where in all these lies the soul? Millions of cells in persistent, indefatigable motion, in a struggle for survival, along with poisons that kill them, burning the verdant and the withered together. After all that, how can one find the energy to cohere? Suddenly I feel as though everything is collapsing at once.

I invert my face over the lavatory bowl and empty my gut completely. Then I empty it more, till there's nothing left to empty, though for some reason I go on retching. Perhaps it will become bearable if I know when it will stop. I feel as though I'm going to expel my intestines into the lavatory. If it goes on like this, maybe I'll vomit up the liver, spleen, pancreas, and other things I'm not even aware of. However, I vomit and nothing comes out but emptiness. I vomit and my eyes tear, as though I'm about to vomit out my eyes too. If I were more sensitive, I might think that something inside me had broken, but I've never been able to weep. It's just meaningless involuntary tears falling pointlessly into a lavatory full of vomit, just another biological process. I decide I'll rest there for a while, my face gazing down, just till I recover my strength. My hands are grasping the sides of the lavatory bowl and their palms are sweaty. I gather my powers and sluggishly raise one, flush the cistern, and the vomit withdraws in little whirlpools and is replaced by clean water. A few bits of vomit rise to the surface again. I observe this because I'm too exhausted to get up. And when I think it's over, my gut explodes once more with a new volcano. I feel as though I'm ejecting my entire stomach but all that comes out is a stream of spittle, which hangs stupidly from my stiff lips without reaching the bowl. I spit it out. I spit out more, just because I want to spit. I calm down a little, then vomit some more. After a while, there isn't even any spittle left, just sounds without sound, a sterile venting, a vast emptiness that divides you from everything that isn't you.

I extend my body over the bathroom floor and close my eyes, depleted, all my strength exhausted. I rest a little before thinking about getting up. Then, the moment I stand, I feel debilitated, as though I'd lost ten kilos at one go.

My mother is standing outside the door, listening in terror. At each new bout of vomiting, she calls out and asks if I'm all right. When I don't answer, she keeps on calling with an

anxiety that is not without reproof, in an attempt to comprehend what is going on. It's a form of reproach she practices
unconsciously whenever I worry her too much. Then, as soon
as I open the door, she helps me to get back to the bed, and
I glimpse her absolute sympathy and desire to make things
easier, so far as is possible, despite which, throughout this, her
eyes are somehow pleading with me not to appear that sick
again in front of her. She knows that my simply pretending to
be better in her presence won't change my degree of pain at
all, but she would accepted the gift of that illusion.

I understood this well, as my condition contained a bitter
reminder to my family of the limits to their own health and the
ease with which, overnight, it could turn against them. I was
sinking into that sickly world where the healthy fear to tread,
even when they're so close to it. Their continual attempts to
comprehend my needs and try to be there for me were a kind
of superficial guarantee against their dread of getting involved
beyond the point of no return. I, in turn, remember how upset
I felt in the ward as I listened to the moaning that came to me
through the next-door curtain, maybe because that person's
moaning was a harbinger of the weakness to which my own
body would one day be reduced.

The following week, my hair started to fall out or, more
precisely, to come off in large chunks as though it had been
stuck on with cheap glue, and when it began distributing itself
dumbly over the ground, the pillow, the chair, and everything
I touched, I shaved it off completely. The moment my mother
saw me with my head shaved, she drowned in a violent fit of
weeping, as though I'd only now been stricken with cancer. I
would sense in her looks her feeling that she was gazing at a
corpse, and I'd seize these opportunities to get into arguments
with her, so as to confront her with that feeling. Little by little,
she became wary of entering the room out of fear that my
irritability would make her cry and she'd send my brother to
look in on me from time to time instead of her.

My brother's style was, in any case, less funereal, though no less irritating. When I informed him, on my return from the capital, that I was sick, he asked, "Do you want me to postpone the wedding?" with the expression of someone who was afraid it would be bad for me if he continued with the preparations, and he repeated the question every time he decided to console me. It was perhaps his only reaction. My sister was standing by his side when I gave them the news. She appeared to be genuinely affected and she went and put her hand on his shoulder and patted it, so that it seemed to me her emotion simply derived from his reaction, plus her fear that he really might go ahead and delay the wedding. I answered him that it didn't call for that and I preferred that things should proceed as planned. The wedding was set for next winter, by which time I might have gotten better as the treatment wasn't supposed to take more than six months. For the first time in her life, she agreed with me and she patted his shoulder again to urge him to accept. The old coolness between us didn't change after I became sick; in fact, it became tenser and more suffocating. All the same, I could rest assured that at least she wouldn't interfere in my affairs and upset me with any excessive concern, in stark contrast to my brother.

When my mother sent him to look in on me, he'd knock softly on the door and in a low voice ask permission to enter, making it exaggeratedly clear that he didn't want to disturb me. He'd enter, sit next to where I lay on the bed, and bring his knees together to emphasize that he'd never crowd me by the way he sat. Then he'd smile his loving, anxious smile that says, "See how loving I am to have come to distract you from your sorrows!" as though I'd been waiting for him to relieve my loneliness. His feeling of guilt at continuing with the wedding preparations didn't help. On top of this, he saw it as his duty to show his concern as a substitute for my father, even though he didn't feel at all comfortable around me, while each fatherly note added more and more to my sense of suffocation at the fake role in which I was supposed to support and encourage him.

One time, he rushed in saying, "Are you devoured by boredom?"—and here I'm not substituting some literary word for a different, vernacular, one as a result of having come under the influence of novels in translation or something of that sort. He really did use that word—"devoured"—thinking that, just because he was aware of my love of literature, I'd enter into the spirit of such talk and it would cheer me up and bring us closer together. I found this extremely annoying. He, on the other hand, kept pretending to be jolly in the face of my scowling silence. When he noticed that his attempt to lower himself to my level was having no result, he asked me, "How are you?" in a serious tone that said, "That's enough joking around. Now let's move on to what's important."

"Not bad," I replied, without turning to look at him.

"How are you feeling?" he asked again.

"Not bad."

"And what's new?"

"Nothing much."

"Are you in pain?"

"Nothing serious."

"What is it precisely that's hurting you?"

"Don't ask."

One might have thought it would end at that point, and that any bastard with an ounce of understanding would stop asking questions, but that shit was determined to ignore my desire for silence, as though it was in my interest to keep answering. When he went on to ask, "Do you need any help?" I replied quietly, "Don't exaggerate," which was enough to cut short any possible continuation.

He sat in silence where he was, knees even more tightly closed, as though his privates had been showing. Like me, he'd carried that expression on his back like a rock since childhood and just hearing it was enough to make all pretense fall away.

Without saying a further word, he withdrew, murmuring incomprehensible prayers, which, despite his good intentions—or, more truly, because of his good intentions—he did not want me to hear.

With the arrival of the third week of treatment, the effects of the toxic medications retreat and the healthy cells, being able to renew themselves faster than the cancerous ones, begin to rebuild themselves. Little by little, the body recovers its appetite and provisions itself with food and blood, and suddenly, from the renewal of its physical strength, it derives spiritual renewal as well. At this stage, the reenergized individual feels he has been brought back to life; in fact, he finds himself in a state of invigoration exceeding that of someone accustomed to good health.

Thus I came to be aware in myself of an inner strength that allowed me to take more independent stands. I locked the door of the room in their faces and even forbade them to go with me to appointments at the hospital, and I told them myself whenever I needed them for any purpose, and only when it required their help, and afterward I dismissed them with gestures delivered with the irritability of a grandfather shooing away a grandchild pestering him for attention. They needed me to show that I needed them but I don't have enough room inside me to take care of the needs of others. My bodily integrity is my permanent excuse for any offense against family relations, and my strongest argument is the weakness of my resistance to infection, since one's immunity is made even lower by the chemotherapy than by the disease itself. After some bargaining, I agreed that they can install a bell on the bed, like the ones on hospital beds, so that I can summon them in case of emergency. This is their only condition for leaving me to myself.

At first, my mother thought that the presence of this bell wasn't incompatible with her insisting on coming every morning to ask me if I wanted anything. As soon as she entered, I'd put on my face mask. Because of my shaved head, my pallor, and my emaciation, my appearance has changed radically, and on top of that my eyelashes have begun to fall out too. All this terrifies my mother enough to keep her at a distance, and perhaps to imagine that this strange body isn't her son's but that of some stranger she's suddenly found occupying a room in her house and whose presence she has, for some reason, to accept and whom she has to take care of whatever his mood. These are the superficial transformations that accompany fundamental change, since the aura that surrounds a person and by which he is normally recognized is turned into something different, to the point that when I suddenly, without warning, see my reflection, it takes me a while to realize that it's me.

In any case, here I am at the end of the third week after the first session, and most of the side effects of the medication have fallen to their lowest point, so that it's now possible for me even to return to my "normal" life. The side effects that remain—headache, loss of appetite, pains in my back and joints, and difficulty sleeping—are nothing new to me. This week the vacation balance that I'd collected over the years ran out. At the start of next week, I go back to work.

Week 19

Seven a.m. I've been awake since dawn, unable to go back to sleep. I turn off the alarm clock before it can let out its sharp ring. I remain lying down for a few extra minutes, then rise and start getting ready. I clean my teeth with a new brush that has soft bristles to prevent bleeding of the gum. I bathe using soap that relieves the itching caused by the sensitivity of the skin to the chemicals; it's my body's way of saying that it isn't easy to get used to such toxins.

I take my time over deciding what to wear. I change shirts one after another to be sure of choosing one that goes well with my hairless head. I put on a new pair of socks and search for a missing shoe that has spent a month in hiding under the bed. I stretch out my body to grasp it and feel the difference in how the air flows in that warm, dark spot. I remain lying there under the bed; I'm filled by an obscure sense that this is connected to a memory from my childhood but one I'm unable to recover in detail. I think maybe I'll remain in hiding there till I go to sleep, next to the shoe. Reluctantly, I take hold of the shoe and stand up again.

Before leaving, I check my appearance in the mirror. I adjust my belt, which hangs below the button on my pants. I insert the metal tongue into the third hole after having first put it into the second. *The kimono sash that used to go around me twice, now goes around three times*—I think of a Japanese poem I read recently, by a poet who is describing her emaciation after waiting so long for her lover, who never comes. And, like a real Japanese person, today I wear a face mask to go to work, the way everyone does on the streets and in the trains of Tokyo, to avoid infection, especially during cherry-blossom season. How easy it would be for me with my mask to fit in, if I were there.

At the traffic signal, an ambulance comes to a halt next to me. I think how convenient it would be for me to have an accident now. The statistics say that a person will suffer a horrible traffic accident at least once in his lifetime. Since it's going to happen whatever I do, it would be good if there were an ambulance next to me at the moment it occurs. In my new situation, any little cut can lead to an emergency, because the bleeding won't stop on its own without medication. From now on, there will be lots of dangers, and I shall have to be alert, as though forever moving through a field of battle.

When I arrive, I wonder if I can—finally!—park in a spot reserved for those with disabilities. I decide not to, so as not to draw attention. I enter via the side corridor that reeks of new paint; I feel as though I'm suffocating as I walk. I remind myself of what the doctor said about the danger of catching any passing infection, and use that to fight my desire to take off the mask. I reach the lobby and wait for the elevator. From the number of smokers in the outer courtyard, I deduce that I've arrived after everyone else. I press the button for the tenth floor, avoiding touching it directly. I check my belt, make sure my fly is closed, adjust the mask over my face time and time again. I'm still filled with the embarrassment of a student who goes to school with a new haircut.

I recall my first day at elementary school. It was very hot but they still held our reception party in the open courtyard. They presented each of us with a hard doughnut and warm juice, and I presented them with tears. The moment my father left me there, I started crying and I went on crying, at the same pace, all day long; I can't remember having cried so much at any other time during my childhood. I cried in front of the principal, the teachers, and the cleaners, but especially in front of the gatekeeper. I wanted to make clear to them that they were mean because they wouldn't let me leave. When we departed at the end of the day, I swore never to return, but finished the school year top of my class. I found nothing in that to make me feel proud.

In front of the department, I discovered that the glass door was, unusually, closed. When I quietly knocked, two persons hurried toward me from inside, though the last thing I wanted was to have attention called to me. One opened the door to its widest and stood there, holding it for me. The other stood there too, staring at me, even after I'd passed him. I took the mask off my face and hurried toward my desk. I wanted to sit down immediately, as one might want to bolt into a hole.

The director with the turkey's wattles was aware of my return day as he'd received a copy of the hospital report as part of the insurance approval procedures. I couldn't help feeling that the son of a bitch had issued alerts to the rest of the employees calling on them to keep their cool and make allowances for me when I returned to work. They were highly professional in their application of these warnings, especially that other son of a bitch, my direct supervisor. Absolutely nothing in his behavior signaled the existence of any contradiction between the mechanical seriousness required by his position of power and the humane concern that the employees under him were supposed to need, as though his kindliness toward me was just another task carried out in obedience to Management's expectations of a model supervisor and their secret criteria for promotion. When I sat down, for example, I noticed that there was no yellow sticker on the screen informing me that I was late. Then he came, in person, to say that I could take permission to go outside at any time I wanted. It wasn't just his voice, whispering close to my ear, that disgusted me, but his hand as well, which he placed on my shoulder with a gesture that said there was still time for us to be friends.

Necktie, next to me, remained well mannered too, avoiding looking at me and restraining himself from making his usual comments about the sounds made by my stomach or interfering in what I was doing on my screen. The two dolts who sit in front of us restrained themselves, when they took their breakfast, from turning around and chatting with him so that they wouldn't disturb me. Even though their excessive politeness was even more annoying, any impolite reaction from me was not an option as I was afraid it would be attributed to an unjustified, childish inclination on my part to exploit their consideration and the fact that they couldn't attack me.

I discovered that here my sickness weighed the scale against me in every situation, depriving me of the weapon that up to now I'd thought I possessed. In contrast to what had happened to me on the airplane, for example, transgression of my due did not result here in self-confidence, or in any capacity for personal victory and the dismay of others; instead, it resulted in kindly initiatives on their part that demonstrated their preemptive readiness to give in and insist on granting me precedence even in going to the bathroom, not to mention the ensuing pitying looks, pats on the shoulder, and unctuous compliments on how great I looked, my willpower, my courage, and so on and so forth, of the kind with which "cancer fighters" are customarily stigmatized. This in itself was a new, unbearable, shackle. I felt how much I missed the now-departed Old Man: he would probably have treated me exactly as before, and perhaps not even have noticed.

I escaped all that by burying myself in the work. Naturally, my supervisor didn't set me any tasks, so I had to catch up on what I'd missed. When I went through the administrative messages in my inbox, I was amazed at the number of decisions that had been passed in a month. I already had an idea of developments during my absence, as the newspapers, television, and communication apps had spread the news: a virus had infiltrated the systems of a number of major companies, not to mention certain government sites, and caused damage to their databases. All of this called for the most extreme level of alertness from these companies to protect their systems, reverse the damage, and prepare themselves for a new level of security that would guarantee that such an incident did not reoccur. The lion's share of the responsibility fell on the shoulders of the sensitive departments, the ones responsible for dealing with these viruses, the IT departments, naturally, at their head.

From now on, every employee had to sign a document granting the company the right to monitor their computer files and internet use, "for security purposes," as they say. There were also new surveillance cameras in all the corners of the department, though "without an employee's participation, the cameras are worth nothing. You are yourself the first and most important surveillance camera. We must all work together and constantly keep our eye on everything that is going on, so that Management can be aware of every jot and tittle, for our aim in the end is to protect you. And what would we do with your secrets, if you're not an agent? What have you to worry about, if you've nothing to hide? Privacy? What does that mean? Don't overestimate the value of your private life! More surveillance means more security. Don't be the weak link through which they can get at us! Aren't you loyal? Do you want the company to lose yet more money? Are you OK with threatening the economic position of the state? You have to act responsibly. Alertness is a duty and the danger is always there. The enemy can slip in through any gap. There are things more important than your trivial private concerns."

There were changes to the department's layout as well. The glass door could now only be opened using secret numbers known exclusively to the employees within the department. The paper files and old ledgers that had accumulated here and there had disappeared and been locked up in safes. Even at the level of the decorations, everything surplus to requirement had been removed, leaving the screens and the faces that stared at them permanently exposed to the cameras and spying eyes. I suddenly thought of the cactus and asked Necktie next to me about it. His face adopted an artificial expression indicating that he was trying to remember; then he asked the man directly next to him. The other looked back and forth between us before pretending to be serious as well, and passed the question on to his neighbor. The question ran the length of the row and then the one after, and the one after, as though it was one of the most important puzzles we faced at work. As soon as they found out that I was the one who was concerned, everyone displayed an excessive amount of cooperativeness in trying to discover the plant's fate. They turned to look at me, one after another, with faces that apologized for failing to come up with the answer, as though they were apologizing for not being able to help me get better. As though the cactus was the last straw, I immediately and definitively grasped the impossibility of my staying there one more day.

Immediately, I printed out my letter of resignation and made my way to the Turkey's office, tapped on the open door, and waited for him to give me permission to enter. He was sitting in his luxurious leather chair with the tall back, busy with a sheaf of papers he was holding, glancing back and forth from one to another as though comparing details of vast importance, and he didn't even raise his head to see who had knocked. His office was so luxurious one felt it must belong to some other building; it had nothing to do with our company's policy of austerity for its employees. Even the walls were held up by decorated wooden panels designed to go with the polished wood with which the desk was topped. In such offices decisions to spy on employees are born, and IT security policies, with their dual goal of increasing productivity and keeping everyone under control, put forward.

When he finally raised his head, he smiled welcomingly and gestured to me to sit. I presented him with my resignation letter, at which he cast a swift glance as he got up and came around the desk, the wattles that hung about his neck quivering with emotion. It was clear that he'd been waiting all his life for a situation of this kind—a human interaction that would add the finishing touch to the perfect picture he had drawn of his fine administrative career. He smiled with his lips pressed together, which made his closed mouth spread far more broadly than normal, and sat down in front of me on the chair opposite, his hands clasped to his chest, the fingers entwined, like those of a wise ape. That smile of his, the way he sat on the same side of the desk as me, all his movements, with the excessive lengths to which they went to emphasize their informality, were attempts to draw my attention to the fact that he was not there to exercise hegemony over me, or try to dissuade me from my desire, albeit he would be obliged to clarify certain obstacles that it would be in my interest to be advised of.

He thus began explaining to me how my resignation now would mean my loss of the medical insurance whose expenses the company currently bore. I could instead take a three-month sick leave, with full salary paid for the first month and half salary for the remaining two, and that this was the most the system allowed; after that, I might return to work if my condition permitted or be transferred to mandatory retirement, if they found they no longer had need of my services. He continued to spell out these compassionate arrangements with pitying emollience, extending his hand from time to time to touch my knee and making repeated alluring gestures, whose purport was "Don't you see? There is room within this system to show concern for every employee."

I could only agree: three months of free medical insurance wasn't something to be refused. Then we would have to see. He got up and stretched out his hand to shake mine, the same smile with which he'd received me still on his face, so I understood that it was time for me to go. Till now I hadn't shaken anybody's hand on the excuse that I might get an infection, but I didn't dare refuse his. Before I could even turn to leave, he had gone back to busying himself very seriously with the sheaf of papers that had been in his hand and which looked far too important for me to distract him from.

I returned to my desk to present the vacation request as the director had told me, filled with fury at having been forced to submit. To make matters worse, I found some of the other employees in the department were on the lookout for me, and I was obliged to depart amid kindly pats on the back, bidding them farewell with a show of gratitude equal to the support they made a show of providing. All of this was totally at odds with how I'd imagined my triumphant exit from the place—with complete disregard, total freedom, and the ability to kick out of the way anything that stood in my path. It seems, however, that when someone wants to leave a place like that, he has to do so in accordance with the requirements of the system, and not without leaving a part of his soul behind.

I sat down at the machine and gazed at it, imitating the Old Man's method for avoiding the others by fixing his eyes unblinkingly on his screen. I gathered together my private files and sent them to my personal email. Then I deleted every trace of them from the computer's records and the company's email. While I was doing this, I received a new message, from an unknown address. The announcement said that I'd won valuable free tickets to an upcoming World Cup of some sort and all I had to do was click on the link to get them. It was a stupid trick, one we were constantly warning the employees about. As soon as one clicked on the link, the hidden virus there would download a small code onto the machine that would send itself on to other machines, targeting the company's servers, where the data was stored, infiltrating and destroying the company's IT systems and spreading continuously, with no other purpose than to cause more damage.

I waited for lunch break so that everyone would leave, and began thinking about it. A virus of this sort wasn't very different from a disease in the way it worked, or so my studies had taught me, and it was precisely from this fact that "internet viruses" got their name. Every virus is a kind of data bundle, and when it infiltrates a given machine, it copies its data into the other's systems as a virus copies its data into the genes of the human cells it infiltrates. I'd read something like that in Sontag's book about illness as metaphor that the girl with the egg in her head had recommended to me. Following this transcription of the virus from one gene to another, the gene's natural function may be distorted, resulting in a mutation, making it potentially cancerous. When the body lacks adequate defenses, this gene substitution in the cell may lead to malignancy, then the same in the cell next to it, then in the one next to that, then in the one next to that, and this leads to cancer, at least in the sense in which scientists first understood it. Impressive indeed that a person can grasp how little it takes to damage an entire system!

As soon as they left for lunch, I clicked on the link and went out, drawing as little attention to myself as possible. The one thing I regret is that I couldn't stay and see my supervisor running around in furious circles, with his wide pants and Skechers, on his face a look saying, "I can't believe this!" This time, my mistake would truly exceed his powers of expression. As for the Turkey himself, I could only guess at what his reaction might be. Naturally, the option of dispensing with my services was out of the question, given my current situation, or not before three months were up at the least. To avoid exposure to any legal accountability as a result of letting go an employee with cancer, they would have to wait until my medical leave was used up, and if they allowed me to return after that, it was always possible that further "mistakes" of this sort might be caused, until it was no longer possible for them to defer to me any longer. There is always a point of no return, whatever your circumstances, one at which you find yourself on the same footing before the consequences as anyone else. Perhaps for no better reason than to test my capacity for nonchalance, I had suddenly found myself determined to pass it.

Week 21

I WAKE SUDDENLY. WHEN I open my eyes, everything looks strange. I see that I'm in a hospital room. I'm sweating, I feel cold, my teeth are chattering. The nurse's dark face suddenly breaks the white of the ceiling. What does he want? He stands over me and calls someone. He continues to stare at me. His anxious face mirrors my plight. The doctor enters the frame of ceiling and the nurse exits it. I see the doctor giving instructions, talking in my direction. After a little, I notice that he's calling to me. Then I cease to be aware of anything.

Time passes. I open my eyes again. I am breathing with difficulty. There is an oxygen mask on my face. Tubes dangle everywhere. It's unclear which go in and which come out. Lots of white gloves, it's not clear which pair is in charge. Someone approaches, takes my temperature, and talks about some virus, a virus that has infiltrated your system, attacked your immunity. Did you pick it up at work? Why did you take off your face mask? Why did you shake hands with the director? Why did you open the link? Did the virus spread from the computer? Another glove approaches. What is it injecting? A tranquilizer. Your body needs it, it says. But you don't trust your body and you don't trust the glove. Is this really your doctor? A nurse? Perhaps he's talking about another patient. Maybe he wanted the room next door and came into your room by mistake. He's saying he's going to anesthetize you. You grumble a bit and then you go away.

You don't know how long you were away. A voice is calling you from a distant place and you're too weak to open your eyes. The call is repeated. It gets closer and closer. A voice wants you to wake up. Through a half-open eye I see the doctor. He insists on my opening the lid all the way. What obstinacy! He asks me what day it is. I don't answer. He keeps talking. I recover consciousness little by little, following the rhythm of his voice. I contracted some infection, then there was fever, then a coma. When did all this happen? When did it stop? I'd always wanted to know what a coma was like; what a pity I hadn't been conscious during it! I'd spent two entire weeks in the hospital, occasionally conscious, or half-conscious, under the influence of the painkillers. My condition is stable now, he says. You have to stay in the hospital to avoid complications. He leaves and I am alone in the room.

For the place that fostered my first contact with the world, I don't find anything very congenial about a hospital room. Even though I've seen them so often in movies and TV serials, things are completely different when you become the prisoner of one. The possibility of leaving your bed exists, but you feel as though you're chained by your wrists to its sidebars. The doors are open, but they might as well be closed, it would make no difference. Everything is available, but you never feel free. I lack the strength to get up and leave, as a man on TV might do.

I lie there all night. The sheets are garnished with a network of tubes that give it a heavy look that makes you want to kick at them again and again. With each movement of your foot to push them off, the covers tighten their grip on you. You're an animal locked inside a car on a stifling afternoon. After great effort, the covers respond and lighten their smothering hold on your body, and even though it's your foot that's hot, you feel that the heat is coming from the steady white light over the bed behind your head. Everything is illuminated by a terrible brightness, as though shade were

162

something dirty that should be eliminated and prevented from building up in corners.

By day, things are easier. The sun's rays streaming through the window give the place a certain naturalness. Is "naturalness" the right word? Things seem more alive as they change in an orderly fashion throughout the day in response to the movement of the sun. Once you've been there long enough, you can work out the time from the quality and angle of the light and how it's distributed around the room.

The dark-skinned male nurse returns by day. I feel at ease with him. He's a gentle soul, kind, and lavishes care on me. When he notices that I'm uncomfortable, he adjusts the position of the pillow behind me. His hand supports my back while he does so. This gives me no pleasure; I'm not sure how my body smells after two weeks of just lying there. He asks me, "Better?" I lie and nod. I don't want him to become aware of the pointlessness of what he does.

After him, the lean doctor returns—always right after the nurse. He stands there in his long white coat with his hands hidden in his pockets. He says I look better. I'm not happy with the speed at which he decides this; I'm also not happy that he's the one who makes the decision. He picks up the test-results board at the end of the bed, giving his opinion additional authority. Everything's fine, he confirms. After a few days, maybe I'll start the second chemotherapy session, he says, and turns to leave. What does he mean, "everything's fine"? What does he mean, "chemotherapy session"? Can't he see me?

I stop him before he can leave. I try to tell him about the pain, the nausea, the fatigue and weakness. I grope my way toward the word, the *mot juste*, the effective word, the word that, when he hears it, will make him realize exactly what I am feeling, the word that, when I find it, will immediately rescue me. He asks me to sum up all the possible descriptions in a number on a pain scale. He points to the piece of paper hanging under the bed light: "How much pain do you feel?"

To answer, you have to choose a number from zero to ten. I have no previous experience on which to lean in making the measurement but there are emoticons that are supposed to help. Number eight shows a crying face with the mouth bent downward, and number ten shows a mouth that is more bent and with tears dripping from the eyes. I feel distaste at the idea of associating myself with these expressions, my usual distaste at exaggeration. I choose number six, a face that looks a little disgruntled, so as to save the higher numbers for pains to come. I deduce from the doctor's reaction that I should have chosen a higher number: the disgruntled face isn't enough to stop them starting the chemotherapy session at the end of the week.

Over the following days, I see a number of nurses. Night shifts get mixed up with day shifts, blood sample follows blood sample, test follows test. The nurses lead me through the corridors, halting me at the nursing station for this department or that, chattering in their native tongue and leaving me sitting in the middle of the corridor while my reception procedures are completed. I have my own wheelchair but I haven't gotten used to driving it yet, only to being pushed in it. I enter rooms and exit them without knowing why I entered or whether I've given the nurses anything useful.

It doesn't matter what they do to me so long as they give the appearance of knowing what they're doing to me; this is what I have concluded. I am injected each day with more transparent bags, no doubt nutrients. Each bears a label with details explaining what it contains, just in case I want to know what is going into my body. I sit next to it doing nothing, except avoiding reading it since I can't yet summon up the appropriate indignation. From time to time I am injected with bags of blood to make up for what I've lost. Bruises have formed on my arms as a result of the lowering of my blood count, the blood struggling to coagulate after each injection. They arrest its liquefaction each time with medications and more injections. Despite this, the blood gushes out, from my nose and through my gums, as though there were no organs left inside my body that still needed it.

I sleep as much as I can, plus a little. As soon as I wake up, my mother is at my side. When I find her crying, I pretend to be asleep, and when she finds me sleeping, she cries. We were never a religious family but she has brought her prayer rug and performs the daily prayers next to my bed. When it's not prayer time, she makes up random additions to the daily prayers that God never authorized and pleads with Him, using any invocations that happen to cross her mind. On that occasion, I heard her reciting the prayer against lightning: "O God, I ask You for the best of what it brings and the best of what You have sent it for and I take refuge with You against the evil that is in it and the evil that you have sent it for." She cried bitterly as she repeated it, to make it seem appropriate to my case.

When she'd finished and turned toward me, the effects of the words of the doctor, which I hadn't heard, could be seen on her face. I pretended I'd just woken up, so she choked back her tears, demonstrating a composure that was supposed to show she had now become strong, for my sake. Her eyes, however, remained just teary enough to show that she found it hard to control her emotions. I wanted to tell her that I was still at number six and she'd do better to hold her tears for the higher degrees on the pain scale. That, though, would have made her cry more.

One day, I was pretending to sleep and she was praying beside my bed. Next thing, I heard her crying and begging God that, if He wasn't going to cure me, He should be kind and take me to Him. I shall never forget how her voice shook at the end of the prayer, as though confirming her preference for the second part of that "if not, then. . . ." I thought it was still too early for that but that maybe I should reevaluate my condition. The problem had changed from my not getting well fast enough to my not dying fast enough. When had this happened, and how? At what moment do the formulae of compassion for a person switch from keeping him alive to putting an end to him? Do I look like someone who belongs to the next world?

I asked her to bring my laptop and some books, and she looked displeased when I mentioned the titles: *Two Losers Stand On a Corner*, *Alone In a Room I Sweep Up the Dust*, and *Love Is a Dog From Hell*. Nevertheless, she brings them to me, sighing, as though the books will make me sicker. They're all modern poetry, easy to read. I don't have the attention span to read a novel or books of philosophy or to follow any extended narrative or sequence of events amid the effect of the medications, the repeated naps, and this lethargy, lethargy, lethargy that clouds all mental energy. Sometimes I can't understand even these short American poems. I search the internet for more Japanese poetry, very short poems the size of haiku.

What a mercy
the turtle can't see
how easily the small bird flies

"What a mercy"—a single phrase that fills me like a dense dream, like a tender, distant, memory; sometimes this is all that's needed to renew my strength. I felt a desire to show the haiku to my mother: this was an esthetic that no one could feel contempt for. But I didn't go through with the idea, of course. Something inside me still felt angry at her for that prayer of hers.

At the end of the week, my breathing was better and my heartbeat was regular again. The female nurse came in the morning and took a specimen to run a blood-count test. The result likewise came back positive for a return to the treatment. She told me I should go on my own, so I propelled my wheelchair toward the long corridor that leads to the Oncology department. The glass side that looks out onto the playground let in large quantities of sunlight, making the corridor stiflingly warm for the time of year. I arrived sweaty and exhausted from propelling the chair, desperate to return to the room from which I'd just come; the mere thought that I'd be going back there at the end of the day removed some of the anguish that accompanies a chemo appointment (I've started to say "chemo," like the ones who are used to it).

In the ward, I spoke to other patients. From one of them I learned that if I put pressure on the doctor, he might let me go home. The others weren't so helpful. There was a nice elderly lady who began talking immediately and with complete spontaneity, as though she'd been briefly interrupted and was picking up again where she'd left off. She told me lots of tales about how she'd been afflicted by the evil eye. All her stories revolved around her envious neighbor, who'd visited her at home every day from the Gulf War to now without once uttering the word "God," and it just so happened that the moment this neighbor started praising her energy, her good health, and her long life, she'd fallen sick. And when she'd called her after she'd found out the results and insulted her and called down curses on her head and beseeched her to say the word "God," all the other woman had done was trade insults and curses with her without ever denying that she was the one who'd caused her to fall sick. Wasn't that proof enough? I didn't know what to reply. She'd remain silent for a few minutes after telling me stories of this sort, and I'd think she had no energy left for conversation, but then she'd suddenly turn and say, "And you? Who made you get sick?" as though asking, "What type of cancer have you got?" I'd reply, "No one," and she'd be astounded. "But everybody knows that cancer's caused by the evil eye!" I began to ask myself whether I ought to feel offended because nobody till now had given any thought to my having been exposed to the eye.

During all my interactions with the other patients, I couldn't help feeling I'd missed something important by making no effort to go over the details of the treatment or listen to the doctor's explanations, while they knew all about them. They were certain that cancer could never be a random accident, or not somehow intended to harm them personally. If it wasn't for some metaphysical reason, then it was tied to modern lifestyles—disturbance of the biological clock resulting from city life, magnetic fields from electricity poles and high-rises, the rays that probably came out of cell phones and microwaves, car exhaust and fast food. Even the fruits and vegetables that were supposed to protect us from cancer might now have become the cause of it, because of the pesticides they were sprayed with.

One of them was obsessed with these lists of things that cause cancer. He used to warn me against them, as though it was an ordinary topic of conversation, so I could protect myself. Then he suddenly realized that I had cancer too and began giving me advice on how to treat myself. He'd say, "To fight this enemy seriously, you have to fill your mind with everything that can make you hate it. It's not enough to attack it just with chemotherapy. You have to want to take revenge on it, destroy it, force it to submit!" It occurred to me that he must have just finished watching one of those war movies that stir up a sense of victory. He shook his fist while he talked, as though delivering a speech before battle, while his other hand continued to grip the metal pole that carried his drip-feed as though he were holding a sword or some pathetic weapon that would perform miracles. As always, there was something about such insistent attempts to create conflict that inhibited any desire on my part to join the ranks of the others.

There was also someone who'd go from patient to patient in their seats and talk to them one by one, offering them advice and pious exhortation. I don't really know if he was a volunteer or a companion of one of the patients who had decided that these too were his responsibility. His conversation revolved around adding pious deeds to one's account so as to reap heavenly rewards later and putting one's life in order before the inevitable end; apparently, as soon as one was stricken with the disease, one was as good as dead and the best thing to do was begin making hurried plans for Paradise. The moment he approached, I drew the curtain around my seat to keep him away. I might not have minded listening to him if I'd had the energy, but I'd reached the end of my limited capacity for socializing.

I wasn't, generally speaking, lacking in faith in God, but I wasn't strongly protective of my faith in Him either. I'd adopted a position that required a stubborn, persistent neutrality, here, in this land which continually forces one to take a clear position on religion, either for or against. Perhaps all it amounted to was that I was delaying taking a stance, just as I delayed clarifying my stance on everything that matters. I did not, however, feel that it was in any way my battle: both sides, in my opinion, lacked spirituality, as does almost every contemporary discourse about religion. I've long thought that people live as though they were God's employees, not his worshippers, as though it was in their power to speak badly of Him behind His back and then pretend to go on with their work.

I spend the rest of the session on my own. I remind myself to bring a book with me the next day, to occupy the waiting time. I wonder what happened to the egg in that girl's head. Had she read Hemingway? Our appointment times no longer coincide because of the postponement of my session this month. I think about sending her an email as soon as I get back to my room.

After the session, I lie down in my room, exhausted. I drink water all day long to alleviate the side effects of the medications and I get up to piss; these are the only activities I undertake. The female nurse is displeased as she helps me to my feet to go to the bathroom, as though my repeated urination was a pure show of obscenity by me to her, or some kind of harassment. She moves slowly, has a harsh voice, and her face is premeditatedly and purposely standoffish and frowning. She might as well be a waitress in a café or an air stewardess, with her manner that gives the permanent impression she has people other than you to serve. When I press the bell on the seat, she comes with a look of thunder, as though to say, "What is it now?" When I remove my face mask, she gets angry and asks me in an irritated way to put it back on so that I don't infect her with anything, and when she reinserts the drip needle in my arm, she does so carelessly, as though taking revenge for my urinating and my coughing. But she's always there, and that's what counts; the other skills are just footnotes. The truth is that I prefer this kind of nurse because, with them, I feel I'm in the presence of an opponent. The ones who rush in on you with an encouraging face that says, "There, there!" put you on guard against allowing anything disgusting to issue from your body in their presence; you definitely don't want to see their kind faces as they hide their revulsion and struggle to look sympathetic while they help you with your most private matters.

After the first day of chemo, I focused my efforts on getting out in the shortest possible time. I was utterly fed up with that room and had decided that the only way to survive was to return to my room at home. I discussed the matter with the doctor and he asked me to wait another week, "for your own good," as he put it. I told him another week in the hospital would kill me but he paid no attention to this excessively exaggerated statement. I immediately felt bad that my need had forced me to seek the doctor's sympathy with such a fervent plea and felt I'd betrayed myself for no appreciable gain. In response, I unsheathed the weapons of my obstinacy against him, to show him my true mettle, which he had failed to appreciate; and after going on hunger strike and threatening not to take my treatment for the two remaining days, he quickly promised me that I could leave if I completed the session without complications. I agreed. It was the second session and I knew what to expect.

For the two remaining days, I increased my intake of liquids, resisted the nausea brought on by the medication, and kept my strength up on intravenous nutrients. I wore my face mask all the time, and whenever I touched anything, I followed it up with sterilizing liquid, as though everything bore some kind of infection. I searched the internet to find out about every tiny thing I could use against the side effects. I ate only things that were light on the stomach—soup, nuts, fruits with high water content, boiled vegetables, and purée. I avoided canned foods, ready-made juices, and anything containing preservatives, as they heat the body and raise your temperature. On the third day, I was tired and nauseous but no more than was to be expected and much better than after the last session. More importantly, I was free of the infection and the viruses.

On the fourth day, the doctor ignored me and I didn't have the energy to confront him. He just came into the room, looked at the test results, and asked the nurse to do a few things, in my hearing but at a speed that implied I understood so much less than he that he couldn't discuss the details of the treatment with me. My extreme exhaustion that day was evidence against me and for the truth of what he had said about remaining in the hospital for longer. This did not, however, make me lose my determination to get out. On the fifth day, I promenaded without my wheelchair, just to prove I could, and I watched out for him, blocking his view every time he passed by, to remind him of his promise. When he informed me that it wasn't time yet, we argued for a bit. I cited my freedom and he cited his experience, and when I confronted him with the facts I'd read on the internet, he moved angrily away, gesticulating in all directions to show how much I was provoking him. At the end of the day, he returned with a piece of paper that he asked me to sign and that said I could leave, on my full responsibility, without completing the week he had recommended for me.

The next day, I went out into the parking lot, where my brother was waiting for me. I think the doctor must have complained about me to him, but he didn't dare start a conversation. We remained silent the whole way, his eyes fixed on the traffic, mine staring into the side mirror; and, for the first time in a long while, I felt at ease with the skinny being that stared back at me. I wasn't in peak form physically, but I'd recently acquired a new form of immunity and it struck root within me, more than at any time before, on my way home: an immunity that made it impossible for anyone to stand in the way of my wishes once I'd made up my mind to pursue them to the end.

Is this what a person feels when they "take the reins of their fate into their own hands"? Is this what it means to "have control over your personal destiny"? Is this "keeping your shit together"? The moment I entered my room at home, I realized that this was what I had to concentrate on from now on: small, well-planned battles, trivial personal victories; these were the ideal way to continue the struggle.

Three

Week 23

AT HOME THINGS WENT MORE or less as I'd planned. I'd eat a small breakfast and kill time in my room. I entertained myself with my phone and my laptop, switching between photo-apps, video-apps, and electronic games and logging onto various social media sites. I took painkillers when I needed them and sometimes just to be on the safe side. I'd imagined I'd get through books I'd put off reading for years but the days passed like a black cloud in my head. Whenever I felt lethargic, I'd read more short poems. When I decided to read something long and serious, I'd go back to favorite novels that I'd read long ago; I found it easier on the brain than reading anything new. Sometimes I'd read children's literature; it can be entertaining, imaginative, and easy to follow—series like *Diary of a Wimpy Kid* and things of that sort. When I'd tired my eyes with reading, I'd switch to television. I'd surf between the news, sports, talent shows, songs, and documentary films about the seas and the forests and the customs of different peoples. I followed everything that was going on everywhere in the world without forming an opinion about anything.

There were times when I was obliged to receive visitors, interrupting the easy regime I'd set for myself. Obviously, they'd hung back from coming to see me in the earlier period because I'd only recently learned I had the disease. Now, though, after enough time had passed for me to get over the shock, it was expected that I should find time for them to cheer me up with their conversations and their concern. I'd put on my mask and pretend to listen to their stock of stories about relatives or friends who'd had cancer and fought the disease. To hear one of these stories is to hear them all, as all of them—glory be!—end in recovery. They reminded me of the meetings at work devoted to stimulating new employees, where the stories were always crowned with success. It would have been insensitive of anybody to come and tell me tales of patients who'd lost the battle and died horrible deaths, but it would have been more entertaining.

Other visitors came to listen rather than themselves take on the duty of chatting. You could tell which they were because of their awestruck demeanor when they came in and the humility they felt before the signs of your illness, at which point you'd realize they'd never before encountered someone with cancer. Soon, though, they'd begin to find humility a burden and begin overwhelming you with questions about your thoughts and your complaints, and urge you to tell your story, as though in the presence of a Buddhist monk imbued with wisdom: no doubt the disease had taught you; no doubt the pain had inspired you; no doubt you now had things to teach about the right way to live. And this at a time when all you could think about was returning to your room and starting a new level in the latest electronic game to which you'd become addicted.

The third type was generally the worst, their most conspicuous feature being that once they'd visited you twice, they thought they owned a fathom of you, and began dipping their bucket into it. One of our neighbors was a visitor of that sort. No sooner did you think he'd used up all his medical advice than he'd come the next day with new remedies and a list of their miraculous curative powers. He was in his late fifties, had ten children and two wives, and a short, neatly trimmed beard that had recently turned black. One might surmise that he knew numerous amazing herbal prescriptions for stimulating the male sex drive. Every day, he'd call at our house in the late afternoon, after the prayer, his belly swollen with lunch and his body oozing so much sweat one feared that the dye from his beard would get over everything. For someone so interested in health information, he didn't look very healthy. This didn't matter, though, because he drank, as he said, lots of green tea, and green tea "burns the fat," which gave you the impression that he was picturing the fat melting and evaporating as he spoke.

His imagination was very literal when it came to his remedies. He'd bring an herbal solution that "disinfects the intestines," and you'd think he was speaking of some sterilizing agent that one poured into a drainpipe to cleanse it of muck, and when he said, "Foods rich in fiber clean the stomach," he'd move his hands like someone scrubbing the inside of a cooking pot with a loofah and getting rid of the hardest-to-reach stains. When I told him I'd no longer be able to see him "because mixing with others, according to the doctor's instructions, could harm my immune system," he came the next day carrying a large bag of onions, which he said strengthened the immune system because they "sweep out the germs", and if his hands hadn't been full with the heavy bag, he would have started sweeping in every direction to confirm the efficacious way in which onions work.

Who would have thought that, as the disease progressed, getting rid of people would become such a difficult task? I couldn't wait for the last of them to leave so that I could go back to my room, but the visits began to pile up, with the connivance and under the supervision of my mother and my brother, and sometimes even due to invitations they themselves issued. My mother believed they were good for getting me out of my loneliness. "Man is called *man* because company brings *man*ifold comforts," she'd say.

"A plague on the one who came up with such a saying!" I'd reply. "May he die of cancer!" They'd shush my tantrum as though I were a child and the next day be welcoming new visitors.

Just a few days ago, a few of my colleagues from work came to see me. They'd found out where the house was from my brother, whose number they'd obtained from the company. Even though I didn't have a strong relationship with any of them, they saw nothing wrong in turning up suddenly at the door of the house. They were the three who encircled me at the office: Necktie, who'd taken the place of the Old Man, and the two dolts from the row in front, who would turn to talk to him so they could quaff from the excellence of his ideas and the charm of his personality. I'd long inspired in him feelings of insecurity; indeed, he surely was suspicious of my sickness, the suddenness of whose appearance must have seemed strange to him. That, at least, was what I sensed the day I returned to work, when he thought I was perhaps hiding behind a weakness that bestowed on me the ability to spy and snitch. None of this, however, prevented him from fulfilling his duty of a visit, since the matter went beyond personal feelings and had to do with his standing as a person who conducted himself appropriately in such circumstances.

These three were another kind of visitor: the ones I used to see daily and who now pretended nothing had changed. As soon as they entered, they delivered such jubilant, laughing greetings that I imagined for a while they must have come for some reason that had nothing to do with my illness. I quickly realized, however, that they were attempting, with this jolly entrance, to control the tone of the visit and set the mood I had to respond to. However, my scowling silence, the deliberately cultivated wretchedness of my appearance, and my failure even to invite them to sit were at variance with their spontaneous impulses and the communicative practices with which they were familiar. They suddenly found themselves faced with a person whom they lacked the tools to deal with, but with whom, at the same time, they had to be friendly.

They sat down, sweating, and began talking about the weather. It was midsummer and the air was saturated with humidity. When one tried to allude to this as he stood up to fiddle with the air conditioning, I objected, saying it had to stay at a high temperature. I hadn't previously meant to open my mouth at all in front of them but I went on, explaining that my body got cold quickly because of the sickness. This was an effective way of unsettling them, since it reminded them of the reality of my illness, which they had decided not to confront directly. We remained silent after that, a feeling of unease, which I watched with great pleasure, infiltrating their overweening confidence. I'd often smelled that same feeling when I'd provoked it in someone else, the way one animal smells that another is feeling threatened.

What this kind of visitor likes to do to recover their poise, once they have finished talking about the weather, is to discuss politics. Generally, their comments take on a tragic, pitying tone expressive of sorrow at all the international wars, nuclear threats, refugee crises, famines, and possibilities of the outbreak of a third world war that exist these days. The more catastrophic the situation abroad appears to them, the more at ease they feel, since all they need to do in order to appear to be shaking their heads over the horrible thing that is happening to me is to shake their heads over those other, distant, horrors, without mentioning the elephant in the room. The political chaos also seems somehow to say, "There are crueler things in this world than just having this disease."

Once this had instilled enough daring in them, one asked for my view on what was going on. I folded my arms over my chest as though thinking and responded that in my opinion the most important issue was global warming. My sole aim, to be honest, was to keep them off-balance, and the forcible introduction of global warming was appropriate since it brought us back to the weather. "I mean all of our activities as human beings that result in climate change. The world is so busy with politics that it takes no notice of all the harm we're causing to other creatures." This provocation had its effect, since a look of disapproval that brought his former suspicions back to life sketched itself on Necktie's face.

"Excuse me. I don't understand. Are you trying to say that the death of a few bears at the North Pole is more important than the death of men?"

"What makes you think animals dislike death any less than we do? They may understand its meaning less but they are no less aware of its danger."

"You must be joking!" He turned to his two colleagues, calling on them to join in with him in rejecting my idea, while they wiped away the sweat and shifted nervously in their seats. "We're talking about genocide, about massacres of innocent old men, women, and children!"

This outburst was his way of showing that his discomfort at the visit had moral foundations. I had proved to him, by virtue of the revolting nature of these ideas of mine, that I was not entirely innocent before death, and that if I had fallen victim to the disease, it might be that I deserved it. This paved the way for the next step: that he would leave and never come back, because consoling a person like me was more than he could stand. That would be wonderful if it happened, I thought, so I deliberately set about stirring up his ire even more.

"What about depletion of the ozone layer, environmental pollution, fracking? Aren't you aware of all the epidemics and malignant diseases these cause?" I kept a straight face but inwardly I was applauding with joy and excitement.

Suddenly, it seemed that my defense of my point of view was motivated by what had happened to me personally, or indeed that I was accusing them and their like of having given me the disease because they didn't care about the effects of global warming. Thus, while they had come to make me feel better, they found that all they'd done was make me feel even more upset, which was highly entertaining. The others began to assure me, in a tone that urged the third to do the same, that they sympathized with my point of view.

"Let's calm down a little. The whole thing's no more than a simple difference of opinion," one said, in an attempt to set things to rights, while the other began shooting reproachful, sideways looks at Necktie. As soon as he became aware that he lacked their usual support, he lost it even more and recklessly flung in my face the famous saying that "The hottest place in Hell is reserved for those who remain neutral in times of great moral conflict." This was the straw that broke the backs of the two camels next to me. One gave him a nudge and the other began muttering into his ear, then pulled him away and addressed him, irritatedly, at the end of the sitting area in words I couldn't hear but whose sense I could guess from their looks and gestures: "How could you tell someone in his condition that you expect him to end up in Hell?" I looked on in excitement at the strangeness of the situation and the intoxication of release from punishment. A moment later, Necktie returned and sat down as though embarrassed, with a false smile on his face, and began to apologize for getting upset, and to try to bring our points of view closer together. I didn't care for this annoying switch as he'd been more amusing when he was on the point of strangling me. I tried to provoke him with every argument I could think of in response to his dumb pronouncement, shaking my finger in his face as one of the camels had done when telling him off. He shook his head and smiled as if to say he disagreed with me to a degree that surpassed belief but he said nothing; in fact, in the middle of my speech he stopped listening. What nobility, what good manners, what gallantry to abandon his superiority for the sake of a sick man's health! Plus, maybe he thought he was granting me a final victory to carry with me to the grave. The others, for their part, continued to calm him down with the look that says, "Let the man die convinced that he's right." They then switched to talking, with passion and good humor, about soccer, going over the latest matches as though this would, by its very nature, sweeten the atmosphere. Finally, they left, apologizing and praying that I be cured. May cancer take them.

The visitors grew fewer and fewer in the face of my distempered mood, which made them uneasy at such a gathering. I had realized that, though I might not have an excuse not to receive someone, I did possess justifications for receiving them with a glowering face: in the second week after the treatment, the dryness and constant ulceration of my mouth as a result of the chemotherapy made me look as though speaking and smiling caused me great discomfort, so they grew nervous when I threw myself into debate and argument against the least thing they said. I found that I could adopt the most extreme opinions, and switch back and forth between roles, as I wished. I had a chance to go as far as I wanted, with nothing to stop me, and I threw myself into it with the bad temper of a child who cannot be punished. I'd worked out that my wretched appearance was my weapon for parrying their kindness and I tried, with the gruffness of an old down-and-out, to appear even more wretched. Little by little, this succeeded in reducing and preventing the recurrence of these visits.

My grandfather was the last person to visit me today, without having told us beforehand that he was coming. We suddenly heard him entering irritably and shouting, as he always did when he intended to rebuke someone for some unguessable reason. The whole house was thrown into confusion by this unusual event. I hurried to him and kissed his hand and his head, while my mother stood there, watching anxiously and urging me to welcome him properly and give him more kisses. The only person with him was his decrepit maid, who was no less stooped than he. The moment I'd taken a seat next to him, she withdrew in her mysterious, ghostly way, and my mother vanished behind her.

I asked him how he was and he said he was well. It disturbed me that his voice seemed sickly and cracked and could scarcely be heard—more perhaps than if he'd answered angrily, with critical, impetuous questions as he usually did. I stared at him a little as he sat there, shrunken and emaciated in his wheelchair, in a silence that might have given one to think that the shout he'd let out when he entered had had nothing to do with him. He seemed thinner than when I had visited him in his house. He asked me about the treatment and I answered that everything was going well. He asked me to tell him if I needed money. I explained that the company's insurance was covering the costs for now and we would see what happened later. He sat quietly for a few minutes, his head bowed. Only his hand, on his knee, shook, as though he were suppressing a reaction his whole body could scarcely contain, and then suddenly his body started to heave in an outburst of tears, like someone who had lost all his lines of defense at one go.

What had happened to the coarse, gruff, soulless old man? Even when he'd called me the week before at the hospital, he'd cried over the phone, and I sensed from the sound of his weeping that he was too weak to put down the receiver. I waited for him to finish, but as soon as his weeping stopped, it would begin again and more bitterly. The thing that puzzled me most, though, was that he didn't hide his tears from me; in fact, it seemed that my presence only made him want to break down further. Nothing I could say or do could console him or encourage him to resist; perhaps all he wanted from me was my presence.

I remember a situation that had occurred right after my father's death, something I hadn't thought of again since. We were all in my grandfather's room after my uncles had told him the news, and they'd brought a doctor with them in case it was too much for him. The doctor inflated the sleeve of the blood-pressure machine around his thin arm, while my grandfather sat on his bed, dignified, silent, his head bowed, and we stood around him. Then suddenly, as though remembering something, he lifted his head to us and I saw that his eyes, for the first time, were brimming with tears—the usual terrifying glassy eyes, but without glasses. He raised them toward my brother and turned, searching the middle of the throng that surrounded him with an anxious look, and the moment they fell on me, they came to rest and the tears gushed. Immediately I lowered my head in a mixture of embarrassment and terror. The feeling wasn't much different as he cried now.

Finally I got back to my room. I lay down, seeking the rest I'd been striving to find all day, but a naïve and sterile, though nonetheless urgent, question posed itself: I was wondering, is the death of a human really less appalling, just because we possess emotions and ideas with which to face it, or is it precisely that faculty of comprehension that makes our death more desolate than anything else in existence? Maybe the best answer is to devote oneself to distractions for as long as possible. Even these questions I could only entertain as a kind of amusement.

Week 25

LITTLE BY LITTLE, MY REGIME settled into a dumb routine. I'd pass the time with computer games and anything that might have been squirted into my phone via social media. I spent hours updating apps, one after another; the moment I'd finished with one, some new thing would have popped up on another. The new television movies and series were in such supply that you couldn't fail to miss some; I'd pile them up, one on top of another, till I'd forgotten which I'd watched and which I hadn't. Sometimes I'd go through an entire television season in a day, that is, the equivalent of nine hours of viewing, a full day's work, but as soon as I'd finished, I'd feel oppressed. I'd switch straight to reading but couldn't do so with real interest. *The Magic Mountain* remained abandoned beside me, the bookmark not yet beyond halfway. Every time I picked it up, I'd cast a look at where I'd stopped, then put it back on the bedside table. I'd finished a novel by Murakami a few days before, not because it was any good but because I found the pages easy to turn, and it was only then that I discovered how much the disease had changed me. If this regime was going to make me prefer Murakami to Thomas Mann, what else might it do to me?

Nothing important has happened during the recent past. I found a new email message from the girl with the egg in her head. She wasn't the sender, it was her elder sister. She'd noticed me talking to her the day we met in the ward, and the egg had told her the details of our conversation and how later we'd exchanged messages, so this sister had felt I'd want to know what happened. The operation to remove the tumor had been a success but complications had arisen: a hemorrhage in the brain, followed by an operation to clean the head, followed by a deterioration in her mental faculties, her memory, and her ability to write and speak. Now she could no longer recognize who was talking to her or had come to see her and, of course, she would no longer be able to correspond with me. Two rounds of treatment, twelve sessions of chemo, a whole year of life with no variety, a life of operations, surgical procedures, organ removals, and doctors' promises that she'd get better, then this.

My situation was better than hers, relatively speaking. I took food that was easy to prepare and to swallow, and I skipped my appointments at the hospital. I used a variety of excuses: if drinking liquids had been effective before in making up for the lack of blood, then why not now? The glass water jug next to the bed had to be full the whole time. Whenever it came close to being empty, I'd press the bell on the bed, and each time my mother would hurry in, as terrified as if every possible emergency had befallen me. I'd simply hand her the jug, with a stony expression and an excessive standoffishness that sought to dampen her overreaction. I asked nothing of her. However, just to please her and to reduce her pressure on me, we'd agreed she should take over this one task. She'd bring the jug back, filled to the brim, in under a minute, then stand for a while as though expecting me to empty its contents straight into my belly so that she could hurry off and fill it up again.

Some things did change recently, especially when we learned that our neighbor wanted to make my mother his third wife. Previously, he'd showered the house with all sorts of foodstuffs and provisions, insisting each time he visited us on talking with my mother to explain to her how she should prepare me the things he'd brought. To her, his remedies always seemed practical and extremely beneficial. Thus, when he told her that beetroot was important for patients with diseases of the blood because it provided us with more red blood cells, this seemed very logical to her, and she began making beetroot juice and tomato soup, and anything else she could think of that was red and horrible, and bringing these remedies to me, one after another, saying over and over that he was a kind, charitable man whose intentions were pure and that I should receive him more welcomingly. When she finally discovered his true intentions, it was a cruel blow to her position. She began driving him away very rudely, via the intercom, after which she would remain rigid with anger because she hadn't figured out his intentions earlier. I took advantage of this to escalate my opposition to all visitors, as though they all had similar objectives for making up to me, and she, given her embarrassment, could only collude with me in not receiving them.

All the same, and despite my fierce resistance to her methods, she continued to receive phone calls concerning me from relatives, neighbors, and friends of the family, including some who repeated their calls time after time whenever they read a news item about a new treatment or heard of a remedy that had helped someone or other who had the disease, even if all it consisted of was camel urine. She'd write all this down and rush to give me the news with such enthusiasm that you might believe you'd be cured tomorrow, and then she'd hurry off to prepare the strange remedies and bring them to me, while I'd listlessly refuse everything she made as though it was all just another soup she'd produced from our neighbor's onions, and she'd throw up her hands. When she insisted, I'd tell her I wasn't an experimental subject for others and she'd get upset and say that was just book talk and I was hiding behind it to avoid making an effort. As I continued to frustrate her endeavors, she began to imagine that I was deliberately postponing my treatment to take it out on her, and this would make her yet more determined to have me cured by the fastest method possible.

Clearly, she wasn't convinced of the passive role I wanted for her. She was, by nature, an active volcano that died down only to erupt later with greater force. If, at some point, she should suffer a lapse of confidence regarding her methods, she'd wait for me, this time, to make a mistake that could harm me and immediately recover her confidence and return to the attack. When, however, all paths were closed before her, she'd confront me by using other people, complaining about me to the doctor and painting a picture for him in which I wallowed in a gloomy, despairing world, and he'd say that that wasn't good because a large part of the treatment depended on the patient's mental state. He'd keep insisting to me that many patients found that a psychologist helped them, and I'd refuse yet again, and my mother would strike palm against palm in despair. We were caught up in an endless duel, in little battles in which the winning side constantly changed but nobody ever lost the war.

When my mother pressured him to do something, the doctor prescribed me an antidepressant, as depression was, he said, a common condition among patients; it was, in fact, virtually a side effect of the chemotherapy. What would have been really useful would have been for him to prescribe me more sleeping pills and painkillers, instead of crap like that, I told him, so he got very angry and said he'd never before come across a patient who was so negligent and arrogant. His words were supposed to embarrass me or whatever. I, in turn, was furious at him and used all available means to make him lose his patience. I kept feeling that, with him, I was the butt of trickery and exploitation, even though he pretended he was telling me the truth at every step. How can anyone trust a doctor? Hardly any of them looks you in the eye when he's talking to you about all the things he's going to do to your body.

In view of his refusal to give me a larger quantity of painkillers, I contacted a friend from college days. "Friend" is very generous: he was just someone who could provide hashish and with whom I'd sometimes smoke his beautifully rolled joints, after which we'd sit exchanging wise thoughts and hold dumb, deep discussions that vanished from the memory as fast as the smoke. I've never in my life had a friend in the true meaning of the word, and I've never felt the lack of one, but hashish, back then, tended to make me somewhat sociable. I didn't use hashish in those days out of any urgent desire, or the craving for a high, it was just what people did during their college years. I tried it the first time because I was searching for the inspiration to write, but after a while its effect became limited to creating a mental cloudiness and casting my body into a state of dull-witted, calm numbness; in other words, precisely what I needed now.

I received him at home while my mother and brother were away. As soon as I saw him, I remembered how in college they used to call him "the horse." He really did look like a horse, with a long, flat face and stupid, sleepy eyes void of any expression. He fitted the description even better now as he had taken to tying his long hair in a ponytail at the back. Fortunately, he still practiced his old hobby, the only thing he did well in life, and which had in fact turned into a profession off which he lived, following his failure to graduate. His joints had become even better and stronger and his prices had gone up too as he imported from distributors of greater probity. At the beginning, we sat in silence, as had been our custom in bygone days, and he gazed at me in a puzzled way, with grave eyes, as though he wasn't sure who I was, perhaps thinking he'd entered the wrong house. When we finished the first joint, which we shared, he said, "You've changed a lot, but I like the bald look. I'm thinking of having my head shaved the same way."

He ran his hand over his long hair, all the way to the end. In a flash, the reel of inanities he'd uttered in all seriousness turned before my eyes, things he'd really meant and expected me to respond to and discuss, like the time he told me, "Girls fart. Did you know that?"

I suddenly exploded with laughter, and he stared at me in even greater confusion as he thought over what he'd said, looking for the mistake. I began to lose more control each time I opened my eyes and saw his lethargic, horsy face and lost expression. After a bit, he joined in the laughter without knowing why and took my bald head in his hands, to get even more witty sayings out of it, and began emitting sedate, robot-like noises, as though I was a creature from outer space. Little by little, I stopped laughing. I don't believe the dolt had even worked out that I was sick, and anyway, it would be better if he didn't know. All I needed was for him to go and spread the news among the rest of my colleagues from my schooldays with whom he was still in contact, and have vast hordes of stoned visitors storming the house.

I bought extra from him and took to smoking in the bathroom, rolling it using the celebrated Shaam brand papers, opening the window, and being careful not to forget to stuff a towel under the door. It became a daily ritual, but no more than one joint a day because my chest couldn't take it any longer. I was found out, of course, because my mother kept hovering around the room, as usual, and yelling, with her ear to the bathroom door, to make sure I wasn't vomiting or in a coma. Suddenly, she knocked anxiously on the door, and when I opened it, the smell overwhelmed her and she went to pieces, because she thought I'd gone back to smoking. I persuaded her that it was special light medical tobacco that didn't do much harm, which was why it had that gentle herbal odor and that, in fact, it was better for my health than the horrible herbs she concocted for me according to the instructions of relatives, neighbors, and WhatsApp housewives' groups. When this didn't stop her wailing, I said she ought to try one herself, it might calm her down a little, and she exited muttering and crying, leaving the bathroom door wide open, and went off to tell my brother and call the doctor. While she was on the phone, I told her to tell him that at least my appetite was a bit better and he could shove his painkillers up his backside. I raised my middle finger, picturing his thin face, which always knew more than anyone else, the tricky, useless, balls-less bastard, and went on insulting him with sedate, robotic noises.

My brother appeared at the door while I was so engaged and laughing with reddened eyes. He got it at first glance and stared at me in silence with glaring eyes; I'd never even realized the faggot was capable of showing such anger. I informed him that in Canada and the USA they provided these things legally to people with cancer, as part of the treatment. I'd seen this recently in a serial about a single widow who sold weed, and thought it was a good point, one I doubted he would have heard before. Despite which, he said nothing; in fact, he kept on looking at me sideways with an expression of disbelief. All it needed was for him to place a bright yellow sticker in front of me the way my supervisor used to. His serious, responsible look reminded me of what was waiting for me tomorrow, and that total absence of merriment was enough to extinguish my ecstasy and make me aware of the pettiness of it all.

I have to be there at seven a.m. for the blood tests, the prepping medication for the treatment, and the antiemetics, which don't provide protection from the gag reflex; more commitments and responsibilities and actions, which, if I don't do them, will place me in the way of what other people have to do. I'd thought that illness would liberate me from that, but it seems all it's done is make me swap the petrochemicals company for chemotherapy. Naturally, this is an excessively artificial connection, but it's difficult to resist the resemblance between the words.

I slept, and woke after midnight. A few hours remained before the third session. I tossed and turned a little in the bed and tried reading, but it was no use. I watched comedy shows that failed to raise a single smile and here I am now, writing, in an attempt to expel the sense of oppression. Even writing, though, can no longer produce the same effect, and perhaps has just changed its goals. I began rereading what I'd written over the past period, but it seemed stupid, trivial, lacking in fluency and honesty, just a lazy effort, full of vague detail and self-importance, when it was supposed in the end to be a consolation.

Is this what isolation means? Is this what I longed to be free of my work to do? Is this the self I'd wanted to become one with? Why had I imagined I'd be like those poets who draw their inspiration from their sufferings, their lack of order, their permanent idleness? Where was the poetry in this never-ending inactivity? Where was the wisdom?

I arrive late, surrounded by a halo of sleepiness. I lie down on the bed in the hospital, trying to get more sleep. The doctor enters in a rush and asks me why I was late. The tests have to be done early and I have a long day ahead of me. He can't believe, he says, how negligent I've been; perhaps he's referring to my mother's call to him last night. He declaims long sentences, then calls the nurse and leaves. I raise my middle finger to his retreating back, before he closes the door.

The nurse enters, needle in hand as usual. I automatically hold out my arm. Do inject me, my dear nurse! Why not? Inject me with whatever you like. Is it painful or painless? That's the only thing that matters. From the shape of the syringe you're carrying, I deduce that nothing more is involved right now than taking a blood sample. One knows some needles right away: just looking at them makes one feel pain.

She stands next to me, holding my hand with the exasperated look on her face that comes from being unable to find a vein in the crook of my arm. I notice that she's the same nurse who used to get annoyed every time she had to help me to get up and urinate and every time I coughed in her vicinity without a mask. She has a distinctive face that seems to be frozen in the act of catching an infection. I wonder what about nurses is responsible for all the sexual fantasies associated with them, what has made them into such fertile ground for pornography. The injections? The cold hands? The level stares? The nauseating smell of hospital food that clings to their clothes? To each his own, but there can be no doubt that whoever came up with these fantasies lived a rudely healthy life. Two or three months of repeated visits to a hospital would have been enough to expel any erotic feeling associated with them from his mind.

She's still struggling to find a vein. My veins no longer show any enthusiasm for putting themselves forward. Some have disappeared altogether, as though they'd taken retirement. All the same, I pretend to lose patience and ask her irritably to hurry up. She obeys and sticks the needle in where it happens to be, even though she knows how painful it will be if she makes a mistake. "Sorry, sir," she says, in a cold, bureaucratic voice, as though she'd suddenly bumped against me in the corridor. Ordinarily, I feel a common bond with employees of this kind, who do their work without dedication, but this time I cry out in protest. In the hospital, you can give full rein to your bad temper and it doesn't matter if it's the fault of the remaining heaviness from last night's hashish: so long as you're a patient in this place, you have an excuse. The nurses are used to it, but there's something about that very imperturbability that stirs up more bad temper.

She sticks the needle in again and doesn't hit a single vein. She tuts in disgust and repeats her absentminded excuse. The third time, she does the same, and I shout at her to give me the needle. She obeys with alacrity, an expression on her face that implies she really wants me to do myself harm. I put the needle into my mouth, like a drug user, and strike the crook of my arm with the palm of my other hand in swift, repeated blows. That's what makes veins rise beneath the skin: I read about it or, rather, come to think of it, I saw it in a movie. Why do we readers always suppose that everything we know we read about in books? Movies can teach you everything from the theoretical point of view, but when it comes to applying the theory in real life. . . . I think I see a vein and I make the injection quickly, before it can disappear. The needle breaks my skin and the blood runs like a river. I shout at the nurse again, as though she was the one who stuck it in. She exits in terror, looking for help. "*Fuck her!*" (I think, in English). Nothing works properly in this body.

Once the hemorrhage has been stopped, the doctor comes in, scowling. His face looks even more severe than it did this morning.

"We shall postpone the session until next week." he says. "We have to give you a blood transfusion to make up for what you lost. Then we'll monitor the count until it stabilizes, and you'll remain here, so that we can give you the necessary care."

I argue with him, insisting on being discharged, and, as usual, we disagree. "Discharge is after four o'clock, but the wound won't coagulate because of the lack of blood platelets, and your immune system will be weakened because of the lack of white blood corpuscles, and your oxygen will be low because of the lack of red blood corpuscles, and the cancer cells . . ." As usual, he has to prove in detail that he's right.

At four o'clock, I'm exhausted and find it difficult to move. I think the doctor was right, but resist. I call my brother to give me a ride and he meets me with a glowering expression that seems simply an extension of the doctor's anger. The moment I climb into the car, he unleashes his pent-up fury against me. The signing of his marriage contract will take place the following week and the wedding festivity a few months later, and he has neither the time nor the inclination to cater to such behavior. While still sticking to the code of conduct for a paterfamilias, he has begun to develop a kind of resistance to me and now sees clearly that I don't merit any sacrifice on his part.

"The days when nobody would say no to you out of concern for your health are gone," he says, and privately I agree with him but say nothing. I content myself with leaning my head back against the seat and gazing at my reflection in the side mirror. The monster whose savagery had once been just a means of self-defense has grown to a point at which it has turned into an instrument of its own destruction and that of everything around it. It appears that the system I've been following, if successful at the beginning, is turning out to prove itself a failure in the long term.

Week 27

A WEEK AGO, WHEN THE doctor explained to me the necessity of my staying in the hospital during the days of the session, I immediately agreed. At first he looked surprised, as he wasn't used to my giving in without argument or opposition or sticking up my middle finger when he turned his back. I took advantage of the situation to make him believe that it wasn't impossible for me to be flexible and understanding if he spoke to me as an equal and rationally. The truth was, though, that I preferred to stay in the hospital this time only so that I could get out of attending my brother's marriage-contract ceremony, which I wouldn't have been able to avoid if I'd gone home.

I've never been very interested in occasions of that sort and I'm ignorant of many of the customs that are observed in them; the only custom that I followed personally was that of avoiding them. It wasn't something to which my family would have attached much importance, but social pressures have increased recently, with the approach of the wedding, and I've discovered that my sickness, rather than lightening the importance of my presence on such occasions, adds weight to it. I am now obliged to be in the picture always, so that my absence doesn't raise question marks that would spoil appearances at the wedding: How can you celebrate with such happiness when the bridegroom's brother is dying somewhere? At the same time, though, the details of the illness had to be concealed as much as possible when I was present and one had to avoid referring to it and asking questions about it except in private, as though it was an embarrassing mood killer that had to remain offstage. It reminds me of something Kafka said in a letter to his friend Max while he was in a clinic being treated for tuberculosis: "Verbally and in public, no one says anything. As soon as tuberculosis crops up, everybody drops into a shy, evasive, glassy-eyed manner of speech."

Thus it was that no sooner had I absented myself from the contract-signing by virtue of being in the hospital than they decided to put on another social event the moment I came out. If I hadn't been so out of sorts those days, and if I hadn't been completely lacking in energy, I would have fought harder but I found myself enervated, my strength depleted, and with no inclination to return to the contest on which I had recently exhausted all my strength. In the past, I had acted with hostility and emotion, as though avenging myself on others just because they were healthy, but when I reviewed that conduct now, I couldn't do so without feeling childish and extremely ashamed.

All the same, I expended some of my energy on arguing with my mother and brother, just so that I could put my position on record and burden them with the responsibility for what might happen if I obeyed the invitation. I used on them, as usual, the argument of my weak immune system: the number of white corpuscles in my blood was close to zero, making me an easy prey for any infection. Also, in addition to the renewed pains following each session, there was that hardening on the right side of my abdomen caused by the swelling of the liver and the spleen as a result, according to the doctor, of the leukemia. Even mentally speaking, I was no longer completely alert, owing to the chemicals in the brain, and I'd noticed some degree of absentmindedness in myself recently. If I left a hospital appointment, I'd forget where I'd left my car; and had I in fact come alone, with my brother, or by taxi? I had to think about it for a while.

None of this, however, earned much sympathy or belief from their side, after my liberal use of some of these excuses on previous occasions. Their reaction took my stratagems into account and was resolute in opposing them. It was clear that their new awareness hadn't been arrived at independently but had developed with the aid of my sister and under her influence; the echo of her words resounded in theirs, while it was easy to trace the projection of her exasperation in the more violent methods they used to pressure me, as though she was warning me, through them, of the moment when she herself would explode in my face. She was determined, having managed the whole thing, not to let me ruin her efforts. It was miraculous enough that those people had agreed to marry their daughter to my hardworking brother and his unconnected family, and any mistake from our side might cause a rift that could never be mended.

With her penchant for grandness and opulence, she could never have chosen people less than they. When, on the day of the event, we arrived at their vast house, we traversed long distances crossing the spacious lobbies to end up finally at our place in the reception hall. I hastened my steps to catch up with my brother as we entered, bearing the pain that surged through my bones, like a jolt of electricity. The entire tribe was there, and my brother and I were like two lost lambs in their midst. As I used to do when young, I followed him and imitated his actions so as to find out whom I should greet with special deference, where I should sit, and how not to refuse a cup of the scalding coffee, which quickly turned my empty stomach.

Some of them asked me how I was, in a normal way, as though they knew nothing about my sickness. One engaged me in conversation with "So! When are you going to get married?" a serious expression on his face. I couldn't tell if it was his way of making a joke. In any case, it was difficult to distinguish among them from any perspective at first meeting; I didn't even know which of them were the most closely related to the girl. As a whole, they seemed like a single person who, through his vast presence, dominated every corner of the place, and this vast presence had customs whose roots spread too far for me to reject its authority. They had distributed symbols of these customs and traditions in every corner of their huge reception hall, to demonstrate their attachment to them. Most conspicuous were the ancient swords and rifles they had hung on the walls, to proclaim that riches hadn't caused them to forget their heritage and their forefathers' way of life, as though, despite all the conspicuous wealth, they'd prefer to live warring with a neighboring tribe over a water well.

The nausea continued to settle slowly inside me. Every time I thought it had reached the bottom, it would surprise me with its ability to settle yet deeper. Nevertheless, I continued turning my head to follow their voices, with the small amount of discrimination I possessed, attempting to appear as much as possible like someone who was following the back and forth of the conversation. Suddenly, one of them started shouting at us to please follow him, bullying every dialog in the world into submission with his colossal voice, and the voices to our right and left immediately began inviting us to stand up, while a new voice came toward us in a hurry to lead us in the direction of another reception hall and the voice of someone else behind us called to us to go toward the dining table, as though afraid we might run away.

For me, being driven to dinner wasn't very different from a sheep being driven to slaughter, knowing it will end up on a platter. Thus I found myself standing in front of a mound of rice and meat, wondering how to get out of eating. My brother read my thoughts, so he tugged on my robe to come and sit next to him at the table, as he wasn't about to lose the respect of his future in-laws because of my lost appetite. The last thing any of them would accept would be for someone to excuse himself from showing due deference toward their hospitality. It would be like impugning their manhood or openly announcing that they had failed to honor you properly.

We sat, encircling the large, shared, round platter, and the moment someone said, "In the name of God!" every hand except mine reached out. Noticing this, my brother raised his head with a reproachful look, urging me on, then tore off a portion of meat and threw it on top of the rice in front of me. Time passed, during which I couldn't bring myself to do more than take up the piece of meat and break it into smaller pieces, while the others wolfed it down with countenances indicative of a serious commitment to digestion and a desire to benefit nutritionally. Soon, however, they took note of my distraction and began demanding, with looks accompanied by knitted eyebrows and without ceasing to chew, that I eat, gesturing with greasy hands toward the dish, as though I didn't know where the food was hiding. When my brother began nudging me to force myself, things got very dangerous, and it wouldn't have needed much for them to find themselves unable to put up any longer with our terrible affront (and only God knows what kind of feeblemindedness would drive someone to refuse their munificence). It seemed to me quite in keeping with this that they might seize the weapons fixed to the walls and drive us out.

I gathered what internal powers I could to suppress the nausea and succeeded in forcing the thing into my mouth, picturing to myself a huge dam set firmly in my belly to protect me from any reflux. It could have been anything—that bitter, metallic taste, which was all that my mouth, poisoned with chemicals, could distinguish—but a piece of meat. It was as though all my taste buds had been removed or swapped by mistake for some other sense. I went on temporizing over chasing the piece of meat with another while trying to make it seem I was eating along with them and began slowly picking out single raisins and chewing them in such a way as to give them the impression that each was a whole mouthful. They too tasted bitter in my ulcerated mouth. Some of those present, however, continued to stare at my hand, watching my serving of rice, which never got any smaller in front of me, then raising their heads to look at me with distaste since the slowness of my rhythm still offended them. I therefore forced myself to eat one piece of meat after another, with handfuls of rice and raisins, well aware of what the future of those morsels would be—and if anyone had a right to feel affronted, it would be the poor sheep that had given up its life so that a man with no appetite, and who would later throw it up, could eat it.

In the bathroom, I curled up and vomited till my heart almost burst through my ribs. My pulse soon started to go down and remained terrifyingly slow. I had barely lifted my head to look at my reflection in the bathroom mirror when I blacked out and my eyes turned up to look at the ceiling lighting. I had no idea what was going on. I found myself lying half-conscious on the bathroom floor and my brother calling my name and banging violently on the door and me being barely able to answer. Nothing at that moment seemed real, or morally justifiable: it wasn't right that a person should fall down like that, like a broomstick, and, indeed, be unable to raise himself again, like a scarecrow thrown over by the wind.

I was still only half-conscious when they gathered outside the door and the murmur of their gallant, collaborating voices began to penetrate. When I was able to make out what they were saying, I got the impression that they must have some experience in breaking through doors, since they set about the matter as if it was as simple as making a hole in one of those Japanese doors made of easily torn paper panels. Soon, the loud report of breaking wood rang out, and the voices, penetrating ever more distinctly through the expanding opening, grew loud. I think I tried to tell them to leave me there for a bit and that I'd get up and leave on my own, but nobody paid attention. Then I felt myself being lifted high, like a corpse at a funeral. The fact of the matter is that I've always lacked social skills and left no stone unturned in seeking ways to thwart people's desire to invite me to their houses. This time, though, I'd outdone myself. What would people say now? They invite you to their houses to show you honor and, instead of rewarding them for their generosity, you die in their midst? Isn't that ultimate bad form?

If only I'd been left in the bathroom, I thought, if only I hadn't been picked up and borne off on people's shoulders, if only my mother had discovered me on her own, the way she might suddenly find some belonging she'd lost or clean up an egg that she'd dropped on the floor! Surely, the seemly thing is for a person to die in his bathroom and be found by no one but his mother. I certainly wouldn't feel any embarrassment at dying in front of her, or in front of the doctor responsible for my birth. Maybe it is fitting only for the persons who saw you enter life to see you leave it.

A day later, my sister invited them to visit me in the hospital, after they'd shown an interest in reassurance as to the results of their gallantry. They had no problem at all with coming together in one big group to fulfill their duty. As soon as they entered, they distributed themselves on the chairs and around the edge of the bed, while some stood. As is my custom when trying to put visitors off, I received them with a brief answer when they asked after my health, and with silence when they tried to continue the conversation. This was supposed to leave in them some kind of embarrassment, some feeling of being *de trop*, and a desire to leave. However, they turned quickly to chatting and discussing among themselves, debating, with the greatest of ease, any subject that happened to cross their minds and showing not the slightest embarrassment at raising their voices till they could be heard outside the room. By falling so rapidly into their normal pattern of behavior, they were confirming that the inconvenience they were causing me with their presence was a trivial matter, not to be taken seriously, and that I would have to accept it whenever they chose to impose it: they had played a role in saving my life, so now they possessed an additional right to be present in it.

I kept my eyes lowered and fixed on some place on the bed, having decided that the safest solution for preserving myself in their midst was to ignore them completely. Their presence, however, was by no means either of short duration or easy to bear; indeed, it extended through the entirety of the visiting hours. Whenever one group left, another would come in, as though someone had urged them to keep an eye out, follow the case closely, and be alert for any eventualities.

The next day, they demonstrated greater ease and agility in addressing me and went further in their efforts to get me to talk and force me to interact with them. "Why are you so quiet? You have to express what you feel, not bottle it up inside!" When I ignored one, another would come and sit down next to me on the other side, making a show of being able to talk to me more sensibly than the one who preceded him by assuring me that by their criticisms they only meant me well, and to help me to get over the evil repercussions I'd created for myself; in fact, the decline in my condition was to be attributed to precisely this uncommunicativeness, as though someone's personality could be what stood between him and his getting better.

It was obvious that they'd been talking about me among themselves, following their visit of the previous day, and the impression I'd made at their party, and that they'd arrived at the following conclusion: I had to change the way I dealt with the disease. Their image of me as its victim didn't sit well with the optimistic narratives of the fighters, who saw a pugnacious stance toward it as the only road to recovery. They, like others, were loaded with continually repeated stories, from the newspapers, radio channels, television, and social media, about people who had defeated cancer through the strength of their faith, or their love for their family, or their nonstop smiling, or by always thinking about roses, or faggoty stuff of that kind, so it seemed that it all, in essence, came down to how you look at things. One told me a story about a famous cyclist who had won a big race in Europe after cancer had spread from his testicles to his brain, because he had the determination, courage, and inner strength to do so; he didn't mention that the same cyclist had been deprived of his title recently when it was discovered he'd been using performance-enhancing drugs. Since people love to repeat, take as models, and draw morals from these heroic stories of salvation, this detail had to be overlooked. None of the similar victory stories simply glorify the power of the survivors to defeat the disease, they also condemn the impotence and weakness of those defeated by it. But who cares what happens to losers?

I was in no state to object, as I remained mentally and physically weak and liable to sudden collapse, and my temperature had stayed high since my fall at their house two days earlier. I realized that that embarrassing situation, the sight of me in a faint on the floor of their bathroom, had provided them with additional freedom in how they could act toward me, and my impotence left me miserably low, even after they'd gone. All this was accompanied by fits of the depression that had been seizing me lately, plus sometimes a kind of feeling of something dropping in the pit of my heart, as the pulses would become slow and widely spaced, like staccato beats on a heavy drum, and I could somehow feel it swelling inside my chest, cutting off any ability to exhale. I convinced myself that there was nothing more to it than my heart getting bigger—literally, not figuratively—which is something that happens in blood-deficiency diseases: they exhaust the heart, which has to work harder, with a lower percentage of blood, to carry out its function and which, little by little, increases in size due to excessive exertion.

When I could no longer find it in my power to put up with the negative impact of their presence day after day, I asked the nurses to bar any visitor who wasn't from my family. The nurses cooperated very well as they'd previously complained of the noise and the congestion caused by this warrior band, who sometimes gathered in the corridors and in front of the nurses' station. When they turned up the next day, at the visiting hour, and learned that they were barred, they showed, for the first time, understanding of my wish and of my need for rest and didn't insist much on entering. All the same, some continued to hover around the room, waiting and watching with all due caution, until one asked the doctor, just like any family member, about me and when the doctor wouldn't respond, they hurried to complain to my family, expressing their good intentions and feelings of affront.

My brother was divided between his feeling of guilt toward them for ruining their party and his feeling of guilt toward me following my fall. He therefore took a neutral position, refusing to intervene between the two sides. My sister, on the other hand, would stand outside the room, refusing to come in and see me, thus proclaiming her allegiance to them, and, as though that weren't enough, would take out her anger on members of the hospital administration. She even asked the doctor to answer any questions they might have, stressing that they were now part of the family and that it was his duty to keep them informed. He was not pleased to have to keep repeating his explanations time and time again but he, like me, was obliged to be diplomatic. I was aware that any additional measure I took against them, after I had barred them from entering the room, would burst the dam of my mother's accumulated anger; she had been successful, thus far, in stopping herself from blaming me for any of what had happened to cause all this chaos, but her unspeaking gestures revealed how hard it was for her to hold back. She began taking sly means of revenge, refusing, for example, to bring me certain books from the house, on the excuse that she'd forgotten them or hadn't been able to find them in my room. She brought only my laptop and even then her looks made me feel that I was a spoiled brat who was always asking for things. Rather than confront me with what had infuriated her, she began directing her energy toward the doctor, arguing with him irritably and criticizing his tendency to go easy on me and give in to my whims, even urging him to make the treatment tougher.

The result of all this was that, faced with the new pressures on us both, a kind of improvement occurred in my relationship with the doctor. Now, at last, we were allies facing a common enemy. I even began taking the antidepressant pills that he'd prescribed for me, though he said they'd take at least two months to begin working. Sometimes I think about how many things I'd do differently if it were in my power to begin all over again. But one mustn't start to feel regret: if one does, one will never stop.

Week 29

I STAYED ANOTHER WEEK IN the hospital even after my temperature had started to go down—"For more necessary rest," as the doctor put it; and since I was there, why not run an MRI? But to be sure we can perform one, we have to do a few tests, which may in turn lead to running some more tests. Tests after tests, and you sign and sign and sign, on pink paper and yellow and blue; as far as you can see, they're all the same. After a while, things get mixed up, and you don't know why this or that test is being run. The only thing you want to know is the summary of the results. "When will the results come out, Doctor?"

But this question is too general. "Do you mean the blood test result? The urine? The bone marrow? X-rays? CTI scan? To be sure of the result from this test, we have to wait for the result from that, and while we're waiting, let's run some more tests."

Today my appointment was with the MRI, which is the most important test, so far as I understand, because it gives a definitive answer as to whether the cancer has metastasized to the rest of the body. I was sitting waiting in a small side room to which one of the nurses had directed me. Then the equipment specialist came in. When you've spent all that time in the hospital looking at the same repeated faces, each of which is associated with some horrible preceding situation, every new arrival is refreshing. This woman came in with her dark grey uniform, which contrasted with the blue uniforms of the other nurses, and a wonderful smile, as though her very arrival had earned me a prize.

She was a young local woman, in her mid-twenties, of a bronzy shade of brown of the kind you only get by sunbathing, and this was the first thing you would notice about her. Her dark bronze color contrasted nicely with the rosiness of her cheeks, which wasn't entirely natural either. When she smiled, her pearly teeth were so white that they looked as though they too had been subjected to polishing and coloring. She wore a white scarf that matched her coat, her shoes, and her teeth, and was embroidered with roses that went with the delicate blush on her cheeks. Overall, one could say that she had a svelte, elegant look that was not, despite this, unprofessional or inappropriate for work, and to underline this idea, she had placed on her wrist an exorbitantly expensive, glittering watch that provided proof that it was perfectly normal for her to be crazy smart when she had a chance to get out of her work things.

She asked me how I was, and I replied I was fine. "And you?" She confirmed that she was fine. Then she asked me to remove any rings, watches, or chains, and as I have never worn any of the latter, I felt as though I'd been preparing for this test my whole life. In fact, I'd never been able to see the point of the wristwatch as an invention. Certainly, I sometimes wanted to know the time, but not to the extent of hanging on my wrist a permanent reminder of its passing. In any case, these days, cell phones did the job. I wanted to put these ideas to her in a serious fashion and see her reaction; perhaps we'd be able to discuss them a little. When you interact with female employees who meet you for the first time in the hospital, you imagine you can bemuse them into thinking you aren't there because you're sick; rather, one adopts the role of some cheerful type who's there for some ephemeral reason and who can get involved in an absurd conversation on the side. This illusion is dispelled, however, as soon as they get to work on you.

She asked permission to put some routine questions to me, as they needed to know, before the test, if the patient was a pregnant woman or had any pieces of metal in his body, as happens when you are hit by a piece of shrapnel, or by a bullet; as soon as you enter the machine, the high magnetic energy is capable of attracting that piece of metal, causing it to exit by tearing through you at amazing speed. While she was explaining, I began imagining my body being cut to pieces inside the machine and exploding in all directions because of some piece of metal inside me of which I had no knowledge. Despite my being just as confident that I'd never been hit by a piece of shrapnel or a bullet as I was about not being pregnant, I began wondering seriously whether that could have happened at some point in my life that I could no longer remember.

She asked me if she could give me the dye-test injection, which was supposed, according to her, to give a clearer picture of the body's organs from inside the machine. Even though relatively new to the work, she seemed to know what she was doing. Then I showed her my arm, with its violet bruises, which had yet to recover from the effects of earlier needles, and she stopped smiling. Even though she tried hard to look as though she was used to it, it became obvious that she hadn't been smiling to be kind but out of fear of being described as ill-bred. A certain embarrassment showed itself in her face as she inserted the needle, and she might suddenly have become aware of the possibility that she might make a mistake. Whenever I asked her to change the way she was doing something, like sticking the cotton wool on my arm after the injection, her face would take on a disconcerted, serious expression; then she'd fix me with a look that said I should be blaming myself because, for example, the place where she'd injected me hadn't stopped bleeding. It occurred to me that she had probably received so much blame from patients that she had taken to preempting it and attacking in self-defense. I had the feeling that if things got worse, her main concern would be to make clear that she hadn't done anything wrong other than to rush to my aid.

Both of us were a little embarrassed when she began helping me—wearing the hospital's short, loose patient gown—to transfer to the stretcher trolley as we were at a level of contact that here only medicine permits. Given my physical state and the stiffness in the right side of my abdomen, it wasn't an easy move. The smell of her perfume was close and everywhere, and she was good-looking enough for me to wish I were more prepared, but I felt nothing toward her since I knew that my chances with her were close to zero. Everything about my appearance in general was a reminder of how far my condition had deteriorated. It had taken a transformation as ugly as this for me to realize that I hadn't been so bad-looking before.

On my way to the examination room, I stole glances at her from my supine position on the trolley. From close up, I could see that her bronze color looked overly artificial. Common sense told me that, given she must live here, she didn't expose herself to the sun on the beaches but probably in one of those artificial tanning pods where you lie down inside and close the lid on top of yourself and its internal fluorescent lamps change your color. My supposition was confirmed when I found that the MRI machine she took me to looked somewhat like such a pod, and I wondered whether she had chosen to specialize in it because of her history with the tanning machines it resembled.

Inside the long pod, within whose belly I was enclosed and which opened only at the foot end, I was stretched out, for the third time that day, after the bed and the trolley, on a new surface. She was sitting somewhere behind a glass window giving instructions, reminding me not to move, as though she could read my desire to raise my head and move my hand to measure the limits of the narrow cylindrical cavity. The machine was making a loud noise but I could hear her voice through an internal microphone. The moment she was done giving her instructions, she elected to remain silent for the rest of the hour that the test lasted. I had to keep silent and completely still throughout that period, like someone having his picture taken in the nineteenth century.

In this silent, blind isolation, my mind flitted among so many different thoughts that I started to panic. It seemed to me that this was how it would be in the grave. But the scariest part of the idea wasn't death, it was that I'd wake up to find myself like that. It does happen that people are buried alive by mistake, or that their heartbeat suddenly returns after the dirt has been thrown on top of them, and then they die again, after hours spent in restless despair, perhaps the worst despair there can be. Where had I read about that recently? Even if it happens in 80 percent of deaths, we wouldn't know it was happening so often because it never occurs to anyone to dig up the graves to gather such statistics, from which it follows that we assume it's rare, which is itself disturbing. And even if it happens at a rate of one percent to a few idiots, I can't trust the intelligence of my body in this, or any other, regard. My body had been foolish enough to let its cells to run riot and get stricken with leukemia, whose occurrence rate is probably less than that of waking up alive in the grave, so there would be nothing to stop it going that far either.

As my anxiety inside the narrow cavity increased, I began, in all seriousness, going through the possible ways of avoiding such a danger. It was a long time since I'd last attended a funeral and I don't remember in detail how burials are performed. Even at my father's funeral, I arrived at the cemetery late, after the prayer, and the crowds around the hole had surrounded it so densely I couldn't see. It would be reassuring if they were to bury my laptop with me, with a fully charged battery, though I doubt that could happen here. That way I could at least pass the time writing and it would end with the least possible amount of panic. When I think of my recent writings, though, it might be better to watch a movie, or a comedy show, or any other dumb crap that doesn't require Wi-Fi.

Suddenly, the source of the idea came back to me. No, I hadn't read about this anywhere. It had been a stand-up comedy show, and the man was talking about his refusal to donate his organs for use after his death and informing the audience that the only thing that could persuade him to do so was the idea that his buried body couldn't change its mind. It wasn't a very original idea, but in my case it was perfect. The more I thought about it inside the cylinder, the more comforted I began to feel, and little by little I felt myself recovering the cheerfulness I'd been lacking recently; actually, it was a new cheerfulness, one that sprang from my having a plan for the grave. It didn't matter what happened in this life, so long as when I died I stayed dead. As to what might occur after that, it was too far into the future to see.

The imaging came to an end without problems, and I was proud of my ability to control my nerves, which was relatively easy for me to do now that I had a guaranteed plan: organ donation. As she was pushing me back to the room, the bronze girl noticed how relaxed I was. She had recovered her fake smile and seemed happy that everything had gone without a hitch. To express her satisfaction, she even asked me, "Weren't you afraid? Lots of patients find themselves terrified inside the machine."

"It was fine," I said. "It's great training for the grave." My answer didn't please her, as it associated her specialization with death, and her peevish mood returned.

"But it doesn't look like a grave. It's in a well-lit room and it's open at the foot end."

I, however, was in a jolly mood and felt like having some fun, so I said, "You're right, it doesn't look like grave. More like a mortuary locker, perhaps."

I smiled to confirm my joke, but she didn't smile back. They get defensive when you talk ill of a medical machine or some test, as though you were attacking the very essence of the medical science to which they belong and which they represent; indeed they feel, necessarily, that it's their essence too.

"Maybe you used to suffer from claustrophobia," she said, trying to make it my fault again, after which she didn't say another word to me, and the moment she'd got me back to my room again, she departed. I too departed, for the comfort of lying down on my bed, as though I hadn't just been lying down for an hour. How pleasant it is to receive services from someone who hates you! No wonder all those sons of bitches of supervisors are so cheerful.

For the first time in a long while, I was enjoying having nothing to preoccupy me. The three months of sick leave were up, and now I had to choose between going back to work and compulsory retirement. My body had made the decision for me and my last bit of tomfoolery with the computer virus had made the task easier for them. Retirement isn't necessarily bad. It was now clear to me that the one disadvantage was the cancellation of the health insurance that was covering the treatment. I'll pay the remaining hospital bills from my service benefits and my savings. There's the house too, which was to be sold after my brother's wedding, even though no one has talked about it since I fell sick. What matters is that I have enough to cover expenses up to the last treatment session here. As to what may happen after that, it's too far into the future to see.

There were two pieces of news, one bad, the other worse. The bad one was that I couldn't sign the organ donation form: my cancerous organs, saturated with chemicals, wouldn't be of much use to them after my death, as the doctor explained, using kinder words than those. He wasn't aware that all I was trying to do was avoid the possibility that my body might recover its enthusiasm for breathing inside the grave. I sensed he was looking at me with a compassion not devoid of respect, impressed by my desire to benefit other patients with my organs, and perhaps thinking he was at last seeing the human side hidden behind my nonchalance.

He remained silent for a while, as his face, uncharacteristically emotional, prepared me for the second item of news. Soon, however, his features regained their usual seriousness and he began explaining, in his headlong fashion, which left no room for objections: "The liver, working as a filter for the blood as it flows through the body, is the organ most vulnerable to receiving malignant cells. The symptoms do not appear quickly and, in the case of secondary liver cancer, they are in any case mingled with those of the primary blood cancer: enervation, lack of appetite, weight loss, nausea, feelings of satiety, fever, swelling of the liver. Taken in combination with the side effects of the chemo, there was nothing worthy of note." He continued to stress it wasn't their fault they hadn't detected it till now.

During his fluent speech concerning the state of my liver, the memory of my father's death eight years before came to me. In my mind, those long days of tests at the hospital, which had never revealed the rise in his liver enzyme levels, had passed quickly. Suddenly, his condition had deteriorated, and he'd accomplished his death with the same ambiguity with which he'd lived his life. In some way, I still carry within me somewhere the feeling that his death was never completed, even though I'd been there and observed everything that happened. This feeling is reinforced by the way in which his chest, with help from the ventilator, went on rising and falling even after his soul had left his body. Lately, and perhaps because of the effects of the chemicals on my mind, I have been subject to dreams about him in which he is again among us, as though returned from a journey, perhaps as an extension of my feeling that his death was never finished. One dream in particular contained things that appeared too real for me to overlook.

Suddenly, we see him coming through the door, his chest stitched up like that of someone who's had a heart transplant and his stomach bloated because of the swelling of the liver. He walks forward, exhausted, his torso naked in the pallid light. He has awoken from death, of that there can be no doubt, and this supposition is supported by the pallor of his skin, which is coated with dust, and his stiff, slightly gaping mouth—the look of someone in urgent need of water, though he doesn't ask for any, perhaps because his thirst is of another kind, a kind that doesn't belong to this world. He hasn't completely recovered his memory yet and he may have found his way to the house without realizing where he was going, but he looks as though he wants to continue his life with us from the point where it stopped. Moreover, he is trembling with fear that he will be rejected, like an animal that slips into a house looking for warmth knowing that it will probably be driven out again into the rain and wind, the storm and the open country. It is the most miserable thing I have seen in my life. We take him by the hand and sit him down, and we tell him everything is all right and we dispel his confusion, then begin comforting him and making him promises and persuading him to start his journey back to where he's come from: he'll just have a little operation there, in that place from which he's come, to recover his health fully, and then we'll receive him as though nothing had happened. He looks from one of us to another, his eyes yellowed by the effect of his last illness, and just at the thought of going back his breath begins to labor. In the end, our lies persuade him, but when he gets up to go out, his new hope does nothing to alter his trembling gait. It is clear from the way he walks alone that he no longer has a place among us, but it has needed some white lies to get him to go back to where he now belongs.

The doctor raised his voice to recapture my attention, stressing the importance of what he was about to say. What he said was that the only possible treatment in this case was radiation. Traditional external X-rays weren't an option because they would soon ruin the liver's healthy tissues. However, it was possible to perform a sort of internal radiation by implanting radioactive isotopes close to the liver. These would emit their rays throughout the coming two months, the radiation growing weaker of its own accord until the end of the treatment period. This means it will be at its strongest in the first week after the implantation and I'll have to stay in an isolation room at the hospital, with the least possible human contact, even with the nurses. My body will be a radioactive mass and even being around me will constitute a threat to others of their contracting cancer.

As this treatment is so expensive, the money will be a deciding factor day after day. And in addition to the symptoms due to the chemotherapy sessions, which have begun to grow stronger as my immunity has declined, there will be from now on the symptoms of the radiation. Then, to relieve all these symptoms, more tranquilizers, more anti-nausea medication, more immunity-boosting injections, more of a mental and physical disconnect from everything going on around my body. In the background to all this, something moves within me, like black dust, chasing away any determination to survive. How much despair do I aspire to endure before I start to listen, at last, to my need to be rescued?

Week 34

I HAVEN'T WRITTEN IN AGES. I was trying to save it up for times when I felt alert, but such times now come only rarely. The effects of the last chemo session, accompanied by the effects of radiation, have made poor concentration an almost constant condition, and I frequently lack any intuitive ability to connect and analyze things. Finding the right word takes too much effort; even remembering the password for my laptop or email is no longer automatic. I often request new passwords, write them down on pieces of paper, and put them into the drawer next to my machine so that it's easy for me to recall them later. Then I have to remember, do I open this program or that when I want to write, or was I looking for something on the internet? I remain perplexed for minutes, unable to remember what I wanted to do or to decide how to perform the next step.

My mind wasn't the only stumbling block. Until a short while ago, I was incapable of writing without my joints swelling. The tightly closed cylindrical bottles of the drugs didn't help much. My limbs had lost all their tensile strength; they were just soft, slender extensions to my body that couldn't push a feather. When I went home the first time, I could only get around using crutches. My feet could hardly support me, and the moment I stood up I realized that it wasn't worth the effort. I soon developed bluish bruises under my armpits from leaning my weight on the crutches. If I tried to do without them, I'd feel dizzy for a few steps. For the last few moments

I'd hold on to walls and door knobs to maintain my balance, and with each new fall or collision, a new bruise would form, in a new place. My skin turned into a map of dark spots, a visual history of each moment of physical heedlessness.

The whole of the first week, I refused to ask for help from the others; it's amazing to think of all the things I forced myself to forgo, just so I wouldn't need anyone. I used on them the argument that it was dangerous for them to be around me now that the implants were in place as my body was radioactive, even if the isolation period had ended. The second week, I had another bone-marrow biopsy to find out how effective the chemotherapy had been so far in destroying the cancer. It was the same biopsy I'd had done to confirm that I had the disease, but this time I couldn't risk traveling to the capital. A needle fifteen centimeters in length in the last vertebra of the back, after which even sitting down becomes an exhausting task. Little by little, the only position I can easily adopt is lying flat. I put on wide, light fabrics and stay in front of the air current, incapable of moving without feeling a current of displeasure running down my spine. Then there was the dryness, the dermatitis, the ulcerations, and the never-ending feeling of congestion in my heart. Pain everywhere, across all layers, in the skin, the bones, the intestines, and the muscles, and pain in the joints and spaces between them. "Pain is the only truth." Many have said this in one form or another; all the same, you don't realize its real meaning until you reach an appalling level of uninterrupted pain.

I can scarcely recall one moment during these past weeks when I haven't been suffering from some corrosive pain that undermines my desire to endure. It's a dog that barks in my body, night and day. I try as best I can to sleep but only rarely does the barking allow me to do so, and it's the first thing waiting for me when I wake, if it wasn't the thing that woke me. The days when I would wake feeling good about my condition are gone; it's a kind of biological gauge whose settings gradually change once you've lived with an illness long enough. Each day you open your eyes, automatically expecting to be in a bad state, even before you begin to think and feel. This doesn't mean friendly familiarity, because you will never get used to the disease. You just forget how things were when you weren't sick.

By this stage, I had excluded the word "cure" from my dictionary for good. Even if the cancer were to be destroyed, the chronic side effects caused by the disease and its treatment have erased any hope of my living a safe, natural life. The constantly renewed realization of this truth is unbearable. Sometimes I feel as though I'm discovering that I have the disease for the first time, all over again.

The depression mounts along with this feeling, and with it come more paralysis and inability to act. Even when my body gained more energy and recovered something of its immunity in the third week, I preferred to stay in bed for most of the day, as though pinned to it by a rock on my chest. I raise the cover, I push it aside, I turn onto this side, turn back onto the other; this is all I have the energy to do. It isn't that I'll be more comfortable if I maintain this lack of mobility, it's just that I feel that if I stand up, my heart will fail. When I touch its place on my chest, I feel the congestion; I feel its complete adherence to the skin; I feel the pulse, the pulse, the pulse, each pulse a contraction in my throat.

I can no longer distinguish when physical pain becomes psychological, or psychological becomes physical. Which whets the other's edge? Everything that affects my body affects my mind too, at the same moment and with the same strength, and vice versa, more or less. Sometimes I look at the drugs set out next to me on the bedside table in their transparent half- or quarter-full bottles, and I think it's easy and within reach. All you have to do is swallow them one after another. I think about it, but completely unseriously, as though I were thinking about making a trip abroad: just a distant possibility that I'd like, but without being at all set upon taking the decision to do so. Finally, I understand the maxim "If suicide weren't a choice, I'd kill myself."

This is how things were most of the time during the month. Only recently, in this fourth week, have I begun to recover something of my old self, now that I'm at the furthest possible point from the previous session and the closest to the next, just a few days away from the whole dilemma staring over again.

As soon as I was able to go out, it occurred to me to visit my grandfather; they said he could no longer leave his bed. I went into his room and found him lying on the sheets, as I'd expected. As soon as he realized who I was, he signaled to me, with a gesture of his hand, to help him sit up. I pulled him by the arm and propped him up with a pillow behind his back, then sat next to him, catching my breath after the effort. He didn't raise his head to look at me, he didn't weep, and he didn't say a word throughout the visit. We just stayed that way in silence, solemnly side by side, like two dangling testicles. Anyone who saw us would have thought we were having a competition as to which could look the more woebegone. But we shared some kind of intuitive communication, and it was enough for us to sit like that for this understanding to be consolidated, without words, without nods, without any kind of patting or hugging, in the consoling way that two old people find comfort at the end of their lives, sitting together, each on his own, on the verge of death.

This was a few days before he died, and I wonder now whether he'd wept so much over the past months because he could see the end approaching. Maybe he had guessed beforehand, without any definite evidence, as though God had informed him through divine inspiration that the hour was close. How often, indeed, had my grandfather resembled a prophet!

I was reading the same long novel by Thomas Mann and finally getting close to the end when my brother called me with the news of his death. The news had reached him via my uncles while he was on a business trip and it was impossible for him to come home, so he stressed to me the importance of my attending the funeral, to represent him. I ended the call and thought about whether it was appropriate for me to finish the novel I had in my hands. What was the maximum number of pages it was acceptable to read after being given news of that sort? Or did everything have to be interrupted, the books thrown aside? Perhaps even putting a bookmark in place so that one knew how far one had read was too shameless.

They decided to have the burial the same day after the evening prayer. There was no reason to put it off. Everything was prepared carefully and speedily, as though he were giving the instructions himself. One round of handshakes after the prayer, then off to the cemetery. Out of the hearse he floated, light and biddable, over the hands and heads and shoulders. There was no confusion: it was the only cemetery in the city and the grave was lit by a spotlight—the only grave in the surrounding area that was lit. Three individuals were there in the hole before him. They received him into it and one exited, then began giving instructions: the head here, the feet there. The second emerged and started handing down bricks, and, when the third came out, there was nothing to be seen of the corpse. Hands threw sand, and sand, and sand, then reached out with buckets, water, gravel, and prayers, and afterward everyone went their different ways and the water soon dried over the gravel and the mud and the grave immediately took on the appearance of the one next to it. That is all the work it takes to commit a body. After ninety years of existence, that's all the time needed to transit from above to below.

Gradually, the cemetery began to empty and take on the appearance of a night with neither top nor bottom: a wide, dark grave left open as a lesson for the living. And once it had expelled the last of its visitors, it seemed as if all that had occurred had done so in someone's imagination.

I was alone in front of the illuminated grave, and my car was at a distance. Nothing stood out above the level surface of the graves. I loitered. I sat for a little. A desire to lie down, to blend into the scene to the utmost degree possible, overcame me. I was still in the grip of a feeling that things shouldn't end so quickly when the watchman came and turned off the light. I felt my way cautiously over the ground to the car using my cell phone's flashlight, then drove, slowly and carefully. The car's headlights lit the narrow sandy track and exposed the surrounding graves in their glare, so that I felt as though someone was going to wake up and ask me to lower them. There was nothing but the sound of the tires on the gravel. I stopped in front of the gate and pondered, as though leaving an underground parking lot, and cast one last long look. I was wondering whether I could guess where my father was in the midst of all those graves. Perhaps it would be possible for me, if I knew exactly where he was, to break through the confinement of the senses, to see behind the veil.

Sometimes, when a man is chatting next to me, or during a TV ad, or while I'm listening to a song, I see things clearly. I see myself lying like that, alone, naked, interred, no sound anywhere nearby. I see it with the same certainty with which I know I shall not die by drowning, for example, or by burning, or struck by lightning, or in a car accident, because some things are sensed by a mysterious intuition before they occur, which is why, whenever I pass out, I'm overcome by a feeling of familiarity. Now, though, in the midst of the total silence, as I gaze at these unmarked graves, why is it difficult for me to believe that this will happen to me one day, maybe soon, in the same way? There is a barrier that stands between a person and the full awareness that he too will end there, and the closer he moves to that end, the foggier his vision becomes.

The doctor had informed me of the results of the biopsy that had been done during one of my last visits to the hospital.

The chemotherapy had destroyed 40 percent of the cancerous cells, though, by that point, it should have destroyed 90 percent. This meant that the treatment, though it might be of benefit in delaying the spread of the cancer, could not be expected to do more than that. Nevertheless, he advised me to continue with a second round as that was the best option to hand: to continue with this abject life just because "there's always hope," as every doctor is obliged to assert. The image of the girl with the egg in her head never left my mind while he spoke of hope.

The only available alternative in such a situation is transplantation of truncal cells. My brother and sister would have to undergo tests, because the cell tissue rarely matches except among siblings. Even if we find that one of them is suitable for donation, the chances of the operation succeeding remain slim at this stage. As an option it isn't much less suicidal than another round of chemotherapy. I asked him to allow me a delay to think, up to the fifth session, next week. After that, I will give him my decision. Whatever the circumstances, I am obliged to go on with the present round to the end.

Before that occurred, I would search the internet as I had never done before. For the first time, perhaps, since I contracted the disease, I searched, desperately, for hope. I read articles, stories, and celebrated books by doctors, scientists, and sufferers; there was no consolation. Even in the specialized medical sources, I found a great deal about the disease and very little about the treatment. After a long history of struggle on the part of science against the disease of the era, the results seemed frustrating: the best way to survive cancer was not to get it. But how to ensure prevention? We don't even have an answer to that. The most we have discovered up to now is that it isn't, in origin, the result of a virus or of external radiation or of any internal agents, as was previously thought. All the above are just danger factors that increase the likelihood of its occurring but whose absence doesn't annul its possibility. The real cause springs from inside, from the genetic structure that is the very source of life.

From the tumorous gene that is present in the cells of every human being, via all the factors that aid it in making the cell cancerous, all the way up to the genetic change that induces the cancerous cell to spread, nothing conflicts with the laws of biology, no attack occurs from outside. And even the process by which the body drives the nail into its own coffin, given that it extends the reach of the cancerous cells via the capillaries, which allow it to grow, nourish itself, and quickly subdivide, thus preparing the conditions for its survival in other organs from those of the original tumor, is the very same process that guarantees the life of these cells in their normal state before the occurrence of the disease. Cancer is simply a natural development originating in the tendency toward growth, and this casual killer is, in the end, none other than life itself, independent of your body and self-sustaining.

Week 35

AFTER THE SESSION, I INFORMED the doctor that I wanted to stop the chemotherapy. The radiation would continue of its own accord until the implanted isotopes ceased to emit radiation, within the determined period, which coincided with the sixth and final session. I didn't meet with much resistance from him. He mentioned that specialized centers in some parts of the world were trying out alternative therapies less harmful to the body, and that even if it wasn't to be expected that they could fight the cancer, they might improve the quality of life of those living with it. By virtue of the fact that they really existed, even though the material resources to take advantage of them didn't, they were options that might soften the blow of my decision for my family, or so at least I hoped.

I told my mother, who could say nothing—she was so terrified and shocked. She immediately made, as is her habit in emergencies, for the telephone. My brother was still away, so it looked as though I'd timed it to coincide with his absence, even though he wouldn't have interfered: it had been clear for some time that how I dealt with my condition was no longer of any interest to him. Since I'd started using taxis to take me to and from the hospital, I no longer owed him anything. In our unspoken brotherly way, we'd reached an agreement: I wouldn't burden him with any responsibility relating to my illness and in return he wouldn't burden me with any relating to his wedding. It seemed he was keeping his end of the bargain admirably, since the expression of terror on my mother's face deepened in response to the shock of his indifference. She immediately put down the receiver and dialed another number, with features yet more distressed but confident this time of getting results. It was clear just from the expression on her face that she was calling my sister.

I was in my room when I heard the rapping of her approaching heels. It took her no time to get to us, but she arrived as chicly dressed as if she had been ready before my mother called. Her hair was carefully coiffed, her headscarf was in her hand, and she was still wearing her abaya, as though she was sure she'd be leaving again soon and had come just for this pressing affair. When I invited her to enter, she walked forward slowly, scrutinizing the room, which she was seeing for the first time from the inside, looking as though she would like to kick at all the mess, or at least prevent her eyes from falling on me. I was facing her, on the bed, in a scene that was out of harmony with the rules of distance that we had maintained so well till now.

"I see you're very relaxed," she said, after a while, and it wasn't clear if this was an encouraging observation or a sarcastic reference to the embarrassment I was supposed to be feeling following my decision. Then she suddenly put her hands on her hips and a joking, reproachful smile sketched itself on her face. "How long are you going to go on like this?" she said, as though urging me with the utmost affection to stop giving in to my whims. By so doing, she reduced the matter to mere naughtiness on my part that she could erase with a feminine gesture in step with my childishness; a maternal gesture demonstrating how cute she found my rebelliousness and her willingness to be more accepting if I would abandon my obstinacy. It was the same hegemony before whose mirror I had so often found myself compelled to back off and climb down.

When she met with no answer, she followed her joking with a little serious conversation, seeking to cozy up to my ideas with cheap moralizing and philosophizing, in a tone that implied she was trying to sound like a book: "Isn't life worth a try? And if it must be death, isn't it better to die with honor?"

I didn't understand what "die with honor" meant. What for? I'd rather die in comfort. I didn't answer, naturally, while her face took on a wounded expression that demanded I think well of her intentions. This faked bewilderment, and her unaccustomed eagerness to hear my reply, increased my desire to exploit this opportunity to push her as far away as possible. I knew, however, that the moment I opened my mouth I would have taken a step down the wrong path and that, inspired by her style, the seriousness of my position, and my limited options, whatever I said would take on that typical whiny tone. Then I'd wait for her to be affected and look forward hopefully to some change in her feelings toward me. To do all that would be to put the ball in her court and accept she had the right to evaluate my justifications. I therefore decided that all I had to do to resist her was to remain silent and end the matter with the least degree of self-betrayal.

"What if I were to donate my truncal cells?" Her eyes shone with an enthusiasm she hoped I would find infectious, and this time she was confident she would obtain an answer. The truncal cells option was ruled out by doctors at this stage, though it remained on the table for any who wished to take the risk. The test results had proved that my sister's tissues were a match for mine, whereas my brother's were not, and this made her the sole suitable donor. Her enthusiasm for it seemed more like a gesture toward peace from her side, as though her readiness to donate was a sign of her having forgiven me for something I'd done to her. While she spoke of this option, she continued to pace the room, her white cuffs projecting beyond the sleeves of her abaya and her black hair bouncing on her back, and she kept repeating that she would subject herself to it for my sake, even though the operation required of her no more than a needle in the vein to gather the cells, which her body would soon replace without the slightest impact on her. For me, though, there was an infinite number of risks of which the possibility of the donor's cells attacking those of the receptor's body was not the most complex, while my current condition, which might not tolerate the stress on my heart and lungs resulting from the transplant, was not the most straightforward. Despite this, she set about twisting the doctor's words so that the possibilities of my surviving the operation appeared to be better than those of its failure.

I would have rejected this desperate option even if my brother had been the suitable donor of the two. Moreover, that she was who she was, and that our relationship as siblings had always rested on bloody combat, made it seem all the more obvious that her cells would attack mine if I allowed them to enter my body. In my mind I began to imagine that, by rejecting her truncal cells, I was simply rejecting the fake bond of blood between us, one that stood in the way of any attempt by her to move beyond hostility, as though it had never existed. I folded my arms over my chest, stressing further my determination to remain silent, in the locked-down manner in which a child who will not forgive its parents for some impoliteness clams up and is afraid to speak in case it appears silly the moment they realize what it's about. Suddenly she stopped pacing and gazed at me in disbelief, as though she had never in her life done anything that could justify my coldness to her.

Once all her affectionate concessions had failed to change my position, she quickly displayed the resentment that motivated her from within and compelled her to spend time with an imbecile like me. Suddenly recovering her loud tone, the one she'd acquired from living in such a large house, she yelled, "Do you know what people are saying?"

When she said "people" she had in mind only her husband's rich acquaintances, whose judgments on my way of dealing with the disease—which, perhaps due to the absence of the Father and, more recently, the Brother, had taken a turn more harmful and more resistant to the insertion of right-thinking into my head—she proceeded to repeat. She may also have added to their judgments something of her own, in that she warned me of the pathetic picture I presented to others and how they would remember me after my death as a failure, the same going indeed even for my family, as though by giving in like this I were sullying their reputation. For these reasons I had come to form something of an indirect threat to their opinion of my brother, since their judgment of me must inevitably extend to include him, and perhaps her too, and for these reasons her heels kept drumming angrily on the tiles, coming and going, while she moved her hands excitedly in an attempt to stress the madness of what I was doing.

Faced with all this, I might at any moment have climbed down and submitted to what seemed reasonable, to her. With my excessive good manners and tendency to follow along, I have always wanted to be accepted by others and avoided as far as possible being an inconvenience to anyone. If I have been tempted briefly at times to go against them, I've quickly come to feel that this will involve risks I shall later regret. The rebelliousness, withdrawal, and independence I am practicing now have always been pictured to me as belonging to a world far from ours, so far that I could never find happiness there. It might be, as my mother saw it, the world of novels and foreign books or, as others saw it, the world of individualism, devoid of family bonds and decent values or, as my sister saw it, the world of complicated personal fancies and weirdness; whatever it was, I needed to make a rapid course correction so that I could join my own milieu, the one in which Fate had decreed I should grow up, and take my place among its ranks, to which one must have recourse since no good could come from such unnatural deviance.

Looking at it from the other side, I had never felt any certainty regarding my present deviance that I was on the right path or that I was entering a battle that might find me at the end on the winning side or from whose loss, even, I might derive any glory. It was useful to me, so as not to allow myself to be misled by my resistance, or attribute to it something that didn't belong to it, to seek the help of what I'd learned from my father's ability to expose exaggerations for what they were. I realized that it wasn't my position per se that was important here but that I stick to it, come what may. I wanted to test my capacity to stand firm. I wanted to acquire this immunity to whatever came from outside. My personal battle with the disease has, from the beginning, lain in this: in resisting all these external judgments, views, and interventions; it is as though my preservation of the self, during a disease that strips one of his identity, is dependent on the continuation of this resistance.

My sister was still pacing the room, yelling at me, demanding that I justify my position, repeating that I was weak because I hadn't exhausted all possible solutions, then stopping and turning toward me to see if she was any closer to making me speak, then resuming her walking in a state of disbelief. In the end, she seemed to tire and her energy to be on the verge of running out, and she took to repeating in a worn-out voice that she would leave me to die as I wished, in a last attempt to stress the weakness of my position. When I said nothing, she took hold of the door as though about to leave, before turning to look at me, her voice shaking prayerfully as she begged me to die quickly and rid them of all the trouble I was causing. She left, slamming the door so powerfully into the wall behind her that it swung open again without closing completely. The pounding of her heels, noisy and rapid, streamed through it as she receded, as though she had resolved never to come this way again.

At her raging exit, my mother called to her but received no response, so she rushed to me in terror to find out what had happened. She opened the door fully and, after one look at me, realized that it was over and there was nothing left to talk about. She continued to gaze at me with tears in her eyes, a panicky, despairing expression on her face, then went out, closing the door quietly behind her.

"It seemed to K then that everyone had cut their ties to him, and he felt that he was now freer than ever before." I recall a passage of Kafka's, from his last novel: "He had fought for and won this freedom, in a way that no one else in his position could have done, and from now on no one might touch him or send him away, indeed, barely even address him. But, at the same time, another conviction, at least equally strong, grew within him: that there was nothing more futile, nothing more desperate than this freedom, this waiting, this invulnerability."

Week 37

IT STARTED WITH A VIRUS in the lungs, just two weeks ago. I'd thought I'd finally taken my fate into my own hands and had organized in my mind the weapons I'd use to resist whatever fatigue or other setback might arise. What can destroy you if you decide to confront everything with total detachment? I thought by doing what I had I'd be protected from falling into the snares of all these influences, but it seems that detachment is just another trick that has to be resisted. How can you talk about nonchalance, or freedom, when something as tiny as atoms of dust can turn your fate, your will, and the activity of your internal organs upside down?

I was alone in the house when the fit seized me. One moment my lungs were working normally and the next they'd decided it was too much effort. Then I lost control of my bowels; it was as though everything inside me had given up and gone slack. I had never wanted to get to the point at which such a thing could happen, never imagined anything so humiliating. Eventually, I called the emergency services, though I'd been putting off doing so until something more serious should happen. Even in this degree of need, I felt I was being a wuss to call an ambulance and would have preferred it if one had passed the house by coincidence on its way to the hospital, so that I could call and wave to it from the window of my room, as though hailing a taxi, and it could stop and take me with it, in which case everything would have happened spontaneously and uncomplicatedly. Instead, everything was weighed down with shit and complication, and I hoped it would be the only time I'd ever meet those individuals, even if they were used to it.

The embarrassment, the goddamn embarrassment, always this embarrassment. No matter how hard I'd believed that I'd reached the ultimate level of nonchalance and encircled myself with lofty battlements of invulnerability and resistance, it took just one attack of embarrassment to bring them all toppling down.

I awake in Intensive Care. Buzzing instruments surround me on all sides. I notice I'm wearing an oxygen mask, which fogs up with each breath. My chest rises and falls involuntarily, thanks to the ventilator. There are curtains separating me from the neighboring beds and another, now open, separates me from the corridor. Nurses are standing there, talking. I try to call to them. Faint croaks dry up in my throat and fail to make it out of my mouth. I don't have the strength to reach the bell on the bed. I feel I've lost contact even with my own limbs.

Suddenly the doctor in charge enters, followed by a nurse. He glances rapidly at the machines and the data. I realize from his body language that he's in a hurry: he has other beds to check on. I look directly into his eyes, trying to engage his attention. If he'd just look back, maybe I'd be able to explain what is happening. If he'd hold the pain scale up to me, I'd point with my eyes to number ten. If he were to ask me something, I could cry. But he only looks at me for a fleeting moment, just enough to register that I'm awake. His face implies that the case is stabilized, but he wants more improvement, which he requests from the nurse, not me. I'm not a person here, I'm a case. Even as he retreats, I follow him with my eyes in the hope that he'll turn around.

The nurse approaches and hovers around me. She feels it's her duty to do something, now that the doctor has swooped. She raises the mask and wipes away some spittle that's running from the corner of my mouth. Her breast rests on my arm and bulges against me, without her feeling the slightest concern. I'm in no condition for thoughts or fantasies, and even if I were I wouldn't be able to do anything about them. It's no different for her than if her breast were pressing against her cat or her dog; she doesn't give even the smallest indication that the situation offends her modesty. Total castration: that's what I feel with her.

She goes out into the corridor again, meets the other nurse, who is responsible for the next-door bed. I hear her murmuring to her that she's tired, in the same tone that she might use to say she was hungry. Then she talks about her son and how she wants to get him into some club or other. I watch her and ask myself, How do they do it? How do they make it look so easy? How does she go about her business in the total certainty that a moment from now she will still be walking and talking and working without any difficulty in breathing? I want so much to imagine myself that way, to bring back all the times I was capable of saying I was tired, while standing on my feet and sighing to the full extent of my lungs, then going on talking. In my condition, I cannot be confident that things that happened automatically before will still happen a little later on.

The other nurse goes in to see the other patient. She pulls aside the curtain that separates us so that she can move more easily around the bed. I turn my head on the pillow in that direction. My heartbeat feels heavy and exhausted from making the movement. I find that he is gazing in my direction. His child's hair is tousled, as though he's just finished playing. His nose is connected to breathing tubes. There is something about his stiff mouth that is unsuited to his age, but his eyes are calm. Neither of us turns his gaze from the other. Only patients can participate in such a look because no one else ever looks at them that way, in the eye. I want to ask him if he's in pain but his eyes answer me that it's too late to ask that. He appears sicker, more dignified, and better informed than I as to the possibilities of death or deliverance. For a moment, I feel he is looking into the depths of my heart. Maybe it's just his expression when in pain, but I perceive in the way he looks at me a certain pity. At the instant he shuts his eyes, the nurse closes the curtain again.

I turn my face to the ceiling. I think of all patients— dumped on beds like this, staring with defeated eyes at ceilings like this, always agitated by the fear that their outward appearance doesn't reflect their inner state, that their features do not convey their pain, that their mouths cannot give sufficiently clear notice of their fears that others rush immediately to save them. I think about this and I understand why some howl like wounded animals.

I think of my father: how, in a room like this, he used to shriek from behind his oxygen mask. No, not because he wanted to be rescued but out of despair at the possibility of such a thing happening. I remember the whine of the heart machine, and the heart rate that went down to zero in a few short seconds; how it agonized him that his chest kept rising and falling after the soul had departed. How it now agonizes my swelling heart.

I think of Kafka, stretched out on his bed in the clinic, when tuberculosis made his throat hurt, so that he could no longer speak, or swallow anything. Wretched Kafka, dying of hunger because they had no feeding tubes available. How terrible those pains, those long, dumb days lying in that state, fully conscious but cut off from everything, knowing that this was how things would end!

I go into an extended fit of weeping that periodically quietens a little only to return with greater force. For something I'm doing for the first time since childhood at least, I'm amazed at how persistently I apply myself to it. When I finally come out of it, I feel a mixture of shame and relief and an even greater numbness: it's unclear whether the nurse has upped the dose of the tranquilizer to calm me down or this is how people normally feel after crying.

Long hours go by under the influence of the tranquilizer. In my semi-comatose state, I notice that the curtain next to me has been pulled back. The machines around the bed are disconnected and the overhead light has been turned down. The sheets and covers are white and new. I feel as though everything that happened, including the child's look and my bizarre outburst, was nothing but part of a muddled, distant dream. This thought relaxes me and I plunge once more into sleep.

The instant that I open my eyes, I am assailed by an unstoppable flood of depression. My limbs are still paralyzed and my body feels cold. I gaze at my surroundings. I call the nurse and ask her with a heavy tongue and a finger that can barely point. She confirms that my young neighbor passed away while I was tranquilized. For a while I say nothing, recalling that final gaze of his. The nurse stands there. I notice that she's not the one who was here this morning. I ask her the time, and she answers that it's midnight. When my silence grows, she lowers the light above me and closes the curtain. I spend the rest of the night awake, alone in that twilight, thinking about things in a brittle state. Something inside me has opened and is seeking more contact, as though one crying fit had been enough to carry me to this fragile place.

But I'd long been without that capacity to communicate, even with God. My uncommunicativeness wasn't completely accidental, due just to my personality: it had taken persistence on my side to keep it up. I'd been born an introvert and subsequently struggled with every defensive instinct I had, year after year, to isolate myself further. I'd trained myself to go without and placed myself out of reach, behind a wall of indifference to others, as though by so doing I could protect myself from anything that might arouse emotion. I don't know what power I thought I would garner by keeping it up throughout those long years; life wasn't easy at all, or without its insecurities, and things kept accumulating, like rust upon the heart, especially the littlest things.

Suddenly there passed before my eyes the reel of events that had embedded within me the frailty of my nature, a nature that could only ever have ended up this sick. Within a few moments, I had burst into tears again.

When I didn't stop, the new nurse stood at the end of the bed and conferred with the other about the possibility of giving me another injection, and with that, I reached the maximum dose of painkillers my body could take. I lay for hours, quiet and numb, like a spent matchstick, as though nothing below my exposed upper body had any knowable presence; as though what lay beneath the sheet was a stiffening corpse. With the little energy I possessed, I sent nerve signals to my toes and looked down to where they were, at the bottom of the bed. I saw them move a little, which immediately made me feel better. This tiny unexpected action of my toes brought back to life a warm scene that I was unable to recall in detail. But how silly are the things that cause a person's feelings to change! How is a man supposed to believe in his resolve, or even his defeat, when he realizes that the soul on which he depends is innately so frail?

In the second week, I leave Intensive Care for the Intermediate Care room. I exchange the oxygen mask for a nasal cannula that forces air into my nostrils via small tubes; the tubes are attached at the other end to an oxygen cylinder that would be portable, if I could move. I sleep the whole day and spend the night lying awake. Generally speaking, my body is in a stable condition, but it has taken on the nature of the room in which it resides: it may, at any moment, move into a more dangerous phase.

The night-shift nurse looks after me. The nurses prefer the night shift because it's quieter: most of the patients are asleep, and there aren't any visitors. This particular nurse is calm and moves slowly and without noise; she may even be asleep herself. Her eyes are dull and have very short lashes and deep-set sockets, and she has a stiff mouth through which it is unclear whether she breathes. Her cheeks are hollow and the wrinkles on her forehead remain stiff and dry, no matter how her expression changes, not that she has many expressions anyway. It's one of those faces that aren't hard to imagine dead, as opposed to others one looks at and which it would never occur to you could enter the dryness of death.

She asks me quietly to raise my arm so that she can measure my blood pressure. Despite her offhand tone, I feel she understands how sick I am. She isn't one of those nurses who have no idea how hard it is sometimes to respond to trivial requests, such as raising your arm, or who ask you lots of question about what medications you've been taking while you're too weak to open your mouth to answer. I think that perhaps she's a patient here herself, a resident in the hospital, so she understands precisely how I feel. Maybe, during her long unoccupied hours, it occurs to her to do something useful, so she comes and does the nurses' work, which she's extremely good at because she's spent so much time here, and when her shift ends she goes back to her bed, which bears her name and the results of her own analyses, fastens to herself the tubes and needles, and for the rest of the day thinks, like us, When am I going to get out of here?

She gives me an indifferent look as she grasps my thin arm and says my blood pressure is low. Her expression tells me I should expel that silly idea from my head and that she's a nurse. All the same, she leaves without making any noise, extremely slowly and with a stoop to her back, as though she were a ghost who might at any moment disappear through the door. If I hadn't seen her open and close it, I would have thought she really had passed right through it. After she leaves, I think they should make more use of such nurses: nurses who look sick. It would be more seemly to keep away from the rooms the ones who move lightly and gracefully before your supine body, which despairs of the possibility of ever again doing the same.

241

As soon as I'm transferred to an ordinary room, I ask to go home. The doctor refuses, arguing that I have to stay till next week to have the last chemotherapy session. When my usual attempts to pressure him have no effect, I ask for the head doctor. They pretend he's busy, so I insist my mother and brother ask to see him. He eventually comes, contradicting all my expectations. He has a kind, extremely cheerful face, with a jolly smile under a white mustache. On the basis of his modest build, he could be a cleaner, except that he enters at a rush, his long medical gown billowing behind him. It appears that there's nothing he likes more than talking to patients, even though he has never actually met me before.

He's one of those doctors who, as soon as he sees you, goes into ecstasies and cries out that you look to be in excellent shape, then reads the results and exclaims, "My my! What health! What life! What a regular pulse! What a wonderful temperature!" and takes hold of your wrist and prods your stomach and does all the routine examinations while keeping up his excited comments: "Your temperature's wonderful and everything's in excellent shape. You're in better health than me! What are you doing here? You should be out there, enjoying your health and your youth. But I understand you completely, you sly, clever lad. You just want to be made a fuss of so you can get some attention, huh?" Then he winks, without pausing in his examination, and says, "What a sly lad! But we're going to have to be careful with the young nurses, huh? Hahaha!" Finally, he puts everything back in place, winks and assures you that you mustn't worry, then leaves and tells your family that you'll die if they don't keep you here longer.

My mother came in and gave me the message. She was carrying my laptop to give to me, as though it was settled that I'd stay and I'd better start adapting. They had agreed with the doctors, on their own, about everything, and I was no longer a party to the consultations going on about my leaving. Discussions were taking place about a further round of treatment too, six more months at least; they'd be looking into all possible ways of forcing me to do it. It's a maneuver hospitals permit when the patient reaches a certain point, which, it seems, I had. I was now about to embark on my sixth session, and I was weaker and less resolute than at any earlier time. I couldn't see any progress ahead, any increase in freedom, only more of the emerging pattern of deception.

Week 39

I WAKE IN A HALO of white light. I feel a layer of cold over my skin, as though it doesn't belong to me. Maybe it's hard to recognize the dividing line at which a person can be sure he has surrendered his spirit. Everything around me is clean and white too but has acquired a touch of the patina that clothes everything that has been used, wiped, and polished numerous times. The walls, the covers, the tiles, the legs and sidebars of the bed, even the lampshade, appear glazed with overuse. It's the second week after the sixth session, approximately the third week since I was transferred to this room. Three weeks in this halo of light, within these walls, and with this smell.

My hands are open at my sides, in the bed, thrust there under the sheet out of pity. I pull them out and hold them up before me, and they look like the claws of an emaciated animal; their pallid color and tattered nails are a good reason to keep them out of sight. The food on the side table is untouched; it seems a bizarre idea to put anything into my body other than via tubes; it seems more natural to vomit than to swallow. The smell emanating from the covered plate is enough to make one ill. Isn't hospital air supposed to be pure? The plate never manages to persuade someone to carry it outside: it's always left where it is until it's time to exchange it for the next meal when another takes its place, as though there's nothing to indicate that I've left it untouched.

I rise sluggishly, holding the feeding pole in one hand and the crutch that was standing next to the bedside table in the other. I round up with my feet the hospital slippers thrown beneath the bed. The moment I stand, I feel nauseous. I walk a little and regain a degree of balance. At the door, I stand, contemplating the room from this unfamiliar angle. The halo surrounding the bed appears greyer, once I'm outside it. I see the shape of my body reproduced on the folds of the sheet, as though I was still lying there. Is that really all the space I occupy? I can calculate my weight loss from the size of the indentations, just as Maritchi-ko could calculate how long she'd been waiting for her lover because the sash of her kimono used to go around her twice, blah-blah-blah. But why bother? At the moments that really count, this constant mimicking of literature vanishes, as though it had only ever derived its power, during moments of ease, from my delusions.

It occurred to me how I used to beg God, consciously or unconsciously, to ensure me a life like this; to punish me with mischievous Fates in return for allowing me to gain from them one true, rich experience. It was the sole connecting thread that I left exposed between us, and how often I imagined, in my overweening folly, that the only thing preventing me from committing a crime, like Raskolnikov, for example, was the keeping of this vow. But whenever I'd see a movie or read a news item about a man condemned to death, I'd imagine myself in his place, envying him the clarity with which his mind must see things. It seemed to me that all those prisoners, despairing of their future, must possess a peephole onto the world in which the self comes into its own and from which inspiration is drawn, that fertile ground where writers find something to say.

The most horrible part, as I now realize, isn't the night before the sentence is carried out, but the long, heavy, not-without-hope waiting. The condemned spends at least six months before execution, long enough for a possible pardon or commutation. But the most horrible thing about that hope is when you realize it probably won't come about, yet it deprives you even of surrender. It follows that you plunge into a fit of don't-give-a-damn, over-the-top behavior in an attempt to distance yourself as far as possible from the fate that awaits you. There is no clarity of mind in such waiting, there are no surges of immortal expressive power, no brilliant intellectual fireworks, no epiphanies ignited by the awareness of death's approach, just an anxious expectation that eats away at the spirit, leaving it tense and hollow.

And here I am, having passed the whole of these last six months in that state. Not once did I feel I was worthy of such a death, of a death that spends its whole time in preparation. Such a death is for thinkers, poets, prophets, and philosophers, and for those who have well-structured last words to say and affecting counsels that change the course of others' lives. I have never once had anything important to say, and when I try to think what would sum up my life all that comes out of my mouth is stupidities. It would have been more fitting if I'd slipped and broken my neck in the bathroom or if the gas cooker had exploded in my face or I'd been hit by a car while looking dumbly in the opposite direction and come to an end right then, on the spot.

I can feel it as I write these words: the self-hatred that rises inside me, like smoke from a burning corpse. This is the only fruit of this writing: the shame that reminds you that you have failed at the one thing you thought you would be good at. It would be better for you not even to try, so that you don't have to confront this truth, in its absolute, acute, and implacable form: the truth that you do not deserve anything better than what has happened to you. I wonder if this is what Kafka felt too when he asked his friend Max to burn everything he'd written; though it's easier today than it was in Kafka's time—meaning the destruction of writings. Today all you have to do is click on Delete All Files, or just leave them as they are on a machine whose password is known only to you and they will stay there, hidden for all eternity.

I pick up the laptop and start messing about in the files. I compress them and collect them into a single folder, then continue my search through the machine. I page through the internet, social media, and games, trying to inspire myself but without success. I end up, as usual, at the news sites. There's a report on a detainee on hunger strike who has lost at least a third of his weight. He describes his condition: "dizziness, intense vomiting, sensory disturbance, bleeding from various parts of the body, failure of some internal organs." In every news item I find tragic signs, in every misery a reflection of my own condition. I leave the page and turn off the Wi-Fi.

I turn on my playlist of songs; I haven't listened to them for a long time. I feel a bit better when "Bohemian Rhapsody" starts. Two minutes in, the song gets to the passage about not wanting to die and I burst into bitter tears. I cry and cry till I don't know what I'm crying about and then I cry some more. However, even keeping that up no longer creates any numbness, just further exhaustion of the lungs.

I sit, unable to do anything. I cover my body and head completely in an attempt to go back to sleep. My mother's raised voice, coming from outside, interrupts me as she again argues with the doctor. She enters, darts a quick look at me, and asks, "Have you eaten?" She lifts the cover, and the smell of the food rushes at my stomach. I turn my head away and empty the content of my guts onto the sheet. She hands me the vomit basin from under the bed and gazes at me, waiting for me to finish. I don't stop until my veins are bulging and my whole body is exhausted. I feel I'm not getting enough oxygen. My mother calls the nurse and leads her to the disgusting scene, as though the nurse were the one who had vomited. She tells her off as she points in irritation to the plate, as though they could have prevented what had happened if they'd taken more care, if they'd forced me to eat.

She asks the nurse to leave. She cleans up around me and gets a new sheet ready without looking at me. She seems angry but doesn't say anything. She puts the vomit basin next to my pillow after cleaning it, thrusting it there with a violent movement, so that I won't forget where it is next time. I watch her with my head lowered and a sideways, half-lidded glance, on my face the exhausted expression a man has after he has just vomited. She goes on moving things about in an irritated way, then mutters, "Why are you doing this?" I'm seized by a feeling of losing my balance, as though I'm about to fall off the bed. A terrible dejection surges inside my chest.

This was how she would always prepare for an attack: holding her tongue and holding her tongue and holding her tongue some more till you feel that at last you've been left alone. But you've only been left alone so that you can push on to the furthest possible point. And when the moment of retribution comes—and it always comes unexpectedly and inappropriately, when you are in your lowest and most vulnerable state—she brings evidence to prove that you deserve what happened and that, in addition, she had previously treated the matter with such forbearance out of kindness. To confirm that she had indeed reached that point, encouraged perhaps by my exhausted expression or by the smell of vomit, she began berating me exasperatedly—"Your brother's wedding is at the end of the week and you're here making everything more difficult. You're refusing treatment, you're refusing food, and you're refusing to show any understanding. You just go against everyone. What do you want? Nobody knows. Perhaps even you don't know. All you want is to spoil all our efforts, without any concern for what we're going through and without any consideration for what I've had to put up with for you and all the pressures from your brother and sister and people and the hospital and your almost exhausted bank balance and—and—and—." It was as though the floodgates had suddenly opened and she was wailing and complaining about everything that was on her mind. A touch of tremulousness seeped into her voice as she said, "I've tried, God knows I've tried. I've spent nights at your side. I've put my whole life on hold because of you. I've done everything I can, and more, and now my health isn't what it was. Do you think you're the only one? I've put up with everything in silence. I've put up with it, and what do you do in return? You spoil everything I'm doing out of stubbornness, and without any explanations, and you still won't say what you want, you still won't, but if it goes on like this . . ."

As she continued to talk, the nausea began little by little to grow stronger, and more of the air in the room became inaccessible to me. That sinking sensation at the pit of my heart was becoming more intense, and I felt somehow friendly toward it, as though I was luring it in. I found myself wanting to stop being a burden, and that appeared genuinely within reach and possible. My death was no longer needed to put me out of my misery but to put her out of hers, and I felt that if I focused all my energy on cultivating my present weakness, I might be able to make it happen faster. And she kept on talking, sobbing with greater stridency, as though urging me on—"I'm not trying to pressure you" and "Your refusal will change nothing" and "You're doing it to yourself"—while in my chest something was on the point of exploding and my heart was swelling and my pulse slowing more and more, till I could no longer make out what she was saying. I felt my whole existence was revolving around some point in my chest, growing denser and shrinking and concentrating itself inside that point, which in turn shrank and shrank till I was breathing through the eye of a needle. Then everything began to vanish.

When I came to, everything in the room was the same. After you've spent such a long time in one place, it's easy to notice any change. Only the resuscitator had been moved a little in its place, giving the impression that it had been recently used and quickly put back; it was hanging in the same place on the wall, but in a hesitant way, as though waiting for me to say thank you. The shift doctor came in with a smile that said, "I saved your life," or "You're lucky to be alive," it makes no difference. I grasped what he told me in staccato phrases had happened: acute drop in blood pressure; decreased flow of blood to the heart; one or two CPRs and the heart begins beating again. "You have to remain calm," he says. "We'll give you an injection to bring your blood pressure back to normal levels, but keeping your nerves under control is very important too." He must have given my family similar instructions because no one came into my room. Their presence wouldn't have been noticed anyway: most of my time passes in semi-consciousness as a result of the amazing quantity of painkillers that have been pumped into me.

I sleep and wake. I make out the dark-skinned male nurse from east Asia. I don't think he remembers me. He notices me gazing at him, while he's checking the machines and the data, and smiles. I tell him of the chest pains and difficulty in breathing. He says we have to improve my low blood pressure a bit. A collapse is natural after a long period of lying down, especially given the anemia that accompanies leukemia, not to mention the side effects of some of the drugs. He explains in detail and makes sure I'm following him closely. His expression is frank and direct, and he doesn't try to evade the possibility of my burdening him further. He's a physiotherapy special-ist too, and he massages my hands and says it's important to energize the flow of the blood within the body. I do a few sim-ple exercises with him. We talk quietly as we do them.

He's fifty years old. He's very fit and has an athletic body. His smile doesn't usually reveal his teeth, as is normally the way with the nurses, but his lips are a little blackened, because of his age and the fact that he smokes. I ask him if he smokes and he says yes and laughs in embarrassment, exposing a row of teeth that are slightly yellowed but clean and regular, as befits a nurse. I ask him if he has never felt the effect of his smoking on his lungs or his heart. Sometimes he gets a cough, he says, just if he smokes too much, and then he runs, to clean out his lungs. As for his heart, the organ that has beaten sixty times a minute for fifty years, he's never had any reason to complain about it. And what does he do in his time off? He exercises, cooks, goes to the market. His wife is there, in his home country, with his two daughters. "They're approximately your age now," he adds. Some days, he goes fishing with his friends; this explains his golden, almost brown complexion. Suddenly, with great warmth and tenderness, I remember the Old Man, and ask him to tell me more. Each weekend, they go out early, in a small boat, him and five of his friends. They catch whatever the sea sends their way, and in the late morning, when the sun has gotten hot, they return. They grill what they've caught and have it for lunch, and in the evening they go home, tired, their bellies filled with what they caught with their own hands. What joy! I ask if I can join them one day and he agrees. Both of us know it's a distant possibility but he's kind enough to leave that window open.

The days passed quietly in this fashion. The female nurse would come by to measure my blood pressure. The male nurse would come to do the exercises. The doctor would check in on me, happy that my condition was stable. My mother would enter, very warily. She seemed to be more cautious about coming in when I was awake than when I had my eyes closed, which is the opposite of when she comes into my room at home. She would move forward slowly, to make sure I didn't object, then sit down and not utter a word. When her tears were too much for her, she'd leave the room in a hurry, as though fearful she'd cause another fit. She would also leave in a hurry when the doctor arrived, as though she were in the way of his work. When the nurse informed her that visiting hours were over, she'd leave as submissively as a well-mannered child, also without uttering a word. Then she stopped coming. My brother told me she was confined to her bed with a fever, as though it were a consequence of what had happened. He took to visiting me daily on her behalf. His wedding had been put off for another week because I was in the hospital, but he seemed relaxed and not resentful. He said he had good news, news that I'd never believe, and that as soon as I came out, he'd tell me. I thought he was just trying to raise my morale as per the doctor's directions.

A whole month had passed since I entered the hospital, and I was feeling as though I'd never leave it again. Then the head doctor came, in high spirits, and gave me the news. Later that morning, I would be leaving, perhaps for good and just like that, the way one might leave a motel on the highway.

Week 40

I WENT HOME WITH MY brother. He brought me up to date on developments. It had become clear that my grandfather had had more money than anyone imagined in that safe, and he'd set aside a bequest to cover the costs of my treatment. It was no trifling sum: the third of the money that one was legally allowed to bequeath to non-heirs. Even though my uncles had received the rest, that third wasn't something they were going to ignore. Some of them hinted at trickery on my part, as though I'd profited from my grandfather's feeling for the disease of which my grandmother too had died. The rest had been more realistic: they'd suggested to my brother that they administer the funds for us and supervise the treatment themselves, in-country naturally, so that I wouldn't be exposed to charlatanry and exploitation.

"Now those bastards remember us," he said, parking the car indignantly and recalling earlier situations with them. I couldn't, for my part, share in his anger as their objection was somehow understandable to me. A decision of that sort was not in keeping with my grandfather's nature, as they knew it at least, and he might not have been in a fit mental state to judge. Part of me felt I'd contracted the disease deliberately to exploit this opportunity. Whatever the case, my brother said as we entered, it would be best if I were to decide quickly what I was going to do with the money to avoid any possible difficulties. He'd let me know the details later; now I should rest and spend a little time with my mother. She was still in bed with the fever, days later.

I made for her room as soon as I'd gone upstairs. She was still asleep. I drew up a chair next to her and sat down. After a little, I noticed the irony: she was in the bed and I was out of it, on a chair; anyone who saw us would imagine that it was always that way. I reached out my hand to feel her temperature, as she had done for me during the months of my sickness, and earlier, when I was a child. I used to hate it when she did so and I felt my hot, sticky forehead against the palm of her clean, plump hand. I left my hand there for a while. Her brow was smooth and unwrinkled; I wondered why I hadn't thought about it that way before. She opened her eyes and gazed at me.

"How are you feeling?"

"OK," she answered, raising herself heavily. Then she added, "I don't want to complain."

I smiled.

"And you?"

"OK. I don't want to complain."

She smiled. The illness had tamed something inside her and given her a degree of gentleness. "You know you can always complain. I'm your mother."

"I know."

It's been so long now that I've spoken curtly in such situations, as though each unnecessary word heralded a descent into mediocrity.

We talked briefly about recent developments in my treatment. I told her that the radiation therapy had completely cured the liver of the cancerous cells, and she welcomed this and beamed. She asked me if I'd heard about my grandfather's bequest and I replied that my brother had filled me in briefly. We were silent for a while. It seemed these pieces of news gave her comfort, and it may be that she began to improve right then. Without thinking, I laid out for her my plan for seeking treatment in Japan. I'd spent a lot of my spare time in the last few weeks researching treatment centers abroad, on the recommendation of the doctor, and, with help from him, I'd reached the conclusion that the immune system treatment there was the most suitable for cases like mine. It wasn't to be expected that it would guarantee an end to the cancer—though there had been cases for which Fate had decreed complete recovery—but it was likely to increase one's lifespan by a few years, with a noticeable degree of health and the capacity to live an independent life, or, in the worst-case scenario, the capacity to live with the disease with the minimum of symptoms.

I tried to appear as much as possible like someone who had resolved to do this a while ago, though in fact the threads of the decision had only begun to weave themselves together as I started to talk. Though she wasn't completely comfortable with it, the fact that I had a clear plan, whose requirements I had already begun to deal with, as I explained, left her somewhat content and accepting. I emphasized to her that this was something I would only do if I could travel alone or, at the most, in the company of a private nurse, so as to deny her any possibility of feeling guilty or that she was abandoning me or whatever that confused feeling had been that had seized her when she urged me, before I got sick, to look for a new place to live. Our house was going to be handed over to its new owners at the end of the month, as agreed, and she'd be moving to live with my brother when he came back from his honeymoon. By that time, all necessary arrangements would have been made, including my receipt of the bequest that would cover the costs of the treatment and of living in Tokyo, plus maybe some tourism in the environs.

At last, I get back to my room. I open the window. I notice how much more space the tower block outside occupies compared to before I went into the hospital. Then, this new housing project had consisted of no more than a few concrete pillars and iron rods. Seeing how much of it is now complete, I realize how much time has passed. It's winter again. The sun is sending its last rays to dye the roofs of the blocks a warm orange, and there's a cool breeze coming in through the window. Standing there, in front of the window, something fresher than the air, warmer than the light, something in the scene that is too large for me to put my finger on, comes to me through the opening. I feel I'm in contact with something that surpasses my limited presence in this place, but it's a feeling that finds it difficult to sustain itself for more than a brief moment.

Nine whole months have passed since I began these diaries. I remember this as I pick up *The Magic Mountain*, which I began on the train, and look through its final pages.

I put the book back on the bedside table and pour a glass of water from the jug, which is full. I place a few painkilling tablets in my mouth and swallow them slowly. My heart rate stabilizes, as though it too had needed water. I lie down on the bed, which has recently been made; its coldness sends a shudder through my pores. I move my limbs so as to feel warmth, reveling in the sound made by their rubbing against the sheets, which give off the perfumed smell of fresh laundry. I wrap myself in them and remain quiet for a while, running my gaze over the contents of the room. The boxes, left as they were since I moved in here two years ago, look ready for another move. I won't have a lot of work to do, I think, before dozing for a little.

When I wake, I feel a sense of peace in my limbs. The sound of the neighbors percolates to me softly through the window, like a burning clot of old memories. I remain lying down for a while, absorbing the warmth, enjoying the pleasure of a regular pulse, of the possibility of turning from one side to the other without great effort. I raise my head and watch a line of ants walking over the tiles, searching for any scrap of food unnoticed when my mother cleaned the room. I watch them and a secret bond of shared weakness grows between these creatures and me. I find myself loath to crush even one with my finger, as I used to do when I was a boy. Perhaps I've become afraid that my evil actions toward them will catch up with me in my next life, or that I'll die, crushed like an ant, in this life if I don't repent for what I did. And who knows? Maybe one day I'll wake up to find that I've been transformed in my bed into a huge insect, as happens in *Metamorphosis*.

I remember that when I was a boy I used to eat ants, just for the experience or I know not what; there is no good reason for doing such a thing anyway. Then I discovered that it was an effective way to attract the attention of the neighbor girls and the new, visiting girls who came to our house with their mothers. They were busy playing and running after one another in their frilly dresses that gave off a smooth rustle, and I was watching them in silence from my usual place on the stairs, refusing to join in out of fear of being rejected, unable to discover the easy ways that make acceptance happen. When one of them noticed me, she came toward me, stood one step below me, and talked to me with curiosity and interest, while I remained sitting in front of her, head bowed, without answering any of her questions. Then, suddenly, I picked up on my finger an ant that was passing close by her foot, put it on my tongue and swallowed it. She squealed and her eyes shone and she ran off to call the others: "Come! Come! See what he's doing!"

The rest stopped running about, approached expectantly, and stood around me, their hot breath panting above me. Without looking up at them, and without saying a word, I picked up another ant and devoured it. Then I stuck out my tongue to prove that I'd swallowed it and they all began shrieking together in amazement and hilarity and some of them cried out in disgust and others asked me how it tasted. I just shrugged my shoulders nonchalantly, like someone who'd tried the silliest things in the world, and they set off running again, with greater exhilaration, shouting with greater joy.

I liked that incident and the success it brought me and felt I'd made an impression on them they'd never forget. Even after they'd told their mothers and my mother had scolded me for what I'd done, I continued always to treat ants as though they had been put at my disposal so that I could show off my strength. So when I sat on the lavatory seat, I'd take the spray and target any ant I happened to see walking at random about the bathroom. I'd spray it from the right and the left so that it would slip on the tiles, kicking out fiercely with its limbs to resist the burst of liquid till it ended up in a corner, to end its life there with the rest of its comrades who had dared to appear in front of me while I was defecating. And when I found one climbing the wall, or walking over the tabletop, I'd blow on it, or flick it with my nail, so that it would fly off far away with no hope of return. When they gathered in large numbers, though, around a bit of food, I'd spray the lot of them with insecticide, and they'd all curl up together, at one go, and their existence would shrink immediately into little scattered dots, devoid of life.

I remember this as I scatter crumbs of fresh food over the tiles, then watch as a few ants gather and eat together or carry it off to their young in their nests. Suddenly the taking of any life, even if it's only the life of an insect, becomes a debilitating action conducive to extreme sorrow. There's no regret, though, in my present sorrow, and none of the melancholy that follows after an antidepressant starts to have its effect. What I feel now is sorrow of a different kind, closer to what one feels after a haiku. There's a word in Japanese that sums it up and has no equivalent in any other language, or so I've read. It's pronounced *mono-no-aware* and it means "the sweet grief felt at the passing of things" or "the emotion resulting from the realization of the inevitability of their passing." So this is my first word of Japanese.

hoopoe is an imprint for engaged, open-minded readers hungry for outstanding fiction that challenges headlines, re-imagines histories, and celebrates original storytelling. Through elegant paperback and digital editions, **hoopoe** champions bold, contemporary writers from across the Middle East alongside some of the finest, groundbreaking authors of earlier generations.

At hoopoefiction.com, curious and adventurous readers from around the world will find new writing, interviews, and criticism from our authors, translators, and editors.